By E E MONTGOMERY

Between Love and Honor • The Courage to Love
Ordinary People
What About Him

JUST LIFE
Just His Type
Just Like a Date
Just in Time
Just the Way You Are

Published by DREAMSPINNER PRESS
http://www.dreamspinnerpress.com

Just the Way You Are

E E MONTGOMERY

DREAMSPINNER
PRESS

Published by
DREAMSPINNER PRESS

5032 Capital Circle SW, Suite 2, PMB# 279, Tallahassee, FL 32305-7886 USA
http://www.dreamspinnerpress.com/

Just the Way You Are
© 2015 E E Montgomery.

Cover Art
© 2015 Catt Ford.
Cover content is for illustrative purposes only and any person depicted on the cover is a model.

ISBN: 978-1-63216-862-7
Digital ISBN: 978-1-63216-863-4
Library of Congress Control Number: 2014921662
First Edition April 2015

Printed in the United States of America
∞
This paper meets the requirements of
ANSI/NISO Z39.48-1992 (Permanence of Paper).

For the Belles: you've been there for me almost from the beginning, soothed my nerves, praised my skill, and told me to get my head out of my arse more often than I can remember. Thank you.

Chapter ONE

JONATHAN SHIVERED in the early morning air but not from the chill. He wrapped his arms around himself and groaned as his wound tugged against the movement. He relaxed slowly as the pain eased. From where he stood, he could see between the two apartment blocks to where the sun glinted off the Brisbane River. Five years ago he used to watch the ferries puddle their way up and down the river, dropping passengers here at Hamilton and across the way at Bulimba. He'd missed that view for a long time. He wondered if he'd miss the house now that he was leaving it.

The house was gray—morning gray, Anthony had called it, but it had always looked like unwashed, neglected underwear to him. The lines of the house were precise and symmetrical, unlike the yard. The front lawn bore scars, just like his chest. They were from his Cruiser skidding to a stop the night Anthony had sent him to kill Mark. His eyes burned as he thought how close he'd come to doing what his boyfriend told him to.

At the time, he didn't think he had any other choice. It was kill or be killed. Literally. By the end of that night, Mark had been the only one left uninjured. Liam's leg had thankfully healed quickly where Anthony had stabbed him. Anthony was still in hospital with a self-inflicted knife wound to the stomach, and Jonathan… Jonathan was done with that life. Anthony's knife in his chest—so close to his heart it was clearly intended to be fatal—had cured him of whatever delusions he'd held onto that let him believe he was in love with the man. Even Anthony's assertions that Jonathan was responsible for him being in a wheelchair since the car accident two years before wouldn't get him to stay.

He was out of it now, or at least he would be as soon as the removalists came and took his stuff away. Then he could begin to heal. The first step had been to learn to breathe again after his lung collapsed when Anthony stabbed him. The next step… he didn't know what the next step after this was. He wasn't going to admit it to anyone, but he was just as terrified now, starting a life of his own—on his own—as he was when he thought he was going to die.

The trembling began again. Dizzy. Couldn't catch his breath. He leaned beside the front door and forced himself to bring his mind back to the here and now and looked around again. There was a new section of fence now, and the Cruiser had been repaired and sat at the curb, waiting for him. His cousin must have had the damage repaired while Jonathan was in the hospital—learning how to make his lung work again after his boyfriend had tried to kill him. He shook the thoughts from his head. He had to stop thinking like this or he'd go mad.

Sleep last night had been impossible. The house had been cleaned, but nothing was going to completely remove the blood splattered on the white carpet. His blood.

A low rumble burbled through the air, and a truck turned onto the street. Jonathan's heart raced. "You can do this," he whispered, although he wasn't quite sure which part of "this" he was talking about. It could be dealing with strangers on his own, or it could be leaving Anthony—finally. He pressed the heel of his hand over the dressing on his chest. Staying with Anthony was no longer an option.

The truck stopped and turned to reverse into the driveway. The high-pitched beeping made Jonathan jump and, to calm himself, he focused on the two men sitting in the cab. The driver looked young and blond, the passenger older and shriveled, his hair sticking out in unkempt tangles.

"Two people. Not Anthony. You're outside, everything's marked. You don't need to go inside with them at all if you don't want to. You can do this." He counted his breaths in and out. The beeping stopped, the engine cut out, and the driver's door opened.

Long, well-formed legs slipped from the cab, by-passing the step completely as a muscled body slid to the ground. Khaki cargo shorts bunched enticingly around a spectacular package before settling loosely around slim hips as the man's boot-clad feet landed on the ground and he stood away from the truck. Jonathan moved his gaze up the body. The worn T-shirt did nothing to hide the trim stomach and prominent pecs and the sleeves framed the rounded deltoids perfectly. Jonathan sighed as he lifted his focus higher to see the man's wide smile.

"You Jonathan Watson?" His voice was low and rich, a dribble of lava over rock. "We're Handy Removals. I'm Ben." He gestured to the man still sitting in the truck. "That's Col. You have everything you need to move ready?"

While he spoke, the other man—Col—got out of the truck and strode toward them. He wore navy Stubbies, the short shorts barely covering what they needed to, and a navy singlet. Both were faded and limp from many washings. Salt-and-pepper hair peeked from the top of the singlet and under his arms. His cheeks and chin sported at least a week's growth of the same mottled hair, but a circle at the top of his head was shiny smooth, framed by the unkempt tonsure. His legs were spindly but loose skin hung on the thighs, indicating a probably recent and significant weight loss. His upper arms told the same story.

"You got dogs here?" It was more a demand than a question.

"No."

"Good. I hate killing dogs."

Jonathan gasped.

"He's not serious. Can you show us what you want moved? We'll get started." Ben grabbed Col's arm. "Come on, Col. Time to move furniture."

"I'll show you the pieces that need loading," Jonathan said. He strode into the house and hurried to the living room. He took a deep breath as he moved into the open space before turning to watch the removalists enter.

"You aren't taking all of it?" The burly man, Col, strode into the room and came directly toward Jonathan. Jonathan stepped back, raising his hands defensively before he realized what he had done and dropped them to his sides. His fingers twitched with the need to lift up and protect his stomach and groin, but he forced them to stay down. Not every man was a violent asshole.

"Col, you're doing it again." Ben grabbed the elbow of the blue-singleted one and pulled him away.

"What? I'm not doing anything, Benny. I'm a pussycat." He jammed his broad fists on his hips and glared at the second removalist.

"I know you are, but you can't come up so close like that to people. Why don't you have a look in the kitchen and see what's there to load." Col took a step back, and—even though Ben was shorter than he was and, in comparison, looked almost effeminate, with gracefully arched eyebrows and neatly trimmed dark blond hair—he grunted an acknowledgement and lowered his shoulders and eyebrows. Ben held his ground and glared at the older man until the last quivering eyebrow hair had settled.

"Fine," Col grumbled. "Stop this bullshitting around and let's get the job done." He turned his fierce stare onto Jonathan. "Are we taking all this?"

Jonathan stepped past the two men as he gestured around the living room and toward the bedrooms up the stairs. "I've put orange sticky notes on the pieces to be loaded. There are also several boxes in the kitchen."

Col strode into the kitchen, muttering. "Bloody orange sticky notes. Bloody queen."

Jonathan gaped after the horrid man.

"Ignore him. Col's in the early stages of Alzheimer's. He's not really such a prick." Ben raised a hand and Jonathan realized, too late, he had probably only meant to clap him on the shoulder. He raised himself from his crouch and lowered his arms but couldn't meet the other man's gaze. He didn't want to see the disgust that would surely be there. Jonathan knew what he looked like. A six-foot-tall black man with broad shoulders and strong jaw, he knew he came across as the potentially violent one of any couple. He was just the opposite. Even though he was much larger and stronger than Anthony, he'd never been able to take control in their relationship. In the early years, taking control had never even occurred to him.

The silence stretched, but the man stayed in front of Jonathan. Eventually Jonathan raised his head to see why he was still there. Hazel eyes regarded him steadily. He was too close, but Jonathan forced himself to stay still, to not step away. If he moved one muscle he'd probably end up running up the street, screaming hysterically. He'd spent a lot of time in the hospital deciding he was going to be in charge of his own life from now on. This was step one.

The perfect eyebrows lowered until they were two straight lines over pale eyes. Sweat broke out on Jonathan's scalp as the need for flight ratcheted higher. Then Ben took a step back, and Jonathan could breathe again.

"The doc said Col will still be able to work for a while. He's good at his job, but you can request another crew if you'd like," Ben said as he held out a tablet and stylus. He jerked his head to the kitchen, where they could still hear the older man's muttering. Jonathan took the proffered equipment and looked at it. "That's what we have on our list to pick up and deliver to the new place. All you have to do is tick off each item as we bring it out and then do the same when we get to the other end. Add anything extra you might have forgotten when you registered, at the bottom there, so we can keep track." He looked at Jonathan for a long time but before the urge to step away overwhelmed him, Jonathan backed up toward the center of the room. "We'll just get started, then. Tick things off as we take them out."

Jonathan stared at Ben's back as he turned and walked into the kitchen to talk to Col, dimly taking in the worn T-shirt and cargo shorts over scuffed steel-capped boots. The shorts sat low on his hips but didn't expose his underwear like so many other people's clothes did. Jonathan appreciated that small show of modesty even as he remembered how the shorts bunched when Ben slid down from the truck. The fabric fitted so well over Ben's hips and butt that Jonathan would have sworn they'd been tailor-made for him, but who would pay for custom-made work shorts?

Jonathan flushed when he realized he'd watched Ben's backside all the way into the kitchen, but he couldn't look away. When the man disappeared from view, Jonathan left the house and positioned himself outside the front door so he was out of the way. As he waited he checked the list. He'd created the list while he was still in hospital and was sure there were things he'd missed that were now marked with a sticky note. He listened to the two removalists discuss the best way to approach the move, Ben's deep baritone providing a soothing counterpoint to Col's strident tenor. At least Col sounded more reasonable now that he was focused on his work. Within minutes they fell silent—then they appeared at the door with a large bureau. Jonathan stepped back farther to make sure he was out of the way before searching for the item on the list and ticking it off.

Jonathan was amazed at how quickly they worked. Within an hour they had loaded everything Jonathan had marked, laid felt between and over the furniture, and tied it all securely, ready for the trip to Jonathan's new apartment.

"How'd we go?" asked Ben. Col stood beside the truck, scowling at Jonathan. Jonathan took a small step to the side so that Ben's body hid the other man from view. "Don't worry about Col. He's hungry but hasn't realized it yet. I'll stop on the way over to your new place and make sure he eats something. He won't bother you anymore." He reached out and took the tablet from Jonathan's unresisting hands, quickly skimming the information. "Okay, looks like we got it all. You want to check inside just in case there's something else you wanted?"

Jonathan shook his head. "There's nothing." Everything he'd marked or packed last night was in the truck. He'd made sure to only take the items he'd chosen and paid for himself. "Do you know where you're taking it all?"

"Sure do. You heading out now?"

Jonathan almost smiled at Ben's habit of starting his questions part way through the sentence but nodded instead. "I'll be right behind you."

"We still need to close up the truck and stop for lunch. You'll have plenty of time to get there before us and open up. That way we can begin unloading straightaway."

"Oh, um, sure." Jonathan waited until Ben moved away before he ducked into the house to check they hadn't left any mess. The sight of the few squares of undisturbed carpet in the living room and the empty shelf in the bookcase tightened Jonathan's throat. He remembered purchasing every piece of furniture, the time and thought he'd put into choosing each item, so that it fitted perfectly in its place and complemented Anthony's belongings. He sighed.

"Maybe it wasn't all for nothing," he whispered to himself. "Maybe it will look just as good in my new place."

His new place. *What a joke.* Jonathan locked up and walked over to his car. His cousin Liam had found the apartment for him while he was still in hospital. Liam had paid the deposit and three months' rent in advance, *and* he'd gone shopping so there would be food in the new fridge he'd bought so Jonathan would have something to eat when he finally moved in this evening. Jonathan hadn't been inside it yet. He didn't think he'd ever even driven through the neighborhood.

He opened his car door and lowered himself carefully into the driver's seat. He'd been discharged from hospital the afternoon before and had spent the entire night packing boxes and putting sticky notes on furniture. His aunt and uncle had left at ten, but he'd continued. He refused to spend even one more night in the house he'd shared with Anthony for ten years.

He leaned his head back against the headrest, feeling every ache and every square inch of his skin, especially over his chest and back. The stab wound was still healing, and his back ached because he'd been using those muscles to compensate for the others that hurt too much. As soon as this move was finished, he was going to take all the pain meds he was allowed, then fall into bed and stay there for at least a week. In his silent apartment.

Taking as deep a breath as his newly-inflated lung would allow him—damn Anthony and his psycho-homicidal bullshit—Jonathan raised his head, inserted the key, and started the car, thanking all that's holy that it was an automatic and he only needed one hand to drive. There was no way his wound would allow him to use his left hand enough to even steer.

The drive across town was an exercise in pain endurance. If Jonathan hadn't already had plenty of practice functioning through severe pain, he wouldn't have made it.

He followed the removal truck until it turned into a McDonald's; after that he blindly followed the directions of his GPS. Weaving in and out of traffic was more strenuous than he'd thought it would be. As it was, he couldn't remember whole sections of the drive. Sweat poured off him as he pulled up to the curb, soaking his back and dribbling down his face to drip off the end of his nose and chin. His chest burned, the muscles around the wound strained beyond what they could comfortably handle this soon after being stabbed. He'd told Liam he'd get a cab and would pick up his car in a couple of days, but in the end he hadn't been able to leave it there. He didn't want anything of his at Anthony's house. Not one thing. Never again.

Now he sat at the curb and watched the truck reverse into the drive like it had at Anthony's place that morning. He wondered how long he'd been sitting there, breathing through the pain, hoping he'd catch his breath soon. If he got out of the car right now, he'd probably collapse. He leaned his head back on the headrest, closed his eyes, and tried to breathe evenly. Deep breaths hurt like buggery so he didn't even try. Worry gnawed at him. Liam was going to kill him if he did any further damage to his lung.

The three-story apartment building was an old one. It wore streaky gray stucco that was probably once white, three concrete steps with an iron railing led to the green front door. There was no security other than a deadlock on the front door and bars on all the windows. His apartment was on the top floor at the back of the building, near the emergency exit. According to Liam, the bathroom had a mold problem and the kitchen smelled of decades-old oil and grease, but the only thing Jonathan worried about was if Anthony would have access. Liam had wanted to find something better for him, but Jonathan knew he'd be able to afford this one, even if it was some time before he found work.

A knock on the window beside him made him jump so much the seatbelt bit into his chest, and he gasped. Frowning eyes loomed inches away and he jerked back, crying out when the seatbelt scraped across his stitches.

"Are you okay?" Ben's voice was muffled by the glass.

Jonathan sucked in a calming breath and hit the button to lower the window. He scowled when it didn't work with the ignition off. He removed the keys from the ignition, released his seatbelt, then opened the door. "Sorry, just woolgathering," he said as he swung his legs around and pushed himself out of the car and onto his feet, hoping Ben would move back some more.

"What the fuck happened?" Ben stepped forward, his hands reaching toward Jonathan.

Jonathan stumbled back but had nowhere to go, trapped between the open car door and his seat. His breathing, beginning to calm after the strenuous drive, ratcheted up again at Ben's proximity. His vision grayed at the edges, and he panted. A whimper escaped when Ben grasped his shoulders and drew him forward.

"Don't. Please."

Chapter TWO

CHRIST. SOMEONE has sure done a number on him. You wouldn't think it to look at him. Who would have the balls to fuck with a guy built like that? Although he's skinny as. Ben should let the bony shoulders go, he knew that, but he couldn't. If there was anyone in this world crying out for some gentle care, it was this guy. Ben didn't know why, but he knew he was the only guy who could do it. *Conceited much?* Yeah, sure, how else would he have been able to work in the mines in western Queensland and still design clothes? It took balls to do that.

Ben drew Jonathan closer and wrapped his arms around him, all the while murmuring in his ear. "It's okay, mate. You're gonna be fine. Just relax. I won't let anything happen to you." He kept his voice low and calm. It always worked on the animals at his cousin Brent's place, even the stupid sheep.

Jonathan began to struggle. Ben should have known he wasn't a sheep. Luckily he had enough sense to let Jonathan go before he put Ben on his ass, especially since Col was striding toward them with a scowl on his face. Ben stepped back and raised his hands in surrender.

"Sure, sure, it's okay. I'm back here. I'm not going to hurt you."

Jonathan's breathing was still harsh, but he seemed calmer now, even starting to get angry. That was good. Angry was better than scared shitless like he'd looked a few minutes ago. Ben glanced over his shoulder. *Shit.* Col was still bearing down on them, and somehow he'd managed to pick up a stick. As Ben watched he raised it over his head. *Christ.* He rushed forward, jostled past Jonathan, and grabbed for Col instead.

"Those bloody ferals will kill you in your sleep, but I'll get 'im first," Col yelled as he fought against Ben. Spittle sprayed from his mouth, globs of it landing on Ben's chin and neck. Christ, he was strong. Col's wife, Lorraine, had warned Ben about Col's reactions to some things if he was late with his medication, but he didn't think the older man would lose it like this while on a job.

"Stop it, Col, or I'll ring Lorraine and tell her to come and collect you."

The fight bled out of him like a severed artery, spurting fitfully for a few seconds before he was limp in Ben's arms. What a fucked-up job this was turning out to be. Ben hefted Col back onto his feet and dragged him over to the truck. After checking he had the keys with him, Ben put Col in the passenger seat.

"Stay there and listen to the music until I finish here. Do you understand me, Col? Do not move from this spot."

Col didn't respond, but Ben couldn't spend any more time with him. He had a client to placate and a truck full of furniture and effects to somehow get up three flights of stairs on his own.

Fuck my life today.

Jonathan was leaning back against the hood of his car. Ben took that as a good sign. If he was still freaked, he'd be sitting in his car in a trembling, sweaty heap like he'd been before. He stopped a few paces away—figured Jonathan wouldn't want him too close.

"I'm so sorry. He's usually good as gold as long as I keep him on task."

His only response was a raised eyebrow.

"Yeah, I know. If I'd just let you be, he probably would have stayed on task, but you've got the keys, mate. Can't do much without them."

If Jonathan's skin was paler, Ben was sure he'd have blushed at that. He dug into his pocket and pulled out a key ring with three keys on it. One was a car key. "I'll go up and unlock." He glanced at the truck. "Will he be all right? I can't offer to help." He gestured to the blood on his shirt. At least the mark hadn't grown much since he got out of the car. Ben still wondered what he'd done to himself, but after the fiasco that was his attempt to help, he didn't dare ask.

Thank Christ he was letting Col's "feral" comment and attack go. He could quite easily have them charged, and Ben wouldn't blame him at all. "Oh, sure. Col will be fine once he gets back on the job. Like I told you, the doc said he's still able to work just fine." *Christ, I hope I'm not talking through my hat.*

Jonathan nodded, then eased himself around Ben, staying out of reach the whole time. Ben's stomach flipped. This time it wasn't what some other bastard had done to him to make him act like a scared chicken; it was what *he'd* done. *Fuck.*

"Look." Jonathan jumped when Ben spoke, and Ben raised his hands again. "Sorry. I'm just... sorry. I didn't mean to make you feel...." *Attacked? Threatened? Like you're incapable of living your own life? Christ on a stick.*

Jonathan ducked his head and hurried up the few steps. "I'll open the doors for you and wait up there to show you where to put everything."

Ben heaved a sigh, then trudged over to the truck and opened the door.

"Come on, Col. Time to move some furniture." He sighed again when Col looked up at him with blank eyes. He'd opened the glove box and taken some papers out. His lap, the seat, and the floor around his feet were littered with finely shredded pieces of paper. One piece clung to his whiskers near the corner of his mouth.

Col held out a fragment. "Do you want some?"

"Yeah, thanks, Col." Ben took the paper from him, then grasped his elbow and helped him down from the truck. "Come around the back and help me with this furniture." He hoped to Christ Col would remember how to do that by the time they started lifting. Luckily as soon as Col saw the neatly packed truck, he clicked over into "removalist" mode and things went smoothly. Ben noted that Jonathan stayed as far away from them as he could, although that could just as easily have been so he didn't get in their way. Ben was pretty sure the slim man was avoiding being anywhere near him.

He'd made someone afraid of him. Usually he'd chat with people while he was working, but words hung heavy on his tongue, thick like an autumn fog. By the time the fog had burned off, his stomach churned with anxiety. Ben remained silent, watchful. They were nearly done before Jonathan showed signs of relaxing. Ben liked to think Jonathan relaxed because he'd worked out Ben wasn't a threat to him.

Ben and Col folded the last felt blanket and stowed it; then Col went to sit in the passenger seat as Ben took the tablet to Jonathan to sign. Ben stood close to him at the bottom of the stairs to the apartment building. It wasn't much nearer than he would normally stand, but it was closer. He pretended it was because Jonathan looked exhausted, a gray cast to his skin making him look like he was barely remaining on his feet. Ben spent the time Jonathan took to peruse the document on the tablet and sign it to consider and dismiss a dozen ways of talking to him.

"Where are you from?"

Jonathan looked up, his brow furrowed. "Hamilton," he said, naming the suburb they'd just come from.

"No, I mean, what country. You're not Aboriginal."

"I'm Australian."

Heat flooded Ben's face. He was probably being racist. Sometimes it was hard to tell what was considered innocent curiosity, a desire to get to know someone, and what was considered insulting.

"I'm sorry," he said as Jonathan finished signing his name. Ben plowed on, even though he was probably making the situation worse. "I didn't mean to insult you or frighten you earlier. It was the blood," he gestured to Jonathan's stained shirt. "It's not something you see every day, and I thought you were injured. Well, you obviously are, but I thought you might need help, and then I thought if I got you talking about yourself you'd relax...." Ben stopped before the rambling took him over completely and he required some sort of verbal exorcism.

A half smile twitched at the corner of Jonathan's mouth, and he shook his head. "I'm fine. It's nothing."

Ben had seen the way Jonathan moved, so he was sure it wasn't "nothing."

"Do you have a dressing? I could put it on for you if you like."

Damn. That was the wrong thing to say. If he'd thought before he opened his mouth, he'd never have said it. Now the fear was back on Jonathan's face, tightening the skin around his eyes and pulling those luscious lips into a tight line.

"Look, I didn't mean...." Ben sighed at how difficult this was. Talking to people and putting them at ease was usually much simpler than this. He looked around as if the apartment building, or the cracked concrete path leading to it, would give him inspiration, even though he knew he should just say good-bye and leave.

"My parents were from Somalia," Jonathan said as he handed the tablet and stylus back to Ben.

"Oh," Ben fumbled for words. "Refugees?"

Jonathan nodded. "From the civil war. They were lucky."

Being a refugee and explaining how difficult it was for his family to settle in a new country probably wasn't something Jonathan, or anyone else, wanted to talk about with their removalist, so Ben accepted defeat in the conversation stakes and looked at his truck.

"You're not going to unpack all this by yourself, are you?"

Bristling offense zapped in the air between them. *Christ on a stick. Could I shove my foot any deeper into my mouth?* "Sorry, sorry." *Fuck.* Ben backed up. "I didn't mean anything by that. Just…." He took a deep breath and started again. "We offer an unpacking service too, so if you decide you want some help, call the office and we'll come out and get you sorted in no time."

Jonathan didn't respond but looked less alarmed than before, so Ben risked a small smile as he went back to the truck. Col was nowhere to be seen.

"Christ. Lorraine is going to have to do something this time." Ben wasn't being completely fair. He had left Col alone for quite a while, and he knew the older man had a tendency to wander off. He ran to the footpath to see Col ambling down the street, peering into each letterbox. He jogged down to him. "Col," Ben said as soon as he reached the older man. "Where are you off to?"

Col looked at Ben blankly. Ben had only known him a few months, but it was unsettling every time Col forgot who he was. "Come on, Col, let's get you home."

Col stepped back from him. *Christ on a stick.* He seemed to be spending his entire day frightening people. "Lorraine called and asked when you'd be home."

"Lorraine?" His eyes brightened, and he looked around. Ben didn't know if he was looking for his wife or suddenly realizing he didn't know where he was. He gently took Col by the arm and led him back to the truck.

"Yeah, she said she was cooking your favorite for dinner tonight." What the hell that was, Ben didn't have a clue, but Col obviously knew because he smiled and increased his pace.

JONATHAN SAT on the couch, stared up at the ceiling, and tried to ignore Liam's strident tones jabbing down the hall and into the rest of the apartment as he and Mark made up Jonathan's bed. It didn't help. He could still hear Liam ranting in the bedroom.

"'Look after yourself,' I said. I know I told him that. And what did he go and do? He drove across town when he knew he wasn't supposed to. Anything could have happened to him. Did you see his chest? He's mangled those stitches again. As it is he's going to have a scar. If he keeps doing it, God alone knows what sort of damage he'll do. He could end up in surgery again."

"He's all right, Liam. You can see that. He's out there resting, just like you told him to. He'll be fine." At least Mark's voice held reason. Liam was off his rocker. Jonathan was surprised Liam was letting loose like this with Mark. Not many people got to see his cousin vent. A smile tugged at his lips. Now maybe Liam would have someone else to focus all his protective instincts on, and Jonathan would have some space to heal and work out how he wanted to live his life.

"He hasn't been looking after himself. You saw—"

Mark chuckled. "You know what I find really funny here?"

"Funny? How can you find this—"

"This is the first time we've made a bed together—hell, almost the first time we've been *near* a bed together—and it isn't even ours. When you come over to my place, we never make it any farther than the couch."

Silence. Blissful silence. Jonathan sucked in as deep a breath as he could and let it out slowly. Perhaps Mark would be good for Liam. *Even if he is Anthony's ex.*

Shit. He shouldn't have thought about Anthony. Now his heart was pounding and tears burned his eyes. Jonathan hated, despised Anthony for what he'd done to him through the years. He hated himself for allowing it, for giving into Anthony's bullying, for staying with him for so long, even though he knew Anthony would kill him if he left. He sat forward, groaning against the twinge of pain in his wound and the cramp in his back muscles.

Today was the beginning of his new life. He had to learn to look forward to things again, but he'd spent so long simply surviving day by day, he didn't know how to do that anymore. Images from the day flitted through his distracted mind, and it was long moments before Jonathan realized every single image was of the removalist, Ben. His bright hazel eyes begging Jonathan to find acceptance and compassion for Col and his strange ways. The way he looked after Col and made sure he ate when he needed to. The way his muscles shifted as he lifted boxes and moved furniture. Jonathan breathed deeply, imagining he could still smell Ben's warm sweat as he maneuvered the bulky furniture through the doorway.

A strident knocking at the front door reverberated through the quiet room. Jonathan jumped and stared at the opening to the short entrance hall, his breathing suddenly labored.

Anthony is still in hospital. There's no lift in the building. He can't get up here.

It didn't matter what Jonathan told himself, nothing stopped the nervous sweat beading on his face or the tremble of his fingers.

Liam's confident footsteps thudded along the floorboards from the bedroom. He glanced inquiringly at Jonathan on his way through the living room. Jonathan managed a slight shake of his head. He wasn't expecting anyone. He watched Liam open the door but couldn't see who was there.

"Oh, yeah, um, hi. I'm Ben, the removalist? Is, um, Jonathan there?"

"Was there something wrong with the delivery? Did you miss a box or something?" Liam asked.

Jonathan leaned to the left so he could see around Liam's wide shoulders blocking the doorway.

"Who is it?" Mark asked quietly from beside him.

Jonathan was so focused on Ben and Liam at the door, he didn't even start at the unexpected question. "It's one of the removalists," he whispered.

"Did they forget a box or something?"

"I don't think so." Jonathan felt silly still whispering, but he wasn't sure if he wanted Ben to know he was there. As soon as the thought floated through his head, he scoffed. Ben had spent most of the day moving him in here. Of course he knew where he was. Jonathan reached out and grabbed Mark's hand. "Do you think he's a stalker?"

Mark looked down at him, a mix of surprise, amusement, and pity in his face. Jonathan dropped his hand and struggled to his feet. Hadn't he been telling himself for the last week—hell, months—that he wasn't going to let fear rule his life anymore? He walked steadily across the room and up behind Liam as he listened to Ben's response.

"No. No, we didn't forget a box. It's just that, well, he looked like he could use some help unpacking."

Jonathan placed a hand on Liam's shoulder. "Thanks Liam, I've got this."

Liam turned to scowl at him. "Jonathan—"

"Why don't you and Mark finish up in the bedroom while I talk to Ben?"

The scowl deepened, but Liam backed off and thumped back into the apartment.

Chapter THREE

WHAT THE fuck am I doing here? He could complain. I could lose my job. Ben took a step back as Jonathan came to the door, intending to apologize and leave, but then he noticed how Jonathan moved. Slow, stiff movements echoed the pain creasing his face, and Ben's heart twisted in sympathy. Before he knew what he was doing, he'd stepped into the apartment and grasped Jonathan's shoulders.

"Christ on a stick, what have you done to yourself now? You should be resting." Ben turned Jonathan around, trying to do it smoothly and gently so it didn't hurt him, then guided him into the living room and toward the couch. "Sit. I'll make coffee. Have you unpacked that yet?" He pressed down on Jonathan's shoulders until he sat, then strode into the kitchen. Everything Ben needed was sitting on the counter, waiting to be put away. He quickly filled the coffeemaker, then opened the fridge to find something to make for Jonathan to eat. He was sure, with how drawn the slim man looked, he hadn't eaten all day. As Ben brought things out and placed them on the counter, he looked up to find Jonathan shuffling across the room toward him.

"I thought I told you to sit. You need to rest if you expect to heal properly."

Jonathan ignored him. "What are you doing here?"

Ben put two slices of bread onto a plate. He pulled the butter and a knife over and began buttering the bread. "I thought you might want some help unpacking everything so you can get settled."

"I already have help." Jonathan spoke slowly, carefully, as if Ben was a dangerous animal he was trying to keep calm long enough to escape from.

Ben used the knife to lift two slices of ham from the packet and placed it on the bread, then added a thin layer of mustard before slapping the other slice of bread on top. He checked the coffeemaker and found mugs in a box on the floor. "Does he want coffee too?" He looked up into the suspicious gaze, then slid his focus behind Jonathan to see the man who had opened the door, with another man behind him.

His heart pounded. He wouldn't be able to bluff his way through this. *I shouldn't be here, and I barreled my way in like I belong here and have a right to take care of Jonathan. Fuck. What's wrong with me?* Ben pushed the plate toward Jonathan, then rinsed three mugs and poured coffee into each of them. *I'll leave, like I should have to begin with.* He focused on Jonathan to say good-bye but swallowed his words at the look on his face. Jonathan was gray with fatigue.

"Christ, will you sit down before you fall down? And eat something. You're too skinny." Ben rushed over to him and, with his arm around Jonathan's waist, turned him back to the couch. Jonathan didn't resist, but Ben could feel him tremble, like every cell was cringing away from him, as his body had that morning when Ben had clapped him on the shoulder.

He spoke to the other man, the one who could be Jonathan's brother. "Will you make him eat something? He's about ready to fall over." Ben pushed Jonathan back into the couch. "I don't know what's happened to you, but it's clear you've been injured. Now sit there and I'll get your coffee and sandwich. You're going to eat it all and then rest." He looked over to the other two men. "Is the bed set up and made?"

"Who are you?" demanded the man who answered the door.

"I'm Ben Urquhart, the removalist. Is the bed made up?"

They nodded, matching bemused expressions on their faces. "Good." Ben turned back to Jonathan. "You can go to bed and sleep. There's nothing that needs to be done here until you've had some rest. How do you like your coffee?"

He was rambling. He was doing his "bulldozer impersonation," as his mother called it. Heat flooded his face. He was making a fool of himself but couldn't stop it. If he stopped talking, they'd throw him out, and if that happened, Jonathan would probably keep working and he'd collapse and— Whatever was in Ben's head wasn't making sense, but it didn't need to make sense right that moment. The imperative was upon him. He almost snorted at the *Star Trek* reference but instead doctored the three coffees the way he was told and delivered them to the men in the living room.

Jonathan still hadn't started eating, so Ben sat beside him and held the plate up. "Here. Eat. You watched me make it, so you know what's in it." He jiggled the plate a little, and Jonathan carefully lifted the sandwich and took a bite. Ben sighed in relief. "Good. You'll feel better once you've had something to eat, and better still after a nap."

As Jonathan chewed, Ben turned to the other men. "Are you Jonathan's brother?"

"Cousin. I'm Liam. This is Mark. Why are you here?"

The plate he was still holding jostled as Jonathan put the sandwich down. He'd only taken one bite. "Don't think *that's* enough, buster. You're going to eat the whole sandwich before you go to bed." Christ, now he sounded like his mother.

"Why are you here, Ben?" Liam's voice was becoming strident. He was losing patience with Ben.

He responded as he jiggled the plate again. With a sigh, Jonathan picked the sandwich up and took another bite. "I told you. I thought Jonathan might need some help, seeing as he's hurt and all." He lowered the plate when it became obvious Jonathan was keeping the sandwich and continuing to eat. "I'm glad you've changed the dressing and your shirt. Is it okay?"

Jonathan nodded as he chewed. Liam answered for him. "He pulled some stitches, that's all. He was lucky."

"Hell, yeah. You're lucky you didn't rip the whole thing apart. Pulling stitches can be a bitch, though. I remember once when I was gored. Every time I bent or twisted to do something, the bloody stitches tugged and ripped. It took forever to heal. You need to make sure you stay still long enough for everything to knit together properly, or you'll be nursing the injury for months."

"Gored?" Jonathan's eyes were huge as he took another bite of the sandwich.

"Yeah. It was the local rodeo. It's the biggest one in the region, except for Longreach. I was doing the clowning and slipped in the hugest cow pat you've ever seen. Fresh too. Got it all up my leg; stank for the rest of the day. Anyway, the bull loved that—me slipping, not the cow pat, although he probably liked that too. He just lowered his head a bit and dove straight in. I can't remember, but my buddies told me I screamed like a girl. Bastards. I'd like to see what *they* do with a bull horn in their bum. I couldn't sit straight for months. Shitting was the pits. Still have a hole in my bum."

Jonathan sputtered over the last bite of the sandwich, then laughed. Ben grinned at him. Christ, he was beautiful when he laughed.

"Well, you know what I mean." Ben put the plate on the coffee table and grabbed Jonathan's coffee to hand it to him. He took the mug and sipped without argument or hesitation. Ben's grin widened, and he sighed in relief. When the mug was empty, he took it gently from Jonathan's fingers. "Good. You look much better already. Now go and get ready for bed while I clean the mess in the kitchen."

He stood, surprised to see Liam and Mark still standing there staring at him. Mark's mouth hung open a little. Ben wandered into the kitchen and began the cleanup, calling over his shoulder. "Go on, Jonathan. You need sleep now. There's nothing here that won't wait until tomorrow."

"Ben, why are you here?" Liam again. Same question.

Yeah, it didn't make sense to Ben either. He turned to look at Jonathan's cousin because that's what he'd always been taught was the right thing, no matter how much he wanted to hide his expression. "I don't know. He looked like he needed some help or a friend. Or both." He shrugged. "I just wanted to check on him, make sure he was okay." He gazed across the small apartment to the bathroom door. "I'll go now I know he's eaten something and will rest." He dug into his pocket and pulled out a receipt for groceries and a pencil stub, jotted his phone number on the paper, and set it carefully on the bench. "Tell him to call me if he wants some help unpacking tomorrow. There's a lot of heavy stuff he shouldn't be lifting with stitches in his chest, and tomorrow's my day off."

He didn't mention he'd have to skip classes to be there, but that wasn't their decision to make. He looked at the bathroom door again, but it remained resolutely shut. He suspected it would stay that way until after he left. Ben nodded to himself, gave Liam and Mark a halfhearted wave, then slipped from the apartment, closing the door softly behind him.

He leaned back against the door for a second and scrubbed his hands down his face. *You're a fool, Ben. Mum would clip you around the ear for the stunt you just pulled.* Chasing after a guy like that. It was wrong. It was blatantly obvious Jonathan had been in a bad place, recently too. Barging in like that could have ended in complete disaster. He was lucky to escape without them calling the cops. He wrinkled his nose at the smoke in the stairwell. One of the tenants must smoke pretty regularly for the smell to linger so much. It was stronger than it had been during the day.

"It's you, isn't it?"

Ben nearly pissed himself at the gravelly voice right in front of him. He lowered his hands and looked at the shriveled leathery face of a middle-aged woman. Smoke dribbled out of her nostrils and drifted under her chin, filling the crevasses in her unevenly hand-tanned neck before wafting around her head. Her gray eyes squinted through the smoke at him, an expression he assumed she had held for many years, judging by the crows' feet beside her eyes.

"It is!" she crowed and pushed her forearm under her breasts. The low-scooped neckline of her shirt showed the perfectly rounded orbs of her freckled breasts as they bulged out from the overtanned, overstretched skin of her chest. "You're the handsome removalist. I watched you this afternoon, you know." Her gaze slid down Ben's body, pausing greasily at his groin and thighs before it slipped back to his face. "You've got the most biteable arse I've seen in a long time."

She took a step toward him. He had nowhere to go with the door at his back, so he stepped sideways and began to sidle around her. "Oh, hi. Um, yeah, we were busy this afternoon and wouldn't have had time to talk or anything." Christ, he needed to keep his mouth shut. Now she was going to think he wanted to talk to her.

A chuckle bubbled in her throat but quickly turned into a liquid cough. She waved the cigarette in front of her face as if that would make her breathe easier. Amazingly it worked. "That's okay, gorgeous. I didn't mind watching you go up and down those stairs at all." Her gaze slid over Ben again, and he barely managed to stop cupping his hands over his cock in defense. "Oh, aren't you sweet. My third husband, Brian-who's-now-Brianna, was just like that when I met him—her now. He was incredibly shy with me to start with. Wait till I tell her all about you tomorrow morning. It's our morning for coffee tomorrow. We still love each other, you know, but when she cut her dick off, I couldn't do it anymore, you know. It just wasn't the same. We're better as friends, don't you think? Of course, if I was still with him—her—I would never have married Kevin-the-drunk-man-whore." She shrugged and turned to keep Ben in her sights as he stepped sideways some more, toward the stairs. The smoke cloud moved with her, a living haze around her head. It made him think of Charlie Brown and Pigpen. She jiggled her breasts again. "He might have appreciated these and had a working dick, but he lent it out to everybody, if you know what I mean—*everybody*. You wouldn't believe the things I caught from that man."

Ben stumbled as he reached the top step.

"Oh, you don't need to worry. It wasn't nothing that wasn't cured with a few shots in the arse. Coulda been, though. That's why I kicked him out. I gotta look after my health." She dragged her cigarette-holding hand through her stringy bleach-blonde hair, scratched a pale mole on the side of her neck, and hacked a solid-phlegm cough.

Ben didn't think people like her existed.

"Are you coming back tomorrow? I know you've probably finished the moving and that, but being here now, I figure you're a friend of his. I met the cousin last week when he took the place. He seems like a right sweetheart too. Queer as folk, you know, but I'll bet with an arse like that, he can dance. I'll get him to take me down to the club one weekend."

He couldn't help it. Honest. He tried, but the image of serious Liam dancing with this woman blew him away. The laughter bubbled up and exploded. She grinned at him.

"There you go, then. I knew you'd see it soon. I'll go and have a chat to Tahlia. She's been cooking up a storm, you know, as a 'welcome to the building' thing. She'll make extra for you, seeing as how you have a sense of humor and all."

Ben stopped his bid for escape and held out his hand. "I'm Ben Urquhart. I don't know what it is, but you remind be a bit of my favorite aunt back home."

"Where's home, love?"

"Mount Isa."

"Ooh, I'll bet there are a lot of men with nice arses in the mine up there." Her gray eyes glowed.

He chuckled. "There certainly are."

"Okay, Ben. You obviously want to head on out. You come back tomorrow. Tahlia will be disappointed if you don't, seeing as how she's dirtied every pot and pan she owns just to welcome you all to the building. I'm Neridah, by the way. Neridah Ryder."

"Nice to meet you, Neridah." He didn't promise to come back tomorrow. That would have taken more balls than even he had, especially after he'd basically stalked Jonathan already. Neridah didn't need to know that, though, and Tahlia, whoever she was, could still give all the food she'd made to Jonathan. He could certainly do with someone looking after him for a while.

He jogged down the stairs. All in all it hadn't been a bad day. Jonathan hadn't slammed the door in his face and had let him feed him, and the crazy neighbor seemed to like him, although he wasn't sure what sort of recommendation that was.

His smile lingered all the way home.

JONATHAN STOOD beside the bed, staring down at the new cover, confused. Liam knocked on the door and came into the bedroom.

"Jonathan?"

Jonathan looked up at him. "What just happened here?"

Liam chuckled. "I have no idea, but whatever it was, at least you've eaten something and can sleep now."

Jonathan turned in a confused circle. "But there's still so much to do."

"Nothing that won't wait until tomorrow. Mum and Dad said they'd come over in the morning and help put things away." He walked over to Jonathan and put his arm around his shoulders. "You don't have to do this on your own. We're here for you, whenever you need us."

Jonathan shifted out of the hold, needing now, more than ever, to stand up for himself. "I have to do this on my own, Liam. How else am I going to learn how to rely on myself? I have to work out who I am now, and I have to build my own life."

"You will, but you have your family to help you." Liam reached around Jonathan and pulled the covers back. "Now get into bed and get some sleep. I'll drop in tomorrow before my shift, and Mum and Dad will be here straight after."

Part of Jonathan didn't want Liam to leave, but if he was ever going to make a life for himself, he had to start getting used to being on his own. "Is Mark waiting for you?"

Liam's face lit with a wide smile. "He is. Make sure you call me if you need anything. Any time."

Jonathan nodded as he pulled the covers up to his chest. "I'll be fine. Go and find somewhere more private to be with Mark." Liam started, and Jonathan chuckled sleepily. "What? This place isn't so large you can't hear conversations from one end to the other. Now go. Enjoy."

JONATHAN STUMBLED into the kitchen just after five in the morning, disoriented. Nothing was where it was supposed to be, not even the window in his bedroom. Neither was the coffee. He scowled as he flicked the light on, then opened and closed cupboards looking for it. Then, in desperation, he opened the freezer to find the canister sitting comfortably in the door.

"Who the hell hides the coffee in the freezer?" he grumbled as he scooped some into the coffee maker. "Liam wouldn't." Then it dawned on him. Ben had said he'd tidy the kitchen after he'd made Jonathan the sandwich. He probably put it there. "Stupid place to keep something you use all the time."

Finding mugs and teaspoons was easier, and he quickly assembled everything before leaning against the counter and waiting for the coffeemaker to finish. In the middle of the counter was a small sales slip, the scrap of paper an incongruous untidiness on the spotless countertop. Jonathan crumpled it to throw it out before he paused. Liam probably left it there for a reason. He smoothed the paper out and examined it. Chicken breasts, shallots, and shitake mushrooms. "What the hell are shitake mushrooms?" He was about to crumple the paper again when he noticed the neat writing down the edge.

"Ben" and a phone number were printed in neat round letters, all exactly the same height and width. If it wasn't for the fact it was obviously written in pencil, he could almost be looking at a printed document. His hands trembled. "He left his number." Why would Ben leave his number? He placed the paper back on the counter and backed away from it, then stepped forward, snatched it up, and turned to toss it in the bin. Instead of letting the paper fall, he opened the cutlery drawer, dropped the receipt on top of the teaspoons, and slammed the drawer shut so he didn't have to look at it.

Ben knew where Jonathan lived. Why not just show up again like he did the day before? Jonathan shivered at the thought of Ben turning up wherever he was, even in his home. He looked around the small apartment. It wasn't home yet, but it was going to be, and Jonathan knew he wouldn't feel that way if people started knocking on the door uninvited. At least with Ben's number, Jonathan had the choice to not call him. A niggling voice in his head said he'd also have the contact information to give to the police if he needed to.

Noise intruded from the hall outside. Jonathan checked the peephole, but no one was there, so he opened the door. The sound of arguing came from another apartment on his floor. Jonathan recognized the tone, even if he couldn't make out the words. Bile rose in his throat, and he had to lean against the door jamb to wait for his head to stop spinning. The argument continued, hovering over Jonathan like oily smoke, seeped into his ears and filled his head with heart-thumping fear. The man wanted something done the "right" way, and the woman insisted it was already done. There was a thump and silence; then the yelling started again, but this time it was different. This time she was angrily capitulating with his demands. There was no reason to believe the man had hit the woman in 4C, but if he hadn't this time, Jonathan knew it was only a matter of time. He'd heard exactly the same types of arguments before. Hell, he'd lived them.

He wanted to go to their door and thump on it until it opened. He wanted to tell the woman she didn't have to accept being treated like that. He took a step outside, then stopped. If anyone had said anything like that to him when he was with Anthony, he'd have told them to mind their own business. Hell, he'd spent years telling Liam it was "nothing." He hadn't wanted to hear what everyone could see so clearly. The woman in 4C probably didn't either. He stepped back into his apartment and locked the door again, resolved to make sure the woman knew he would help if she needed it. There wasn't much else he could do.

In the hallway, a door slammed and heavy footfalls trod down the stairs and away.

Jonathan picked his coffee up to take a sip and jumped, nearly dropping the mug, when the phone rang, the sound startling in the quiet of the morning. Scalding coffee soaked through his T-shirt and made him gasp. He slammed the mug down on the counter, lifted his shirt away from his skin, and dove along the counter for his phone.

"Who the hell would be ringing at this hour?" His breath caught. Ben. He knew it was Ben. God, was he going to gain a stalker before he'd even got rid of the bastard who'd ruled his life for the last ten years? Thumb hovering over the disconnect button, Jonathan made himself look at the caller ID displayed on the screen.

"Liam. Thank God." He swallowed the small disappointment as he shifted his thumb and answered the phone. "Liam. What's wrong? Why are you calling so early?"

"Oh, sorry, I didn't realize the time. Just wanted to check in to make sure you're okay."

"It's not even six o'clock. Did they change your shift at the hospital?"

"No, I was just up and wondered how you were settling in."

"I repeat, it's not even six o'clock. There's no settling to be done yet—not until I've woken up properly and had at least one cup of coffee."

"I can come over and give you a hand."

"I thought Mark was staying with you last night."

"He did."

"And? Where is he now?"

"He's asleep, of course."

"Where you should be. I'm fine, Liam. I'm going to rummage through a few boxes today and rest a lot, just like the doctor ordered. Your mum and dad will be over before lunch, remember? You don't need to check on me every five minutes. Now go back to your man and wake him up *properly*."

"Are you sure…?"

"Very sure. I'll call you later today and let you know how I'm getting on, okay? I won't be going out. I have plenty of food, plenty to keep me busy, and plenty of opportunity to rest. You don't need to worry about me."

"But—"

"Go back to Mark, Liam. Bye." Jonathan pressed the disconnect button and tossed his phone on the counter before picking up what was left of his coffee. He put it down again with a groan, then stomped into his bedroom and changed his shirt. After moving all day yesterday and now the coffee on his shirt, he'd have to wash so the bathroom didn't begin to smell like an alley behind a gym. The last thing he wanted to do with all his aches and pains, some from his injury and some from the move, was laundry. By the time he returned to the kitchen, his coffee was cold and he had to start again.

He drummed his fingers against the counter as he waited for the coffee to filter through.

"Ah," he sighed. He put his mouth to the edge of the mug, enjoying the fragrant steam wafting over his face, and—tipped it down his front when the doorbell rang. "Fuck!" He slammed the mug down on the counter and cringed when the china cracked and hot coffee leaked from the bottom. He ripped his soaked shirt off, gasping as his wound tugged. He tossed the shirt on the floor and rubbed his burning chest before checking to ensure the dressing hadn't been soaked too.

How the hell did Liam get here so fast? I told him not to come over. He strode to the door and flung it open. "You should have given Mark a blow job instead of—" *Fuck.*

A short, slim woman stood in front of him. Her dark hair floated around her in a twisted cloud that concealed half her face. Faded blue eyes gleamed up at him. Her gaze flickered over his bare chest, and a rosy hue infused her cheeks. She lifted up a triple-decker Tupperware container. "Hello. I thought you might like some croissants for breakfast. I made them myself."

Jonathan shivered as she spoke. She wasn't angry or frightened now, but she was definitely the woman he'd heard in 4C. His gaze traveled over her, but he couldn't see any bruises and she moved easily.

She pointed to the middle container. "There's cheese too. I made that last month. And there's some ham as well"—her finger moved to the top container—"I didn't make that. I bought it at the deli over on Ramsay. I also put in a small container of mango chutney from last season." She pushed the containers toward Jonathan, and he had no option but to take them from her.

"Oh, um, thank you, and I'm sorry for—for—"

"Oh no, it's nothing. I'm Tahlia Ross from 4C. Neridah met your friend Ben yesterday. I watched him from my window while the fruitcake was in the oven. He was very organized with the move, wasn't he, and kind to come and help again last night?"

"Good morning, Tahlia. I'm Jonathan Watson." *Does the woman know it's barely six o'clock and most sensible people would still be in bed and not baking croissants and delivering them to neighbors? Is that how she deals with the fighting?*

"Yes, I know. I asked the man who helped Ben yesterday. Mr. Anderson was lovely, but I hope his family is keeping an eye on him. I think there's something missing there, if you know what I mean." Her gaze slid down his chest again, barely pausing at the bandage before focusing squarely on his abdomen. With his hands full, Jonathan had no way of covering himself except to hold the containers a little lower. "Make sure you eat a full breakfast. Moving is hard on you, and I know you still have a lot to do today." Tahlia stepped back and gestured down the hall toward the open door of apartment 4C. "I have bread rising for lunch, so I'll get back to that. There's a vanilla slice for morning tea. My great-uncle brought the recipe back from the Great War. Of course it's the French version—the original one—not the Italian one. The Italian one only has one layer."

Finally she seemed to run out of steam, but Jonathan wasn't game to take a breath in relief for fear she'd start up again.

"Thank you, Tahlia." He held the containers aloft. "I'll just go in and have breakfast, then."

She beamed at him, her hair bouncing with the effort. "I hope you enjoy it. And make sure you eat enough. You're very thin. Kyle eats a lot, but he's twice your size—" She stuttered to a stop. "I mean, not that he's fat or anything. He's really muscular but big, you know." Tahlia clamped her mouth closed and inhaled deeply before continuing with a sunny smile that didn't reach her eyes. "I'll bring morning tea over around half ten. Neridah will be up by then. You don't need to worry about anything except getting yourself settled." She strode down the hallway as she spoke, the hem of her long floral skirt flipping against her calves with every step.

Morning tea? Neridah? And Tahlia had thrown him so much, he hadn't offered to help *her*. Maybe it wasn't the way he'd thought it sounded. It was probably just a normal argument—he wouldn't know how to recognize normal anymore.

Jonathan stepped back and carefully closed the door. Then he threw the deadlocks closed as well. What the hell kind of... hell had Liam found for him?

Chapter FOUR

JONATHAN SAT on the floor and opened another box labeled "kitchen." Inside he found a hodgepodge of china, glassware, and cutlery. "Why the hell...." Jonathan suddenly remembered taking everything that was in the dishwasher and jamming it into a box with tea towels haphazardly wrapped around the more delicate items. He carefully lifted each item out, and winced when a glass collapsed in his grip.

In all, three glasses and one plate were broken, but Jonathan thought he'd got out of it easy considering the way he'd packed it. He grabbed the bundle of cutlery and stood to add it to the drawer with the rest. It came straight from the dishwasher, so he wasn't going to be bothered washing it again.

The crumpled receipt with Ben's number on it caught his eye as soon as he opened the drawer. He snatched it up and shoved it into his pocket with his phone. If Aunty Faye found that, he'd never hear the end of it. A knock sounded at the door as he dropped the last of the cutlery in its place.

"I thought there was a bloody dead bolt on the front door. How the hell does everyone make it up to the third floor and to my door without buzzing me?" He threw open the door, ready to blast whoever it was, but gulped his words back instead.

His Aunty Faye smiled at him, her tight blonde curls bouncing as she bustled forward and drew him into a careful hug. He bent over to wrap his arms around the diminutive woman who'd been mother to him since he was ten.

"Oh, baby, I'm so glad you're okay. You're looking much better than last time we saw you." As she spoke, Faye walked forward, effectively pushing Jonathan back into the apartment. Behind her came Uncle Bruce.

"Come on, Faye, let the boy go so we can get inside and start work. You don't need to smother him."

Jonathan stepped back out of Faye's arms and steeled himself for Bruce. Sure enough, as soon as Faye moved aside, Bruce enveloped Jonathan in a bear hug. "It's good to see you home, son." He sniffed and stepped back. "Now what can we do to help you get settled?"

"Oh, Jonathan, surely this isn't the best Liam could find for you." Faye turned in a slow circle in the middle of the living room, taking in the small kitchen and short hallway to the only bedroom and bathroom.

"It has everything I need, Aunty Faye. I don't need a lot of room and, until I find a job, I'm not going to be able to afford a larger place."

"That's nonsense. After ten years with that man, surely you're entitled to half of what's in the bank accounts, at least. And if not, then we'll help you." She spun in a circle again. "You can't stay here."

Jonathan turned imploring eyes to Bruce, who stepped forward.

"Now, Faye, you leave the boy alone. He's just come out of hospital and out of a bad relationship." *Thanks, Uncle Bruce, for that reminder.* "He probably wants somewhere small and cozy for a while." *Dear God, could they make him seem any more pathetic?*

Faye glared at Bruce, whose black gaze, so similar to Liam's, stared steadily back. Eventually she sighed and flapped her hands at her sides.

"All right, all right, I'll back off." She pointed an accusing finger to Jonathan. "But you're not allowed to mope forever, and the minute you think you want something a little larger than this, you let me know."

Jonathan had been naïve to think the rest of the morning would be filled with quiet busyness, the three of them unpacking and putting things away with familial harmony. Faye took over the kitchen, rearranging everything he'd already put away so that it was in the "right" place. Bruce began opening the boxes in the living room and was currently filling the bookcase with Jonathan's books and the few ornaments he had brought from his… Anthony's place.

"You don't have to do this. I can put everything away once I find a place for it."

"Don't be silly, baby. You're injured, and we love doing this for you. I'll make sure everything is in the right place so you can find it easily when you need it." Faye took a stack of plates out of one cupboard and put them into another. Jonathan looked to Bruce but received only a shrug before his uncle emptied another full box onto the kitchen bench for Faye to find the "right" place for the contents.

Jonathan opened and closed his mouth a few times to stop her, but she looked so happy to be helping him, he snapped it shut and retreated to his bedroom. At least there he could choose where things were to go without Faye telling him it was the wrong place or Bruce insisting he should be the one to do the work.

It only took so long to hang his clothes up and fill the drawers, but he sat on the bed and stared at the shadows on the floor rather than go back into the main part of the apartment. Their familiar and comfortable bickering soothed him, and by the time the doorbell rang, he thought he was ready to be around people again.

"I'll get it," he called as he strode from the bedroom, forestalling Bruce's headlong dash for the door ahead of Faye. They both stopped in startled comprehension that this wasn't their home and their competitive rush to see who was at the door wasn't needed.

"Hello, Jonathan," said Tahlia. The heavenly scent of freshly baked bread assaulted Jonathan's senses, and his mouth watered. "I made some cinnamon scrolls to go with the vanilla slice for morning tea." She took a step forward, forcing Jonathan to give ground. As she crossed the threshold, she said, "Have you met Neridah from 1C?"

Neridah followed Tahlia into the apartment and immediately went to Faye. "Oh good, you found your way up all right, then." She looked over the small dining table nestled between the coffee table and the kitchen bench. "How about we clear this off, then we can have a nice chat over Tahlia's buns." She picked up a box from the table and gave it to Bruce with a wink. "Put that somewhere, will you, love? Tahlia, you put the kettle on for us and grab some plates. We'll have this ready in a jiffy."

Jonathan stood near the bookcase and watched the four people in his apartment introduce themselves, then bustle around each other as they readied the small space for what could only be considered a tea party. *They work well together*, he mused, like they'd been doing the same thing for years and each now knew their role. How would they react if he suggested they do it somewhere else? He was getting twitchy, and there was nowhere he could settle to find the quiet peace he needed. His apartment and his life had been invaded.

"So you're our Jonathan's parents, then?" asked Neridah.

"Now we are," said Faye. "We're his aunt and uncle, but he's been with us since his parents were killed."

Jonathan winced at the familiar look of devastation that entered her eyes as she said that. It wasn't only his parents who had died in that car. Faye and Bruce had lost their youngest son too. Jonathan imagined he could still hear the snap of Dom's neck as the car rolled and the roof slammed into his cousin's head. He touched the side of his face, where he could still feel the slide of metal as the roof of the car collapsed in. A graze had been all Jonathan had to show for the force of the metal that destroyed his family. He was the only one who'd survived.

There'd been so much grief and so many "if onlys" from everyone around him, he knew he was being punished for something he'd done or not done. There was no other reason for them to leave him.

"Come on, Jonathan, you can't stand there all day," said Tahlia. "Sit down and I'll bring you a cinnamon scroll. Neridah's made the tea, so you just help yourself to that. Oh yes, that's perfect," she said as she surveyed the table Faye had set.

Jonathan stood in the entrance to the short hall leading to the bedroom and bathroom, reluctant to take even one step forward to accept this invasion. The idle social chitchat they'd already begun had no meaning in the world he knew. It wouldn't help Jonathan at all. He needed to get his life sorted so he could work out where he was going from here, what he was going to do with his life now he wasn't part of a couple. The last two years had been so terrible and so busy caring for Anthony, Jonathan had no idea who he even was anymore. He didn't know how he was going to find that out, but he knew it wouldn't happen while sitting down to tea and buns with his parents and neighbors.

"I'll be just a few minutes. I want to go down and start this load of washing." He'd seen a sign to the laundry downstairs on the ground floor when he'd arrived yesterday afternoon, so he grabbed his laundry hamper and quickly let himself out of the flat before Aunty Faye could finish her sentence.

"Jonathan. Are you sure you should—"

He closed the door, leaving four startled faces behind. Footsteps came close to his door. Jonathan gripped his laundry hamper and ran down the stairs before anyone came out to see what was happening.

Doing boring laundry at least calmed Jonathan's breathing and eased the squeamish trembling in his stomach. The noise of the machines crowded out other sounds until even his thoughts were calm. Usually Jonathan put his clothes in the washer or dryer, then left them to retrieve later, but the only place he could go right then was back to his apartment. With his meddling aunt and uncle and strange neighbors. He stuck it out until the first load was switched into the dryer; then he trudged back upstairs. The hallway was silent. He opened his door and stepped inside.

"There you are. I told Bruce you wouldn't be avoiding us." His aunt bustled over to him and led him to the heavily laden table. "Look what Tahlia brought with her."

"I thought it was just the cinnamon buns," he said weakly. He was sure the table groaned under the weight.

"It was, but then I started talking to Faye and realized she liked the same foods I did, and since I've been baking all morning, I thought I'd just run back and bring a few things over for you all to try. Don't think you have to eat it all." Her hopeful expression belied her words.

Jonathan slumped into his seat and watched as Aunty Faye and Tahlia placed items on his plate until it was piled high. He smiled weakly at them, knowing he'd never be able to eat this much but not sure how to get out of it without hurting their feelings. He picked up a small pink muffin and took a bite. The groan of delight that swept through him took him by surprise. *My God, what did she do to make them taste like this?* He looked up to see Tahlia beaming at him.

"Do you like that? I hoped you would. You look like a raspberry and white chocolate kind of person. I think the extra cream in it makes the flavors explode in your mouth. It's so much richer."

He nodded at her as he took another bite. This was divine. He wanted to reach for another one, but his plate was full of so many other things, it would seem rude not to try them too.

Half an hour later, his stomach was about to burst. He leaned back in his chair and contemplated how difficult it would be to continue with the work still needing to be done. Across the table, Tahlia sighed happily as she stood up.

"I'll just start getting lunch together, then. Neridah, would you pack all this up? It'll be good for afternoon tea." She smiled at everyone, then rushed from the apartment and down the hall to her door.

Lunch? Jonathan glanced at his watch. It was nearly midday now. When was she planning on lunch? And how did she expect anyone to eat anything else after all the food they'd just eaten?

"I'll just…." He didn't know how to finish the sentence in the face of his aunt's and uncle's curious expressions, so he fled to his room and shut the door. "Crap. There's no way I'm going to get anything done today." He burped. "God, lunch. No way." He flopped down on the bed, wincing as his stitches pulled at the swift movement. How was he going to get out of this? He'd hurt their feelings if he told them to go home. He shifted on the bed, the sound of crinkling paper distracting him from his thoughts. He twisted and shoved his hand into his pocket to pull out the paper.

A grocery receipt. He hadn't been shopping. *Ah.* He looked at the number on it. What would happen if he rang Ben? The man had offered to help him move. Would he consider giving him an avenue of escape? Jonathan grabbed his phone and entered the number. His stomach churned, but not from all the sweet food he'd consumed. His breathing increased, his heart raced, his fingers trembled. He knew what that was. He was scared. Terrified. Of a man he didn't know.

No, that wasn't right. He was scared what had happened with Anthony would happen with Ben, but when he was with Ben, he'd felt safe. Except for at the beginning, when Ben went to clap him on the shoulder. And when he'd knocked on the car window. Those times weren't about Ben being violent, though. That was Jonathan reacting because of Anthony. Ben had never threatened him and had been nothing but kind and calm. He'd treated Col well too. Jonathan sucked in a deep breath and hit Send. He focused on calming his breathing as he listened to the phone ring. He was just about to hang up when Ben answered.

"Hi, sorry, I was in class. It's Ben here."

Of course, Ben didn't know Jonathan was at the other end of the line. He could hang up now and the other man would be none the wiser. Jonathan could stay safe.

"Hello?"

He couldn't just hang up. That was rude. He opened his mouth to speak, but instead of a word, the only sound that came out was a squeak.

"Hello? Who is this?"

"Jo-Jonathan," he whispered.

"Jonathan?"

Oh God, Ben didn't remember him. He'd made a complete fool of himself. But still he didn't hang up.

"Jonathan Watson."

"I know who you are, Jonathan. Are you all right? You sound funny."

"Oh." He cleared his throat. "No, I'm fine. I just…." He was lame. Totally lame and probably coming across as pathetic and needy and… lame.

"Are you all right? What's wrong? Are you hurt?" Ben's voice changed and the odd echoey sound of his voice stopped. His breathing changed too. He was running. "Are you home? I'm coming now."

Jonathan sat up and met his shocked face in the mirror above his dresser. Ben thought he was hurt, and he was coming to him. His lips spread into a totally ridiculous and unexplainable smile. "I'm fine. There's nothing wrong."

The pounding footsteps over the phone slowed but didn't stop. "You're sure you're okay?"

"Yes."

A sigh. "Good. I'm glad." The footsteps stopped, and Ben's breathing began evening out. "So…."

Oh yeah. Jonathan had rung him, and Ben was wondering why. "I'm sorry. I didn't mean to interrupt what you were doing."

"I told you I could help you if you needed it, remember? Is that what you need? Is one of the heavier pieces in the wrong place? I can come over and move it for you." Jonathan heard a thud, then a beep and a car door being opened. A few seconds later, the car door *thunk*ed closed, cutting off all the outside noises.

"No, everything's fine." God, how could he say he was feeling smothered by his family and neighbors and needed to escape? Why didn't he just get in the car and drive away if he needed to escape so badly? Oh yeah, the whole not being able to drive thing. He'd ignored it yesterday and was still feeling bruised and battered enough that he wasn't going to ignore it again. He wasn't an idiot. "It's just that…."

"Jonathan, honey, did you know there are several glasses missing out of your set? I'll start a list for things you need to replace. Oh, sorry,

I didn't realize you were on the phone. Who are you talking to, dear?" Faye's eyes narrowed in concern.

"It's a friend of mine." He sighed as her lips firmed in disbelief. "It's not Anthony, Aunty Faye. I promise."

"A friend?"

"I'll be out in a minute, Aunty Faye," he said firmly. Apart from not wanting to talk about this now, it was rude to have a conversation with someone when he was on the phone with someone else.

"Of course, honey. I'll be just out here."

Great. Now she was going to hover outside his bedroom door to make sure he was safe. He loved his family, but sometimes they smothered him.

"Sorry, Ben," he said on a sigh. "Look, I'm sorry I disturbed you. This was obviously not a very good idea. I just—"

"You just wanted someone to take you away from your loving family for a while." The rumble of a car engine had replaced the silence of before.

He huffed a laugh. "Something like that." *Exactly like that.*

"Well, I'm your man. I'll be there in about fifteen minutes. That'll give you time to think of an excuse that will satisfy your family."

"Excuse?"

"From what I just heard, your aunt is a bit protective of you. She's going to want to know where you're going with a man she's never met before."

"Shit."

Ben laughed. "I always tell my mother I'm going out to buy condoms. That stops any questions she might have."

Jonathan sputtered. "I can't tell them that! I've only just... I'm not looking for.... God, I can't even think straight after that."

"You have about twelve minutes to work it out, babe. I'll leave it up to you if you want to meet me out front or introduce me to the family." The connection cut off, leaving Jonathan in the silence of his indecision.

He dropped the phone onto the bed and scrubbed his hands over his face. "God, what have I done?" He jolted upright, hissing at the pain but otherwise ignoring it. "He's coming here. Now." He strode to his dresser and flung open the top drawer. "God, what am I going to wear?" He grabbed clothes he'd only just put into the drawers onto the bed, discarding each item as he shook it out. He swore and flung clothes.

"Jonathan?" Aunty Faye stood tentatively in the doorway, watching his frantic clothes-tossing with wide eyes.

"Faye! What am I going to wear?" God, he was panicking. He threw himself back onto the bed and covered his face. "God, I'm going mad." He shot to his feet. "He's going to be here in ten minutes." He grabbed a pair of jeans and the first T-shirt his hand landed on, then strode to the bathroom. When he emerged, Faye was gone. He shoved his wallet and keys into his pockets, grabbed his sunglasses, and rushed into the living room, hoping he was quick enough to get downstairs before Ben arrived. He stopped short at the end of the hallway when he heard his aunt's lilting laugh. "Crap." He took a hesitant step forward into the living room.

"There you are, Jonathan. Ben's just been telling us what you have planned for the afternoon. You didn't tell us you wanted to see that new Marvel movie."

"Oh." He looked frantically at Ben, who smiled serenely back at him. "Is that the one we're going to see?" he asked weakly.

Ben checked his watch. "Yep, and we'd better hurry if we want to make the next showing." He turned back to Jonathan's aunt and uncle. "It was nice to meet you, Mr. and Mrs. Watson." He nodded at Neridah, who was still packing the leftovers from morning tea. "Neridah." They all beamed at Ben.

Jonathan followed Ben to the door. "Jonathan?" his aunt called. He turned back and met her suddenly serious gaze. "Call if you need us."

He sucked in a breath against the sudden tightness in his chest and nodded.

As he turned away, she spoke again. "Oh, don't forget we're leaving tomorrow. It'll probably be a few days before you can contact us, but Liam's there if you need him."

Jonathan walked back to his aunt. She came into his open arms, and he held her close. "I love you, Aunty Faye."

"I love you too, honey." She pushed back from him and smiled tremulously. "Have a good time. We'll get this sorted for you, then head on home."

They were on the landing with the echo of the door closing behind them before Jonathan made another conscious decision. His feet stalled and his heart rate increased. He'd lost control of his life. He'd had one night. Just one night when he thought he'd taken charge again, but it was all an illusion. His family had taken over his apartment, his neighbors had taken over his eating habits and—he scowled at Ben— he'd handed control of his social life to a stranger.

Chapter FIVE

THEY DROVE in uncomfortable silence. Jonathan fidgeted in his seat, hating that he was using Ben to escape his family and neighbors. He should have a deeper reason for wanting to spend time with the blond man, but he probably wouldn't recognize it if he tripped over it. Since Anthony, his emotional responses were shot. The trembly churning in his gut was probably nothing more than indigestion after eating so much at morning tea. Once upon a time, he'd thought that feeling was attraction.

Ben pulled into a parking spot around the corner from the suburban theatre. He turned off the car but didn't move. "We don't have to do this if you don't want to," he muttered.

Jonathan jumped, his twisting, nervous hands finally separating. "Oh God, I'm sorry. You don't want to be here. I didn't mean to—"

"Stop." Jonathan jumped again at Ben's firm command. "I wouldn't be here if I didn't want to be, but it's obvious you're not comfortable."

"I'm sorry." Jonathan cringed as yet another apology escaped him. "I don't know how to do this."

"Do what?"

He flapped his hands. "I don't know! I don't know what I'm doing."

"You're going to the movies with a new friend." Ben's voice sounded just like a vet's "calm panicked animals" voice. Jonathan sat in silence as Ben got out of the car, more sure than ever that this was a monumentally bad idea. He jumped when Ben opened the passenger door and waited while Jonathan stood and moved away from the car; then he locked it and led the way into the theatre.

"Is that what you are?" Jonathan asked tentatively as they waited to buy tickets.

"A friend? I'd like to be."

"Just friends? Nothing else?" *More than friends* was dangerous. He hoped he hid the emotion in his voice. He couldn't tell if he felt wistfulness, longing, or relief. Whatever it was, it was enough to want to stay near Ben and hope Ben felt the same.

Ben grinned at him.

"Friends," he whispered as he poured himself a large blue Slurpee to drink during the movie.

There was just one problem. It had been so long since Jonathan had a friend, he didn't know what to do or what to say.

The movie was a good idea. There were enough explosions that he could ignore everything swirling through his mind and enjoy being entertained for an hour and a half. Ben was a fun companion. Most people just sat and allowed the movie to entertain them. Not Ben. He was a fully involved participant, jumping if an explosion shocked him, laughing out loud when something funny was said, and slapping Jonathan's thigh when he was thrilled that something he knew from the comics was recreated on screen or some dialogue brought in a character from another movie. He was totally connected. By the third light slap, Jonathan's heartbeat had settled, and he'd begun to think the small touches were normal—almost.

At the end of the movie, they blinked their way back onto the bright footpath and headed to the car.

"You want lunch or something?" asked Ben. It was after two o'clock.

"God, no. I'm still stuffed from morning tea." Jonathan walked a few steps, then turned back, guilt churning his stomach. "You haven't eaten, have you? God, I'm sorry. That was really thoughtless. Where would you like to go for lunch?"

"Why do you always apologize?" Ben snapped his lips closed at the end of the question as if he hadn't meant to ask.

"Oh." Jonathan took a small step back, stricken. He'd had a new friend for less than two hours, and he'd already done something stupid. This wasn't going to work. Anthony was right. No one could possibly want him. "I'm sorry," he whispered before he turned and raced down the street.

"Jonathan!"

He was an idiot. Ben's footsteps slapped the pavement behind him. Jonathan increased his speed. So did Ben.

"Jonathan! Wait!"

Jonathan slowed, feeling ridiculous for running like that, but he couldn't make himself stop. Ben's footsteps slowed too. "Jonathan!"

They ran down the street. Jonathan pressed his hand against his dressing, holding his wound as still as possible. Ben's truck was left way behind, and they'd have to go back to it before going home. If it was any other situation, Jonathan would be laughing his head off. Ben chasing him was different to the way Anthony had pursued him. Anthony always punctuated his pursuits with insults and punches. Not Ben.

"If I'd known you wanted some crazy-ass exercise after the movie, I'd have worn joggers instead of boots," he called from behind.

Nope. He couldn't hold it in. He laughed.

Ben called him again. "Hey, wait up. I don't want to run to the bloody Gold Coast or somewhere."

Jonathan stumbled and looked behind him, smiling. Ben grinned at him. Jonathan tripped again and landed on his ass on the concrete sidewalk, gasping at the sharp pain when his wound tugged.

Ben ran to catch up, no longer smiling. "Are you okay?" he asked.

Jonathan flinched as Ben dropped to his knees beside him and froze, hand out, nearly touching. "Are you hurt anywhere?"

Jonathan huffed. "Just my bum." He ignored the burn that shot through his wound at the impact. He rolled and pushed himself to his feet, groaning as he rose. He rubbed his buttock. "Crap. That's going to bruise."

"What about your stitches?" Ben indicated Jonathan's chest.

Jonathan checked his shirt. There were no telltale red stains on it. He pressed his hand over one side of his chest, frowning at the heat and the pull. It ached like a bitch but wasn't stinging like it had when he'd torn the stitches. "I think it's okay."

"Move your shirt out of the way. I'll see if there's any blood."

Jonathan hesitated, then lifted his shirt, slowly exposing the expanse of his smooth dark skin.

Ben breathed deeply a few times, then gingerly lifted the corner of the dressing. His breath caught.

"What? It's not bleeding again, is it?" Jonathan's voice was higher than usual, half panicked.

"No, it looks fine." He pressed the edge of the dressing down and left his palm over it. "I just expected it to be bigger, you know, after all the blood yesterday." He paused, his hand still on Jonathan's chest. "It must be deep."

"Yeah," he said quietly.

Three heartbeats later, Jonathan stepped back and lowered his shirt.

Ben stared down the street back toward the theater. "You right to walk back to the truck?"

Jonathan didn't reply but turned and walked in the direction Ben indicated. Ben followed.

An impenetrable bubble of silence engulfed them as they walked back down the street toward where Ben was parked.

"I have enough food at my place to feed a small country, but if you want something to eat without Neridah or my family watching every bite, we could stop at a café or something." Jonathan didn't want to go home yet, but it seemed a waste to leave all that food uneaten.

After a long silence, Ben turned to Jonathan.

"What?" He clamped his mouth closed and considered running again, but dismissed it immediately. Ben would just follow like he had before. Damn, he'd said the wrong thing again.

"A café sounds good," said Ben. "There's one not far from here that does old-style burgers, with real meat and beetroot on the salad."

"You—I—you—" Ben couldn't really want to spend more time with him after the stunt he'd just pulled.

"Yep, you and I." Ben grinned. "At a café to eat food and drink coffee or whatever." He continued walking. "That's a great idea."

A sigh of relief escaped Jonathan before he could control it. "Good."

"You sound surprised."

Jonathan shifted, but he remained silent for a long time. Finally he decided to just say it. Ben was his friend—he checked his watch—of two hours and twenty minutes. If Jonathan wanted that to continue, he'd have to relax. "I'm not used to being able to suggest things."

A muscle in Ben's jaw jumped before he replied. "Suggest away. Just remember when I get this hungry, I head straight for the food. You'll have to hit me upside the head and make sure I don't forget to ask if you want something too." He stopped talking and swallowed.

That sounded… permanent. Jonathan's stomach flipped again. He couldn't do permanent. He glanced at Ben as they walked and was surprised by the look of consternation on his face. Perhaps Ben didn't do permanent either. That would be good, but he had to say something to lighten things up. What was it Ben said? Oh yeah….

"What about brain damage?"

"What?"

"If I'm always hitting you upside the head, you'll eventually suffer brain damage."

Ben burst out laughing, and he slapped his hand on his thigh. "Yeah, I'll have to do better if I'm going to avoid the brain damage." They reached Ben's truck, got in, and Ben drove into the light traffic. They were silent the short distance to the strip of shops where the café was, but Jonathan didn't mind. The sight of Ben's lingering smile brought an answering smile to his lips. Maybe he could do this friends thing after all.

Ben pulled into the small car park in front of the café. Jonathan turned to him when he didn't move to get out. He couldn't turn down the wattage of his smile at the look of happy anticipation on Ben's face. "Wait till you see these hamburgers. No way will you be able to resist."

Jonathan did resist the hamburger, but when Ben turned his plate so the chips were closer, he stole a few. He groaned at the flavor. "These are great. The note on the menu says they make their own garlic salt from dried garlic they grow themselves." Jonathan took another chip and enjoyed the contrast of crunchy outside around the perfectly cooked, fluffy potato. "The first time I ate chips was when I went to live with Faye and Bruce. They were frozen ones Faye cooked in the oven—nothing like this."

Ben looked surprised. "I thought Faye and Bruce were your parents," said Ben. "They treat you like a son."

Jonathan grinned. "Yeah, they do. Always have, I guess, even though I didn't make it easy for them."

"Really? You're so quiet and agreeable. I can't imagine you any other way."

Jonathan stared out the window at the heat shimmer above the cars outside. "I used to argue about everything." An echo of the devastation he felt at that time shivered down his spine. "I was so angry when my parents died."

"Now you're sad."

Jonathan returned his gaze to Ben. The need to talk to him, really talk, like deep-and-meaningful-bare-your-soul talk, bubbled up like indigestion. He brushed the salt off his hands and stood. "I can't—I'm just going to…." He fled.

The bathrooms were clean but tiny. Sweat beaded Jonathan's upper lip, and his fingers trembled under the stream of water. He stared at his reflection: the whites showed around his dark eyes. What was he thinking, to tell Ben all of that? That sort of soul-stripping exposure was exactly the kind of thing that scared brand-new friends off. Jonathan didn't have so many friends he could lose a new one.

He'd lost his last friend about two years after he moved in with Anthony. Ty had stuck around for a long time but eventually it had been easier, both for him and Jonathan, to stop trying. There'd only been his family since then, and contact with them had been sporadic in the last couple of years. Except for Liam. Liam had ignored all of Anthony's machinations and visited anyway.

Jonathan dried his hands and returned to find Ben waiting for him inside the café door.

"Okay?" he asked. "Panic over? You look like you're ready for a break."

Jonathan sighed as he followed Ben to the car. Ben was a steamroller too. Jonathan opened his mouth to release some of his exasperation, even if he sounded rude and ungrateful, when Ben spoke again.

"So what do you want to do? Are you ready to face your family again, or do you want to go for a drive around or something else?" He turned an earnest gaze to Jonathan. "We can do whatever you want."

Okay, not so much of a steamroller. Jonathan's chest felt full and tight. It had been a long time since someone had treated him like he was capable of making a decision for himself. Not even his aunt and uncle, who loved him like one of their own, gave him choices like that. He scrubbed his hands over his face, not that it made any difference.

His head was filled with white noise and he couldn't see through it. All he could hear in it was *Useless, useless, useless.*

He couldn't decide.

At all.

"Home," he whispered. "I want to go home." Even if he didn't know exactly where that was right now.

"No problem. Hey, did I tell you about the first time I drove anywhere here? Mount Isa is a pretty big town but it's still just a town, nothing like Brisbane with all its traffic lights and roundabouts and tunnels. I kept getting in the wrong lane over the Story Bridge and ended up at Wynnum about four times. I wanted to go south, not east. Even after I finally worked out which lane I needed, I took what my mum calls the 'scenic route.' It took me nearly two hours to travel about five kilometers…."

THEY STOPPED outside Jonathan's apartment building, and Jonathan realized his aunt and uncle were still there. He couldn't take Ben upstairs. His aunt would latch onto him and grill him. She'd have them engaged inside half an hour. He couldn't let that happen again. He'd introduced Anthony to them on the second date and moved in with him after the third, and Anthony had been a total disaster.

Jonathan flung the car door open and practically fell out. "Um, thanks for the movie and stuff." He leaned down into the half-closed door. "Bye." The door thudded when he pushed it and Jonathan scurried up the path and to his building.

"What the fuck?" Ben called out. Jonathan fumbled with his keys but eventually got the front door open. He went inside and locked it again, then peered out through the glass pane. He slumped against the wall when Ben drove away. They'd been having a good time—at least he had been—but it couldn't last. He waited in the silence of the foyer until his breathing eased and the ache of loneliness settled in his gut. Then he trudged upstairs to his aunt and uncle.

"THERE YOU are, honey. What movie did you go and see? It must have been a long one to be gone so long. I told Bruce you were fine and wouldn't be that long. You must be starving. That nice Tahlia from down the hall brought over the most amazing salmon quiche for lunch. I'll just get some for you and—"

"No, it's okay. We ate after the movie." And Jonathan hated quiche. Anthony always insisted on eating it for Sunday lunch.

"Oh, that's why you took so long." She turned toward Bruce. "That's why they took so long—they ate after the movie."

"Yes, dear. I heard." Bruce stood from his seat on the couch and fished his keys from his pocket. "Let's go."

"Go? But Jonathan just got home." She turned back to Jonathan. "You've only just got home from hospital, Jonathan." She flicked a look around the apartment. "Are you sure you're ready to start dating? Already?" She turned to her husband. "We haven't visited with him yet."

It wasn't the hospital stay that was bothering Faye. It was the fact that Jonathan had only just left Anthony. "It wasn't a date, Aunty Faye. We just went to a movie and ate afterwards." He trailed off at the end when he realized it might have been a date.

"I think you should give yourself time to get over Anthony, especially since he's been so awful to you."

Awful to me? The bastard stabbed me. He wanted to say it but he didn't. A decade of suppressing his opinion and never saying what he was thinking was difficult to break. Jonathan stepped away from his aunt.

"Come on, Faye," said Uncle Bruce. "It's time we went home and left Jonathan to settle in properly."

"Is he coming over tonight? Is that why you want us to leave?"

"I haven't asked you to leave, Faye, and no, he's not coming over."

"That's good. I really think you should take some time, Jonathan."

"Faye." Warning threaded through Bruce's voice. *Thank you, Uncle Bruce, for trying*, but Jonathan knew it wouldn't work.

"We haven't visited with him yet, Bruce. Don't you want to—"

"We spent all morning with him, Faye. We can come back after our holiday and visit again. He's fine." Bruce raised his eyebrows at Jonathan until he nodded. He grabbed Faye's handbag from the couch, gripped her at the elbow, and strong-armed her from the apartment.

Jonathan dropped bonelessly onto the couch and scrubbed his hands over his face. He loved his family, he really did, but they were all so bloody protective of him, he never had a chance to make a decision for himself. Just like Anthony—except for the whole bashing, screaming, manipulating, and stabbing thing, of course. He sighed and stared around the room.

His second night in his own place, and he still didn't know what to do. Thanks to Bruce and Faye and, he supposed, Tahlia and Neridah, all his belongings were unpacked and put away. Faye had probably even gone through everything Jonathan had left jumbled on his bed and put that away too. He didn't know what he thought about his aunt taking over his life like she had when he'd still lived at home, but there was nothing he could do about it now.

He got up and wandered through to the kitchen, opening and closing doors to peer inside and see where everything was. Sometime soon, he'd need to know how to find things in his own home. The fridge was stocked full. Containers and plates of sweets from morning tea battled for space beside a quiche, salad, and cheesecake. He slammed the fridge shut and turned. A bag of bread rolls languished on the counter.

His bathroom sparkled, the towel different from the one he'd used the night before. The laundry hamper was empty and the linen cupboard neatly packed. He didn't recognize most of the towels or sheets and assumed Faye had bought new ones for him. He'd only brought one new set each with him from the house. His bedroom was spotless. All the clothes he'd tossed around earlier that day were now pressed and hanging in his wardrobe or folded neatly in color-coded piles in his chest of drawers. He sighed and wondered why he didn't feel more grateful. Faye was just trying to help. He opened his bedside table to find three new bottles of lube and several boxes of condoms.

"Fuck. Goddamn it, Faye. You say I shouldn't be dating, then you stock my bedroom with enough bloody condoms to last a slut a year." Unless it was Bruce. Or, hell, maybe Neridah from next door. She'd seemed particularly focused on Jonathan's butt. Surely she wasn't brazen enough to leave condoms here in the hope she'd get some action. His stomach churned. *Oh shit.* She probably was.

He considered the contents of the drawer again. His boys shriveled, as if trying to climb up into his body at the thought of a nude Neridah in his bedroom. He slammed the drawer shut and returned to the living room.

Before he got further than deciding he'd watch television, his phone rang. It'd be Faye, for sure, to tell him where everything was. He snatched it up and answered without checking the display.

"Thanks for the condoms, but I don't think I'll use that many this week."

"You fucking asshole. You're already cheating on me?"

Only luck had him landing on the couch rather than the floor when his knees gave out. He pressed trembling fingers against his lips to stop the frightened whimper burbling through his body from escaping. "Anthony."

"Of course it's me. I'm your boyfriend. Who else would be calling you?"

He darted frantic gazes around the room, unable to focus on anything until he saw the front door. He pushed himself onto shaky legs and checked the door was deadlocked, then slid down the wall to sit on the floor, his head on his knees, the phone clamped tightly against his ear. "You're not my boyfriend. We're finished. I told you I was leaving you."

"You're not going anywhere. You owe me."

"I owe you nothing. Not anymore." Jonathan wanted to hang up, wanted his life to continue blissfully Anthony-free.

"Bring me some pajamas. These hospital things are too rough for my skin."

Was it attention, then? Is that all Anthony wanted? No, that was never enough for him; there was always something more that Jonathan had to be aware of, had to protect himself and his family against. He forced himself to pay attention to what Anthony was saying. "You're paralyzed. How can you tell they're too rough when you can't feel anything?" Belatedly he checked the number. It wasn't Anthony's. "Whose phone are you using?"

"One of the nurses'. I need those pajamas before bed. Bring the red ones."

"No." His voice trembled as violently as the rest of his body. He pressed his back against the door to minimize the shudders flowing in waves through him. "I'm not your boyfriend."

"Don't talk rubbish—"

"Don't ring me again." Jonathan very carefully lifted the phone away from his ear and disconnected the call. Then he went into Settings and blocked the number with trembling fingers. He lowered his head to his knees and pressed his eyes against the bones until it hurt. He couldn't breathe, couldn't draw air into his lungs without his lips quivering and tears leaking from his eyes. He gripped his knees harder, curling into a tighter form, trying to get Anthony out of his head. Out of his life.

He was still curled on the floor five minutes later when the phone rang again. Jonathan jumped and nearly dropped it. Panting, he checked the number and frowned when it showed a number he didn't recognize. Would Anthony have been able to get another phone so quickly? With shaking fingers, he answered the call.

"Jonathan, it's Ben."

Jonathan released a shaky breath. "Ben." Not Anthony. Every muscle relaxed, and he rested his head on his knees as he listened.

"Yeah. I wanted to let you know I had a great time this afternoon. It was good to go out and just relax, you know. You're good company."

Jonathan's muscles tensed again. He breathed. *In, out, in, out.* That was almost word for word what Anthony had said to him after their first date.

"Jonathan?" Ben paused, but Jonathan stayed silent. "Are you okay?"

That jolted Jonathan out of his fugue. "Yes, I'm fine. Thank you." Being polite was necessary, or Ben would fly into a rage and scream about not being appreciated.

"Good." Ben's voice sounded different now. Quieter, more tentative. "Um, I was wondering if you, um, if you wanted to do it again. I mean, maybe not the same thing, like a movie and stuff, but maybe dinner or something."

Jonathan stood and checked the deadlock on his door again, then carefully, quietly slipped the security chain across. He turned all the lights out, then stood carefully to the side of his living room window and peered through the gap between the blinds and the window. He couldn't see much, just the alley between the buildings and a patch of the road out front. Cars drove past, but there were no people standing around. Nothing moved.

"Jonathan?"

Vaguely, he realized Ben had been talking. "Where are you?" He couldn't see him in the narrow gap.

"At home. Did you want to meet tonight? I could come over."

"No!"

Silence greeted his outburst, then Ben spoke again. "Jonathan?"

"I have to go." He fumbled his phone as he tried to stab the right button to disconnect the call, then tossed the phone onto the couch and backed away from it. "I can't do this. Not again."

Chapter SIX

JONATHAN PACED all night. Into his bedroom to check the windows, same in the bathroom. Back to the front door to check it was still locked, to the window and the narrow view outside. The night remained quiet, but he couldn't relax. Anthony wasn't going to let him go. Liam was wrong. Moving out wasn't going to be enough to get away from him, whether he was in a wheelchair or not. The man was in hospital after stabbing himself and he'd still managed to get to Jonathan.

Faint noises carried from the other apartments on his floor just after dawn, and he put his head on the arm of the couch and closed his eyes, allowing his exhaustion to claim him.

His ringing phone woke him two hours later. He sat, groggy, and peered at the screen. Another unknown number brought Jonathan's heart to pounding. He groaned and answered the phone. As he said "Hello," he realized he shouldn't have answered it at all.

"You'd better be on your way with those pajamas, you bitch, or you'll pay for it when I get home."

Jonathan froze, inside and out. When dizziness threatened, he slowly released his breath and carefully lowered the phone so he could see its face. He disconnected the call with a trembling finger, then gently placed the phone on the coffee table. He sat on the edge of the couch, counting his breaths in and out. After two breaths, he surged up and checked the locks on the doors and windows before taking up his position at the window again. "You don't need to do this," he told himself. "Anthony's still in hospital, and he doesn't know you live here. No one in the family would have told him. You're safe."

Talking to himself didn't help. His breathing was too rapid, his fingers trembled, and sweat ran down his spine in terrified rivulets. He cried out and jumped when the phone rang again. He turned to stare at it as it lit up and vibrated its way across the coffee table until it bounced off and landed on the carpet. He waited, fingers of one hand pressed against his lips, preventing the terrified wailing that wanted to escape. His other hand pressed against his chest, holding his heart in and his feet to the floor. Finally the phone beeped, indicating a message.

He stared at the phone, but when it remained silent, he picked it up and checked the missed calls. *Ben.*

"I thought you were a nice one," he whimpered. He frantically pushed buttons to listen to the message. Liam would tell him to delete it unread, or un-listened-to, but Jonathan needed to know what Ben had to say.

"Um, hi, Jonathan. It's Ben. Look, you obviously don't... or maybe you're busy, I don't know. Did I do something wrong? Look, I just... do you want to go out again? If you do, give me a call. If I don't hear from you...." He sighed. "I'm sorry."

Jonathan cradled the phone in both hands and held it close to his chest. "Oh, Ben," he moaned. "You sound like a nice man, but so did Anthony, and I can't do this again." His voice echoed through the empty room, and Jonathan heard the insecure whining in it. He put the phone down and sat up straighter. He looked around, again checking the locks were engaged and the curtains drawn tight. He was safe. Anthony couldn't get him here.

A small voice whispered *Ben could*, but he pushed it away. Thinking like that wasn't normal. Living with Anthony hadn't been normal, but he wasn't there anymore. He was beginning a new life, and that meant he had to begin new thinking. So....

"Don't be such a punce, Jonathan Watson," he said out loud. "You can't assume everyone is like Anthony. You can date Ben if you want to. Even if he turns out not to be the one, there's nothing wrong with taking time for yourself after the end of a bad relationship." He stood. Hearing it said out loud made it better. "People do it all the time. So that's what you can do. You can find out who you are now and build a life. Then you might meet a nice man who'll be kind to you." He scrubbed his hands over his face. "God, now you sound like Aunty Faye, not a grown man of twenty-nine."

Someone knocked on the door, and Jonathan jumped, an embarrassing squeak escaping before a second knock. *So much for the new, brave Jonathan Watson.*

"Jonathan?"

Tahlia. Jonathan strode to the door and unlocked it but left the chain on, even though he knew it would be useless against a determined intruder.

"Hello," Tahlia said with a tentative smile as soon as she saw Jonathan behind the door. She carried a container similar to the ones already stacked in Jonathan's fridge. Behind her, Neridah grinned at him, her ever-present smoke cloud swirling around her head.

"I thought you'd like some buttermilk pancakes with my special caramel sauce for breakfast."

Jonathan closed the door and released the chain. He couldn't refuse his neighbor through a partially opened door. That it was a mistake to open the door became apparent immediately as Neridah surged forward, pushing Tahlia in front of her. Within seconds they were in his kitchen.

"Tahlia, I still have a lot of food left over from yesterday."

"Do you?" she said distractedly as she unpacked her containers. "That's good."

"You can have it for lunch, can't you?" Neridah asked. "What have you got?" She opened the fridge and began pulling out the stacked containers, lifting the lids as she placed each one on the counter. "Ooh, are those crêpes suzette? When did you make those, Tahlia? I missed out."

"I didn't realize you liked them. I'll make you some tomorrow if you like."

"I can't do tomorrow. I have to go and pound that stupid Kelly's head into the pavement. She married Lindsay as soon as the ink on our divorce papers was dry and refused to listen to me then. Now she's found out what a lazy ass he really is, she wants me to talk to him and get him to do more for her. Why does she think I divorced him? The lazy bastard wouldn't listen to me. He's not going to listen to her or any other woman."

"I think you're amazing, Neridah. I don't know any other woman who still keeps in touch with all her exes."

"That's because you don't know any other women who have exes. All your friends are still married to their first boyfriends, just like you are."

Tahlia's face flushed as she opened a door to pull out plates for breakfast. That wasn't where he'd put the plates when he was unpacking. The women seemed to have forgotten he was there, even though they were in his apartment.

"Here you are, Jonathan," Tahlia said as she handed him the plates. "You set the table, and we'll be ready to eat in just a few minutes. Neridah, can you put the kettle on? I'll start the tea, then I'll serve."

The phone rang just as Jonathan's butt landed in his seat, and he shot up again, heart pounding. His chair fell over as he stumbled back from the table and glared at the vibrating phone while he tried to catch his breath.

"Aren't you going to answer that?" asked Neridah. "Would you like me to get it?"

"No!" He rushed forward and snatched the phone up. Another unknown number. He answered the phone.

"Don't you ever hang up on me again."

"Stop calling me."

He didn't think Anthony heard him, because the other man didn't stop talking. "I want those pajamas, and I want you here to visit me within the next hour. This isn't negotiable, Jonathan. You owe me."

"Stop calling me," he said again as he walked down the hall, away from the women's curious gazes. "I'm not in your life anymore, and you're not part of mine. Don't call me again."

"That's not your decision to make, you bitch. You put me here. This is your fault, so you have to fix it."

"Stop calling me, Anthony, or I'll call the police."

"You wouldn't dare."

Heart pounding, fingers trembling, Jonathan disconnected the call, turned the phone off, and put it in his top drawer. Then he curled up on his bed and pulled the pillow over his head. He pulled the pillow down tighter against the side of his head, but all that did was cut out all the quiet sounds of his apartment and emphasize his panicked breathing.

"Jonathan?" Tahlia's tentative voice was much closer than he wanted, especially through the muffling pillow. "Your pancakes are getting cold."

"I'm sorry, Tahlia. I'm not hungry right now. Can you and Neridah please close the door when you leave?"

"Oh. Of course. Don't worry. We'll take care of everything."

"Thank you," he said through the pillow, because he was taught to always be polite regardless of what was happening in his life.

He waited, listening intently, but didn't hear the front door open and close, as it would if two people left his apartment. When he couldn't stand it anymore, he dragged the pillow off his head and turned his face toward the door. Cutlery clicked against china. Voices spoke in hushed tones. Jonathan sat up and stared at the door, his mouth open.

They were still there. They were eating their breakfast at his table, in his apartment. A burst of smoke-roughened laughter made him jump. He stood then stormed down the hall to find Neridah and Tahlia sitting comfortably at his table, half-empty plates in front of them along with steaming cups of coffee.

"There you are," said Tahlia as she pulled an empty cup toward her and filled it from the pot. "Have some coffee while I heat your pancakes."

Neridah pointed to the chair between her and Tahlia.

Jonathan sat. "What—?"

Tahlia placed a heaped plate in front of him. "Isn't a stack three?" he asked.

Tahlia looked at once mortified and scandalized. She reached over for Jonathan's plate, then snatched her hand back. "Oh... um.... You wouldn't be satisfied with three. Look how tall you are, and you're far too thin. You make a start on those, and if you're still hungry after, I'll go and fetch some of my muffins. I made some lovely raspberry and lemon ones yesterday. Of course, they're better straight from the oven, but they're still nice the next day." Her panicked rambling faded away, and she sat abruptly and continued eating in silence.

Jonathan stared at the food on his plate and tried to work out if the grumbling in his stomach was because strangers had invaded his home and taken over his life, or if he was just hungry.

"It's been such a long time since I've had someone to appreciate my cooking." Tahlia wrinkled her nose at Neridah's eye-roll. "Oh, I know you like my cooking, Neridah, but you don't eat more than a sparrow. And Kyle"—her voice wobbled—"likes what I make for him, but he never...." She put her cutlery down and took a deep breath before looking up at Jonathan. "You show a totally different type of appreciation." She smiled at Jonathan, her face an odd mixture of anticipation and begging.

He ate his pancakes.

"You know, Tahlia, there's that new exhibition at the Gallery of Modern Art. I'll bet Jonathan would love to see that." Neridah turned to Jonathan. "Do you like modern art? We could all go together. Some of the sculptures there will blow your mind." She leaned closer to him. "Totally anatomically correct, you know, and you can see so much of the detail, even with the strange materials they've used to make them."

"Neridah, why do you always have to embarrass everyone?"

"I don't embarrass everyone. You're not embarrassed, are you, Jonathan? It's just bodies. The male ones are very interesting. There's a whole section devoted to buttocks. You wouldn't believe—"

"Neridah, you stop that right now. I don't want to hear about buttocks or exposed anuses or anything else. I heard enough the first time around."

Jonathan ducked his head to sip his coffee and hide the smile threatening to erupt. They were odd, and he wished they weren't around quite so much, but he was beginning to really like his neighbors.

He was enjoying his second cup of coffee, while Tahlia smiled at him and Neridah cleaned his kitchen, when there was a knock on the door.

"I've only lived here two days. How can I possibly have so many visitors already?"

"Don't sell yourself short, dear. I'm sure there are a lot of people who'd love to spend more time with you, not just Tahlia and me."

Jonathan's good mood vanished. The only person who wanted to spend time with him apart from his family, who wouldn't call this early in the day, was Anthony. Even though he told himself Anthony was still in hospital and couldn't get up the stairs anyway, he couldn't catch his breath. He recognized the symptoms. He'd read enough and heard enough from Liam to know what it was. Not just fear. Good old terror. That's what Anthony always reduced him to: basic caveman nervous responses. He clenched his fists and counted his breath in and out three times.

"Who is it?" he called through the door.

"It's me."

Liam? What was he doing here so early? He opened the door to find Liam scowling at him. "What's wrong? Why aren't you answering your phone?"

"My phone?" Jonathan looked over his shoulder to his bedroom door. "My phone is turned off."

"Why?" Liam pushed past him and stopped short when he saw Tahlia and Neridah standing in the kitchen, curious smiles on their faces.

"Hello, gorgeous," said Neridah. "You're just in time for coffee. You and Jonathan sit in the living room, and I'll bring it through."

Liam turned to Jonathan, a question clear in his gaze. Jonathan shrugged at him and went to sit on the couch. "What's wrong?" he asked. "I thought you couldn't come over until the weekend."

"I couldn't, but you didn't answer your phone."

Jonathan sighed. His cousin didn't need to say anything more for Jonathan to know he was waiting for an explanation. Ten years of panic and worry vibrated between them. "Anthony called," he said quietly. "Three times from different phones."

"Fucking bastard." Liam surged to his feet. "I thought he was still in hospital."

"He is. I think he's borrowing phones from patients or staff. The first time he said it was a nurse's phone."

"Fuck." Liam pulled his phone out and hit speed dial. "Barry, this is Liam. We have a situation with a patient." He quickly explained what was happening. "I know we can't stop him borrowing patients' phones, but we can damn well make sure staff don't enable his abuse." His scowl lightened as he listened to Barry. "Thank you. I'll be in shortly."

For some reason, Liam's quick-as-lightning response irritated Jonathan far more than his nosey, intrusive neighbors. They just cooked for him and wanted to talk to him all the time. Liam was trying to run Jonathan's life, just like Anthony had. Not exactly like Anthony—Liam would never hit Jonathan—but he was still taking control. Jonathan straightened his spine to stand taller. "You don't need to constantly ride to the rescue, Liam. I'm a grown-up. I can look after myself."

Liam scowled at him. It was the same scowl that had always accompanied the words "Don't be an idiot" when they were children.

"Fuck you," said Jonathan as he took his cup back to the kitchen, where Neridah and Tahlia had finished cleaning and were shamelessly eavesdropping.

"I have to get to work," said Liam from behind him. "Go and get yourself a new phone number or, better still, a new phone. That way you'll be able to keep all the messages Anthony leaves—in case you need them. Take a cab. You can't drive yet."

"In case I need them?" Jonathan's heart pounded, his throat dry with fear. Suddenly his calm, if unusually social, morning was destroyed. "Do you think he's going to try again?" *Try to kill me?*

"Hopefully he's not that stupid, but it makes sense to be prepared."

"Thanks. That makes me feel loads better." He didn't know where to put his hands. They floated shakily around in front of him, then behind before he finally took control of his body again and shoved the trembling digits into his pockets. He felt marginally more in control, even with the nervous sweat beading on the back of his neck.

"I'm just saying." Liam pulled Jonathan into a rough hug, dislodging Jonathan's hands from his pockets. "I'll call again when I finish my shift."

"You don't need to do that." Jonathan decided he was finally going to live his own life. Even though nothing seemed to be resolved with Anthony, no matter that he'd thought it was over, he didn't want to involve Liam anymore. It was bad enough that Anthony had stabbed Liam when he'd tried to kill Jonathan. There was no way he'd put Liam in the firing line again. It was his fucked-up life, and it was his fucking job to fix it. "Don't you have a new boyfriend to go see?"

A blinding smile broke out on Liam's face. "Yeah, I do. He's staying over at my place again tonight."

"Wow. That's, what, three nights in a row? You're really serious about this one."

"What do you mean 'this one'?" Liam walked to the door and opened it. "It's not as if there've been a constant string of men through my life."

"Sure, Liam. If you want to totally forget your twenties, you go ahead. I'm just saying, I won't be forgetting with you." It felt good to tease Liam again. Jonathan hadn't felt safe enough to relax that much in—he sighed—a lifetime.

"Fuck you," Liam said but he was grinning. "You should check out uni courses while you're arranging your new phone."

Jonathan rolled his eyes, wondering if Liam would ever accept he was an adult. Then he grimaced. With all the years he'd spent allowing Anthony to treat him like shit, probably not. At least not until Jonathan started acting like one. He'd been talking about going back to uni for a few years now, so refusing to go just because Liam was the first one to think of it was childish and self-defeating. He nodded at his cousin.

"Give us five minutes and we'll go with you," said Neridah from behind him.

"What?" The two women stood in front of him with matching, beaming smiles. Jonathan was torn between smiling back and wondering what the hell he thought was nice about the interfering biddies.

"Liam said you couldn't drive, so I'll drive you, and Tahlia needs to go to the shops too." Neridah raised her eyebrows at Tahlia, who checked her watch, then grinned conspiratorially and nodded. "Good, then." Neridah brushed past Jonathan, who stepped back to allow her and Tahlia to leave. "You can wear those jeans. They make your butt look great."

Jonathan slapped both his hands on his buttocks to hide them from Neridah. She laughed.

"We'll be back in five minutes." Side by side, the two women ushered Liam out. Neridah pulled the door closed behind her, the click a clear message that Jonathan wasn't to leave without them.

He leaned against the door once they'd left, knowing he only had a few minutes before they'd be back. He'd never get rid of them. They were lovely women, even though Neridah stank of cigarette smoke and Tahlia flitted around with a nervous tension that was disturbingly familiar, but he really didn't want them babysitting him all the time. That's what it felt like. They were treating him like a child, and so were his aunt and uncle and Liam. The only one who had treated him like a human being, an adult capable of living his own life and making his own decisions, had been Ben.

Ben scared him.

No, that wasn't right. Ben didn't scare Jonathan. Anthony scared Jonathan, and the thought that Ben might be the same scared Jonathan. The man himself was… wonderful. He was calm in the face of a crisis, and he treated others kindly. He was funny and interesting and smelled... divine.

And Jonathan had brushed him off and not answered his calls.

He was an idiot.

He shoved his wallet into his back pocket, picked up the keys from the bowl on the kitchen counter, and left his apartment, thinking if he was fast enough, he could get away before Neridah and Tahlia noticed.

"Oh good. We won't have to come get you, then," said Neridah as she walked through a cloud of smoke toward the stairwell. She linked her arm through his and dragged him down the stairs.

Tahlia followed them. "My cousin has just started work at a computer shop. I know they have phones too, but I don't remember what the shop's called. It's very clean, though, and everything is painted white."

The remainder of Jonathan's morning was more of the same kind of insanity. At least they stayed in the waiting area when he went to the bank to open his own account and transfer half the funds from his and Anthony's joint account.

Just before lunchtime, Neridah drove them into the car park at the university.

"Ooh, I've never been to a university before. Do you know where you're going? We should come with you and have a look around." Neridah turned to Tahlia. "Tahlia, this could be your chance to check out cooking courses. Do universities do that? You'd like that."

"They don't do cooking here, Neridah. They do doctors and lawyers and stuff. Is that what you're going to do, Jonathan? Are you going to be a lawyer now?"

Jonathan stepped out of the car and breathed deeply of the still air. The ladies were kind, but they never shut up, and Jonathan craved some alone time. Anthony had always been around but, apart from when he was demanding something, he was quiet.

"Jonathan?"

"No, Tahlia, I don't want to be a lawyer. I'm not sure yet exactly what I want to do. I have a degree in business administration, but I don't want to work in business. I was thinking a museum would be nice. I could be a curator in a museum." He held his breath when he finished talking. This was it. They'd criticize and belittle until the last thing Jonathan wanted to do would be anything with a museum. Or anything else.

"So you'd get to see all the orsopheguses from Egypt up close. They'd probably let you touch them, even though no one else is allowed to. Oh, and what about that airplane, you know, the one Bert Hinkler died in. Would you be able to sit in that? Wouldn't that be wonderful, Tahlia?" Neridah linked her arm with Jonathan's.

Tahlia, arm linked with Jonathan on the other side, nodded sagely. "I think it would be a wonderful job."

Jonathan snorted. It was nice not to have all his ideas shot down as soon as they were spoken, but their easy acceptance didn't feel comfortable yet. "Let's go and collect a prospectus." He was smiling as they headed to the administration block.

It wasn't the usual thing to actually visit a university to find a prospectus and discuss course options, but Jonathan didn't want to do it online. He had been feeling closed-in in his apartment—fuck, he'd been feeling closed-in for years—and he wanted to see if he'd like the environs of the university before he decided to go ahead. His plans were so nebulous that it wouldn't take much for him to change his mind.

An hour later he'd almost completed an application for a Masters of Museum Studies, then changed it to Physiotherapy, and was wandering around the campus with Neridah and Tahlia. Most of the students were much younger than Jonathan, but there were a few his age and older.

"I think this will work," he said quietly, a smile tugging at his mouth. The idea of being here, studying and working toward a different future, one that he'd chosen on his own, was a heady feeling.

"Oh look, there's Ben. And he's wearing totally edible jeans. Let's go and say hello to him." Neridah tugged on Jonathan's arm, and as soon as she spotted Ben, so did Tahlia. Neither woman slackened their hold on him enough for him to slip his arms away, so Jonathan was dragged along with them.

"Ben! Ben, wait up," Neridah called, her smoky voice foghorn loud in the semienclosed courtyard outside the refectory.

Ben turned and frowned, then grinned, then frowned again. Jonathan's stomach twisted into nervous knots. What would he do if Ben ignored him? Jonathan wouldn't blame him. After the way he'd acted the last time they were together, Ben probably thought Jonathan was too high maintenance to bother with.

"Hello, ladies," said Ben when they were close enough for conversation. "What brings you here?" He nodded at the women, but his gaze soon landed on Jonathan and stuck.

Jonathan was sure if his skin was pale like Ben's he'd be bright red, just like Ben was. "Hello, Ben," he said. "Are you a student here?" He nearly slapped his face at the stupid question.

"Yes, I'm doing a history degree with a major in textile conservation. I've just finished a tutorial and was going to grab some lunch before my next lecture."

"Oh good. We'll join you. I'm starving," said Neridah. "Jonathan's been dragging us around town all morning."

Jonathan gasped and glared at the grinning, unrepentant woman.

"I wonder what their food is like?" said Tahlia as she wandered toward the counters, still dragging Jonathan with her.

Ben fell in with them. "Most of the food is pre-prepared, Tahlia. I don't think you'll find anything as good as you make."

"That's sweet of you to say so, Ben. I don't get to eat out very often, but I always learn something I can use at home."

Neridah humphed. "Usually something you'd never do."

"Even that's useful," Tahlia agreed serenely. "What would you like for lunch, Jonathan? You hardly ate anything at breakfast." She stopped walking, tugging Jonathan to an awkward stop beside her. "You don't like"—she leaned closer to whisper—"*junk* food!"

Jonathan's laugh burst from him and bounced around the large room, drawing the attention of several groups near them. He leaned down to her and whispered conspiratorially. "Sometimes, Tahlia, I'll even eat at…. *McDonald's*."

She gasped and stepped away from him. Then, noting the grin on his face, she slapped his arm. "Oh, stop it. No one would eat *there* once they've tasted *real* food."

He didn't correct her and made a mental note to never bring anything from that particular fast-food restaurant home. Neridah would probably check his garbage and report back to her. Jonathan paused deliberately and closed his eyes. His breathing was even, his mouth was stretched in a smile, his head was clear. *This*, he thought. *This* is happiness.

"Ben, you can sit with me so we can get to know each other better." Jonathan snapped back to the moment in time to see Neridah latch onto Ben's arm and drag him to an empty table as she called over her shoulder. "Tahlia, choose something for us, will you? You'll be the best judge."

Tahlia beamed up at Jonathan, and he led her to the display cabinets. He directed her around scattered chairs, as attentive as he always was with his aunt when she dragged him out to shop for shoes. As much as he was enjoying the moment, he hoped this activity would be less painful than shoe shopping and wouldn't last as long.

Chapter SEVEN

ANTHONY GRASPED the nurse's forearm. "You'll help me, won't you, Vaughn?" He turned pleading eyes to Vaughn's cool blue ones. "I just need Jonathan's address so I can send his things on to him. It's not a big deal."

"You know I can't give you personal information of other patients."

"You won't be giving it to a stranger. He's my husband. He's just staying with a friend for a while until he recovers enough to come home and look after me."

"He could give you the address next time he calls."

Anthony spread his lips into his most beguiling smile. "Of course he could, but I told him not to come in until he was perfectly well again. All that traveling will only delay his recovery." He tightened his grip on Vaughn's forearm. "Of course, I could always tell them about your visit here last night and how you made sure I was *very* relaxed so I could sleep well."

"I didn't do that."

Vaughn stepped away but Anthony was faster. He gripped Vaughn's penis hard. "I can describe very clearly exactly how big you are," he said as he traced the outline of Vaughn's balls. "And then there's the matter of my drugs being short each time."

Vaughn froze at the mention of drugs. *Got him.* Anthony smiled.

"I'm sure they'd be interested in what you're doing with them." He released Vaughn's balls, then patted his arm and sat back. "Just get the address for me so I can send some of his things around to him. I have to do it today or he'll get in the car and drive, and you know he's not supposed to be driving yet." He turned the wattage on his smile up a notch. "I don't want him injuring himself trying to do something he's not ready for."

Vaughn sighed and shook his head. "Okay, okay, give it a break. He's registered for physio. I'll look up the address on the system next time I'm on the desk."

"Thanks, Vaughn. It will make things so much easier. For Jonathan."

Chapter EIGHT

BEN MOVED the container of sugar packets to the middle of the table, then slid it again a little to the right. He sighed and shifted the container again. He should excuse himself and leave. Jonathan didn't want him here; he didn't want anything to do with him. That much had been made perfectly clear when Ben had dropped Jonathan off the day before and when Jonathan wouldn't respond to his calls. He flicked a look at the counter where Tahlia and Jonathan were peering into the display cases, then pushed the sugar away and sat up straighter. He glared at Jonathan's taut ass, clearly defined in those tight jeans, even this far away. Yep. It still got to him. And so did the man. They'd had fun when they'd gone out, and Ben wanted more of it. If Jonathan didn't want to see Ben, then he could damn well say so.

Decision made, he finally turned to Neridah, who sat beside him with a smirk on her smoke-wrinkled lips.

"Tell me about yourself, Ben." Neridah smiled widely and fluttered her false lashes. It was disconcerting to see her face clearly, without the haze of smoke that usually acted like a soft filter and muted the deep vertical wrinkles on her cheeks. "I bet with all the moving you do, your muscles are solid." She lifted one hand and traced a fingertip down his bicep, so lightly he could have imagined it if it hadn't made him shiver.

He sat back in his chair, moving his arm away from her touch. "There's not a lot to tell. I moved down here to go to uni, and I work as a removalist to pay my way."

"Where are you from?" Neridah leaned over the table, her forearms folded underneath her breasts.

Ben searched frantically for Jonathan and Tahlia, but they were still at the counter choosing their food. "Um—"

"Do you have a girlfriend?" Neridah shifted her forearms so her breasts jiggled, almost spilling out of her low-cut T-shirt.

"No!" He looked over to Jonathan again, willing him to turn around and see his distress. Jonathan's focus remained solidly on

Tahlia. When Ben returned his gaze to Neridah, she was smiling. *Oh God, is that supposed to be enticing? She's older than my mother.*

Neridah laughed and leaned against the back of her seat, her breasts flopping back into her T-shirt. He sighed as the fabric covered the loose brown skin. "You should see your face, love." She reached across the table and patted his hand. He couldn't stop the automatic snatch to remove himself from her.

"Oh, um, I'm sorry, Neridah. It's not that you're not, um—" God, he couldn't say it, not even to make her feel better.

"Oh, stop it, Ben. Don't burst a vessel. I know I'm no spring chicken, but I like pretty young men, and you're certainly pretty." She pouted, then licked her lips in a way that had Ben swallowing bile and trying not to show it on his face. She shrugged. "It was worth a try. You'd be surprised how often it works, especially if I wear some gaudy jewelry and offer to pay for lunch." She jiggled her left hand to show off a large diamond ring.

Ben stared at her. There was nothing in his head to say in response to that. Not one thing.

"We've all ended up with salad sandwiches," Tahlia said as Jonathan slid a tray onto the table. "It was the only thing I could be sure was made fresh. Everything else looks like it's been sitting there since the ark was built."

Jonathan's chuckle drew Ben's attention. The relaxed, happy look on his face held it. The man was so gorgeous, Ben had to watch him as he unloaded the plates, put the tray aside, and held Tahlia's chair for her. Gorgeous and thoughtful. "The pasta didn't look too bad," he murmured as he slid Neridah's plate toward her before placing a mugachino next to it.

"That pasta had been boiled for so long, it had congealed." Tahlia settled into her seat. "You wouldn't have been able to tell if you were eating pasta or rubber. I'll make real pasta for you for dinner tomorrow night. A proper semolina pasta that doesn't need to be dried for a week before cooking."

"You're making it from scratch? Not even buying a packet of pasta? Isn't that a waste of time?" Ben asked, surprised. He'd always thought his mother was a pretty good cook—she always made her pasta sauces herself—but she never made the pasta.

Instead of being insulted, Tahlia laughed at him. "You're in for a real treat tomorrow if you've never had homemade pasta before. Just you wait. You'll never want to eat any other kind again."

It looked like he was invited to dinner. He grinned at her even as he was dismayed at the stunned look on Jonathan's face. If he spent more time with the gorgeous man, he'd be able to ask Jonathan about what he wanted to study and why and, maybe, find out why he ran hot and cold all the time. Too bad they wouldn't be alone.

The ladies kept the conversation going, but Ben couldn't have said what topics were discussed. He responded when one of them asked him a question, but the rest of the time he watched Jonathan. Every time the man looked like he'd stop eating, Ben tapped the table. He tried not to, but it was like he channeled his mother whenever there was food around. He was lucky Jonathan took it so well. Whenever he did it to his brother these days, Jack punched him.

"What time is your next lecture?" asked Tahlia when Jonathan was eating the last of his sandwich.

Ben glanced at his watch and surged to his feet. "In about two minutes." He pulled his wallet out of his pocket. "I have to go. How much do I owe you for lunch?" He looked between Tahlia and Jonathan, not sure which one had paid.

Jonathan shook his head. "Don't worry about it. You can buy next time."

Next time. Ben grinned. "Count on it." He shouldered his pack. His day suddenly seemed like early spring—bright and crisp and full of promise.

"Don't forget dinner tomorrow, Ben," said Tahlia. "You don't need to bring anything."

Ben's grin was so wide it felt like it would split his face. "I'll be there." He looked directly at Jonathan. "Thanks for lunch. I'll see you later." Jonathan smiled, then seemed to remember where he was and who he was with and coughed slightly, then nodded.

Adorably awkward. Perhaps it wasn't hot-and-cold. Perhaps Jonathan was just shy. Ben couldn't wait to find out.

JONATHAN WASN'T sure how he felt about Ben coming to dinner. On the one hand, the need to see more of him clawed at his insides like a ravenous wolf. On the other hand, drawing Ben into his life or getting drawn into Ben's was a bad idea—no matter how good it felt.

Three missed calls from an unknown number during the morning had fear still skittering through him and his gaze darting into shadows as Neridah drove. He knew it was Anthony, even though it was a new number and only his family and the hospital physiotherapy department had it. He scrubbed his hands over his face and tried to think logically. Maybe he should go back to Anthony. He knew what the score was there, knew how to survive. He moved his shoulders, feeling the pinch of stitches nearly ready to be removed, and forced himself to remember that survival hadn't been that easy at the end.

What he was trying to do now—start a life of his own—was hard, seemingly impossible. He closed his eyes, tempted to ask Neridah to take him back to Anthony's place.

The car hit a pothole. The stitches pulled again. Jonathan pressed against the dressing and breathed through the pain. He blinked rapidly to clear the burning tears from his eyes. Going back wasn't an option. Living with Anthony was no longer a matter of dealing with his bullying or dodging punches or flying objects. Living with Anthony now would be a fight for survival.

Jonathan wanted to live.

He huffed out a surprised breath. He did. He really did want to live. The realization blistered every other thought from his mind. He wanted to live.

He looked at Tahlia's serenely smiling face and cracked the window a little to dissipate the lingering smoke smell from Neridah's hurried cigarette before getting into the car. He wasn't sure about his new neighbors, not their involvement in his life, and particularly not their coming to dinner. It seemed like he didn't have a choice about that.

Was he making friends? Against his moodiness and silence, could he really be making his own friends? His breath caught. He would have friends that Anthony hadn't chosen and approved of beforehand. He'd have friends he could see any time he wanted.

Tahlia turned and smiled. He smiled back and he knew— *knew*—he wouldn't be punished for it.

He had friends. Automatically he began to justify why they wanted to be friends with him. He supposed Tahlia was lonely, with Kyle working such long hours, and the meals were spectacular. He wondered why she didn't get a job as a cook.

Neridah was something different entirely. She was a weird combination of slutty cougar and über-compassionate friend. Even though she kept hinting she wanted inside his pants, he was beginning to think she'd run the other direction if he accepted.

And then there was Ben. Jonathan knew he hadn't loved Anthony for a long time, but it had only been a few weeks since he'd escaped. Maybe he should find another man to go out with, because he really didn't want Ben to be his transitional guy. It was cute the way Ben fussed over him, but what was with the food? Every time Jonathan stopped eating, Ben would subtly and not-so-subtly get him eating again. Like he was the mother duck and Jonathan was the duckling to be fed and nurtured. He didn't seem to be pushy with anything else, though, so Jonathan had let it pass. He'd even enjoyed the attention, knowing that even though Ben had been talking to Tahlia and Neridah, he'd still noticed exactly what Jonathan was doing.

Perhaps he should be freaked out by that sort of attention, after Anthony, but it was actually quite nice. Ben wasn't trying to manipulate Jonathan into doing something for him. He just wanted Jonathan to eat. Anthony hadn't cared if Jonathan ate. Anthony had only cared if Anthony ate exactly what Anthony wanted to, exactly when Anthony wanted it.

Damn all this soul-searching. What other people did or didn't do couldn't matter anymore. Jonathan had to work out who he was and take control of his life, probably for the first time ever. He needed a plan—a goal. The first thing he was going to do was start jogging again. He used to love the quiet solitude of his early morning runs. He rubbed his palm over the dressing on his chest. Perhaps actual jogging would be out of the question right now, but surely he could at least walk around the block.

Neridah pulled up outside their building. "I'll drop you off here and go and park the car."

"Of course," he replied as he opened his door and got out to open Tahlia's for her.

"I don't need you fussing about me, but thank you." Her cheeks pinked as she spoke.

Neridah leaned over the seat to speak through the open door. "I know you don't, Tahlia, but Kyle's due home this afternoon. I'd feel better if Jonathan was there with you until I get back."

The soft pink that colored Tahlia's cheeks deepened. "Thank you," she said as she turned toward the building. He closed Tahlia's door and led her into the building as Neridah drove away.

Chapter NINE

"I WANT you to work for me." Anthony watched Vaughn's face closely as the nurse arranged the blanket over him. The doctor said he'd release Anthony if he arranged for at-home care.

"You're already one of my patients, Mr. Porter."

"I told you to call me Anthony, and I want you to work for me when I go home."

"I have shifts here at the hospital."

"You've already told me that's on a casual basis. You can come home with me and live in."

"You don't need full-time care." Vaughn stopped fussing with the pillows on the other side of the bed and gave Anthony his full attention. "You know your injuries aren't as severe as you've led people to believe."

"Bullshit. I suffered spinal injuries and a head injury in the car accident two years ago. That's bloody serious."

"Of course it is, but your spinal cord wasn't severed and the bruising and swelling has long since repaired."

"Don't tell me it wasn't severe. My career is ruined."

"That wasn't because of your back. The tremor in your hands is from the head injury."

"You don't know what you're talking about. I can't draw and I can't walk. That's the end of it."

"Okay, you're settled for the night. Is there anything else I can do before I leave?"

"Yes! You can work for me full-time and move in with me. You owe me that much."

"Owe you? How do you work that out?" Vaughn glared at Anthony. It wasn't a look Anthony was used to. Jonathan usually looked guilty and agreed. But bloody Jonathan wasn't there, and Anthony needed to get out of here so he could track him down and bring him back home. He was running out of time. Jonathan had to withdraw the attempted murder charges so he could get on with his life.

Anthony backtracked. "I can pay you a lot more than you're getting now. You just need to be there and help me."

Vaughn continued his tidying of the room and didn't respond. Anthony flopped back into his pillows in exasperation. "Jonathan would do what I wanted and wouldn't argue about it."

"Jonathan isn't here, is he?"

Vicious bastard, pointing that out, even if Anthony had just been thinking the same thing. Anthony scowled at Vaughn, but it didn't have any impact.

"What about your physical therapy?" Vaughn asked.

"It won't work. I can't walk and I can't draw." Did the bloody man never listen?

"You can't walk and can't draw—yet." Vaughn came to the edge of the bed and looked down at Anthony. His short, spiky light brown hair glinted gold in the light from above, and his blue eyes looked darker in his shadowed face. "If I come to work for you full-time, you'll have to agree to go to all your PT sessions and do all the exercises in between, right up to your court date. You'll have to do exactly as I say. It's going to be a lot harder now than it would have been if you'd started two years ago." He stepped back and raised his eyebrows. "Those are my conditions."

Negotiations. That was something Anthony knew how to do. He considered carefully what his counter-offer could be. "You have to drive me around wherever and whenever I need it. I need to go and see Jonathan." Jonathan would be lost without Anthony. "He must be frantic in that pokey little place he's in now. I have to get him out and bring him back home." *And get him to drop those stupid charges.*

Vaughn regarded Anthony silently for so long, Anthony began to squirm. He hissed as his wound pulled with the movement. Vaughn leaned over him.

"Let me check the drainage, then you can get some sleep." As he spoke, he pulled Anthony's pajama top up and lifted one corner of the dressing to peek under at the red skin held tightly together by a series of neat black stitches and the tube that ran from it to a bag under the bed. "That looks fine." He pressed the dressing back in place and lowered the pajama top. "I'll be back in the morning to help you shower."

"But I want you to work for me full-time."

"My shift has finished. I have to collect some clothes and other things and let the hospital know I won't be available for any shifts for a while." He tucked the blankets in and checked Anthony's water glass and medic-alert button was within easy reach, then stepped back. "I'll see you in the morning."

Anthony sighed in satisfaction as Vaughn turned the light out and closed his door. He listened with a smile as Vaughn walked down the hall. He laughed and punched the air. Vaughn would be back in the morning, and he'd work for Anthony, and together they'd get Jonathan back. And maybe—maybe—Anthony would do the stupid PT Vaughn was insisting on. He was tired of being stuck in the wheelchair anyway.

THE SUN had barely risen when Anthony was shaken awake.

"Rise 'n' shine. It's a new day, and you have exercises to do." Vaughn grabbed the covers and threw them to the bottom of the bed.

"Fuck off," Anthony grumbled, reaching down for the blankets but hissing when his stomach wound pulled.

"Not today. Today the drain comes out, and then I'm going to help you with your exercises and shower and breakfast. We'll take it easy until your stitches come out. After that the doctor will be around, and once he sees you've been up and working on getting better, he'll sign your release papers. Then we're going for a drive."

Anthony stopped struggling. "A drive? Good. I need to see Jonathan and tell him I'm home now so he can come home."

"Are you sure that's what he wants?"

"What are you talking about? It's his home. He belongs with me, and I'm going to make sure he remembers that."

Vaughn responded by sliding his arm behind Anthony's shoulders and sitting him up. His other arm wedged itself under Anthony's knees, and suddenly Anthony was lifted out of bed and carried toward the bathroom. "What are you doing? You don't have to carry me. I can use the chair. I'm supposed to use the chair."

Vaughn shrugged, jostling Anthony against his chest. "It's much quicker and easier for me to carry you to your shower chair. It's not a problem."

Anthony stopped struggling, and once he was settled in his shower chair with Vaughn washing his hair, he relaxed. Vaughn was a good choice. He'd look after him like Jonathan had until Jonathan came home. He leaned forward as Vaughn began scrubbing his back. Perhaps he'd keep Vaughn even after Jonathan returned. The nurse could sure do a mean back scrub.

IT WAS still early when Anthony arrived at the building where Jonathan was hiding, but just early enough, because less than a minute after Vaughn turned the engine off, Jonathan slipped from inside and slowly jogged down the street, his hand pressed firmly over his chest.

Good. It should hurt you, after the way you've betrayed me.

Vaughn opened his door.

"What are you doing?" Anthony asked.

"I'll call out to him so he knows we're here."

"No! No, let him go for his jog. He must be lonely and bored," Anthony mused. "He hasn't been jogging for a long time." Not since the accident, when Anthony needed him all the time. He hadn't been lonely or bored then.

Vaughn closed his door, and they sat in silence as Jonathan jogged around the corner and was lost to sight.

"Follow him and see where he goes," said Anthony.

Vaughn stared at Anthony for several seconds before starting the car and driving after Jonathan. He stayed almost a block back all the time, Jonathan's tall, dark body easily seen from a distance. Anthony was glad Vaughn stayed silent. He'd followed Jonathan before but never with someone else. His stomach squirmed as he thought about the conclusions Vaughn might be drawing from their actions, but Jonathan needed Anthony to watch over him.

"He's young and naïve. He'll never survive unless I look after him. He just needs a bit of time on his own. To recover."

Chapter TEN

JONATHAN OPENED the door to Ben's knock, and they stared at each other. Was this a date? More so than the movie the other day? Is that why nervous bubbles skittered through his body and clogged basic functions? He cleared his throat several times before he found his voice. Even if it wasn't a date, Jonathan knew he didn't want to fuck this up a second time.

Ben hefted the box he carried. "I wasn't sure what anyone drank, if anything, and I thought something soft would be nice."

"That's a great idea," said Neridah from behind Ben. Jonathan started, not having noticed her and Tahlia in the hall. Neridah leaned her chin on Ben's shoulder and grinned at Jonathan. The bottles in the box Ben held clanked against each other.

Tahlia handed the ubiquitous stacked Tupperware containers to Jonathan as she nudged Ben inside in front of her. "Kyle said he'd come over soon. Is it all right that he's coming too?"

Jonathan narrowed his gaze, trying to work out what was so different about her from the day before. She looked the same, just more… no, less…. It was like she was suddenly slightly transparent, almost not there at all, and shrouded in a thick blanket of nervous energy.

Ben shrugged as he walked past and put the box of drinks down on the kitchen counter. Neridah followed and grinned as she took Tahlia's Tupperware containers from Jonathan. "No point in you just standing there with these. We'll sort it out." She followed Ben and Tahlia into the kitchen, where Tahlia clanked around with Jonathan's pots and pans.

Jonathan stood just inside his doorway and watched his neighbors and his… removalist?… take over his kitchen. Ben poured a drink for Jonathan and brought it to him. His fingers touched the back of Jonathan's hand when he handed him his glass, as if to make sure Jonathan held it firmly. Or perhaps it was just to touch. It seemed intimate enough to Jonathan that there could be a private message included, although he didn't know what it could be. Neridah sidled up to Jonathan as he gazed mutely into Ben's eyes, the glass clutched between them.

"Oh, brilliant. I'd love a drink." She bumped against Ben as she turned back to the kitchen, knocking him closer to Jonathan and jostling the drink. "You stay right there. I'll get it."

Jonathan was tempted to do what she said and stay right where he was. This close, he could smell the clean soap scent of Ben's skin, and a sudden yearning to lean down and nuzzle against Ben's neck overtook him. Ice clinked in the glass between them. Ben came closer, his hazel eyes intense.

Tahlia's voice broke the spell. "Neridah, do you have a tin of chickpeas at your place? I think hummus on thin toast would be a nice starter." When Neridah left, Tahlia opened and closed cupboard doors, and soon the counter was covered completely with pots and pans and utensils, ready for her cooking frenzy. "Oh dear. No blender." She came over to Jonathan and Ben and grinned at them as she removed the glass from Jonathan's hand. "I'll just pick up a few things from my place. You two relax for a few minutes. We'll have dinner on the table in no time at all."

Jonathan wondered if the ladies would hang around after dinner until Ben left, or if he would get some time alone with the intriguing man. He returned his gaze to Ben to find him staring at him with his mouth open, a look of total incredulity spread over his face. Then he burst out laughing.

"What kind of freaky hell have you moved into?" Ben tried to whisper, but his laughter made the words rush out in uneven spits and spurts, like a teenage boy's first attempts at adulthood. "There's a tin of chickpeas on the bench right next to the blender."

"They probably mean well." Jonathan kept his voice even, but his face was burning.

"Yeah, I get that, but neither of them have any idea about personal privacy, do they?" He sobered. "Unless that's the way you like it?"

Jonathan shrugged. "They seem really nice. A bit like my family, you know, all invasive and bossy but loving you just the same." He stepped closer to Ben. "Sometimes, though, it would be nice to have some private time," his whispered.

Ben stood on tiptoes, bringing his lips closer to Jonathan's. "Mmm, sounds perfect."

Jonathan leaned closer and let his fingers tangle with Ben's. "Perfect," he said before he lowered his head and pressed his lips against Ben's. Ben's groan drew him nearer, and he wrapped his arms around him and pressed against his body. The solid cushion of Ben's pecs pressed just under Jonathan's nipples, tiny pinpoints of desire that instantly fractured his breathing. He wrapped his arms around Ben and shuffled closer still, desperate to feel their bodies together all over, from knee to shoulder.

Ben groaned again and tugged Jonathan's shirt from his jeans. The cool tips of his fingers on Jonathan's heated skin brought goose bumps to the surface, and he shivered. Jonathan ran his hands down Ben's back and cupped his firm buttocks, lifting him and pressing their cocks together.

Ben snatched his lips from Jonathan's. "Yes. God, yes," he panted as he lifted one leg and wrapped his foot behind Jonathan's knee to grind against him more firmly.

The shrill of the telephone made them both jump. Jonathan stumbled and almost fell when Ben hopped, unable to put his leg down fast enough to gain his balance. The phone rang again. Jonathan considered not answering it, but Ben had already moved a few steps away and leaned against the wall, trying to catch his breath. Jonathan snatched the phone up and swiped the screen to answer it without looking at the display.

"Is he in there with you, you bastard? You're mine! Don't forget it."

Jonathan fumbled the phone before putting it back to his ear. "Anthony?"

"I don't share, remember. Stay away from him if you don't want him hurt."

Fuck. Jonathan looked around frantically. *How could he know?* The curtains were open. Someone else had opened them, because Jonathan knew he damn well didn't. He was on the third floor. No way could Anthony see. Even so, he rushed over and pulled them closed, then fussed with the edges, pressing them against the wall beside the windows, all the while holding the phone against his ear. Anthony still ranted, but Jonathan didn't hear any of the words.

"I thought you were still in hospital."

"Of course you did. I nearly died and you didn't visit me once, you bastard."

"Visit you? Why the hell would I visit you? You're certifiable, you know that?" In a small part of his brain, Jonathan was horrified at his words. This was Anthony he was speaking to. It was Anthony who had broken each one of Jonathan's limbs at various times, just because Jonathan disagreed with something he'd said. Or dinner was late. What would Anthony do to him after this? How did he find out where Jonathan was living now?

"I'm not crazy!" Anthony screamed. "You owe me, and this is how you repay me, by abandoning me and taking up with some sleazy guy."

Jonathan gasped and stared at Ben in horror. *He knows. Anthony knows and he'll come after Ben.* He disconnected the call, tossed the phone aside, and rushed to Ben.

"What's wrong?" Ben grasped Jonathan's elbows when Jonathan grabbed his shoulders and began maneuvering him toward the door.

"You have to go." He pushed Ben closer to the exit.

"Go? Why?" He looked around as if something in the apartment would give him an idea what was going on. His gaze landed on the phone that listed precariously between a seat cushion and the back of the couch, like the couch was devouring it millimeter by millimeter. "Who's Anthony?"

"I'm sorry, but you have to go." He couldn't explain about Anthony. He'd look like a loser, although that was probably the least of his worries. He was so far out of his depth with everything that was happening around him, but he absolutely refused to allow anyone else be put in danger because of him. He pushed Ben again, forcing him over the threshold and out of his apartment. Behind him Neridah and Tahlia stepped into the hallway from Tahlia's apartment. Neridah carried a bowl of crackers and Tahlia a small bowl of what Jonathan assumed was the hummus. Behind Tahlia a broad-shouldered man stepped into the hallway. Ben turned to them as well.

Jonathan stepped back into his apartment and slammed the door. He twisted the deadbolt and put the chain on with shaky fingers, then fished his keys out of his pocket to double lock the deadbolt. He squealed when Ben knocked.

"Jonathan?"

He pressed his forehead against the cold surface of the door.

"Jonathan. Open the door."

"What did you do to him?" That was Tahlia.

"He didn't do anything, Tahlia. He's too nice to do anything bad." Neridah's voice of reason and calm floated eerily in the air. "Aren't you?" Jonathan chuckled silently at the way Neridah's voice changed from gentle and caring to deeply suspicious in a heartbeat.

"I didn't do anything. The phone rang. It was someone called Anthony, and Jonathan freaked out."

"Oh dear."

"What are we standing around here for? I thought you said there'd be food and beer." He recognized the timbre from the argument and assumed it was Kyle, Tahlia's husband.

"Jonathan? Open the door. Tell me what's wrong." Jonathan expected Ben to sound angry, but he didn't. He sounded hurt.

"Is he the one with the beer?"

"Kyle, they're our new neighbors."

"What? They shouldn't give us beer as a how-do-you-do?"

"Jonathan," said Neridah. "We have the hummus for starters, but Tahlia's not going to be able to finish dinner if you don't open the door."

"Jonathan, just tell me if you want me to go or stay. Whatever you want. I just need to know." Ben's voice was very close, like he was leaning against the door trying to speak just to Jonathan without the rest of them hearing him. A hot tear slid down Jonathan's cheek. Ben seemed so nice. Why couldn't Jonathan have met him before Anthony, or after him; any time, as long as Anthony wasn't around.

"Jonathan?"

He shoved the key into the dead bolt and unlocked the door, then unlatched the chain. He opened the door to four pairs of eyes, gazes ranging from impatient to worried.

"Do you want me to leave?"

Jonathan flicked a look at the others. The only other one who looked like she wanted to leave was Tahlia. No way did Jonathan want to be left with all of them and not have Ben to make it interesting and exciting. He reached out and grasped Ben's fingers. The smile he received in response was blinding.

"About time. Bloody queers and women always have to have their little dramas to make sure they stay the center of attention." Kyle pushed past Jonathan and Ben and glared at the dark television. "Don't tell me you don't even watch the football."

"Kyle!"

"What?" He turned to look at Tahlia. "Come on, babe. You know us men bond over football and a few beers. I'm being neighborly." He faced Ben and held his hand out to shake. "G'day, I'm Kyle."

Ben shook Kyle's hand but glanced at Jonathan as he did so. Jonathan noticed his neighbor didn't offer to shake his hand. He shrugged at Ben and walked into the living room. He'd been dealing with people who didn't want to touch his black skin all his life, and it had become worse once he came out. He wasn't the one with the problem. Jonathan tried to ignore Kyle's rudeness for Tahlia's sake, but if it continued he'd tell the odious man to leave.

He sat on the couch and observed the others, wondering why his apartment was filled with people, none of whom he'd actually invited over and only one of whom he wanted to spend time with. He was obviously still letting others control his life, but he didn't know how to stop it without being rude. Tahlia and Neridah were sweethearts, and Tahlia looked like she needed a friend. He relaxed back into his seat.

"Tahlia, do you need any help in the kitchen? I'm pretty good at following instructions," said Ben.

Kyle snorted as he flopped into Jonathan's favorite recliner and raised the footrest. He held out his hand. Tahlia blushed as she scooped up the remote from the coffee table and placed it in his hand.

Tahlia beamed at Ben. "Oh no, thank you. We can manage. You just sit there and relax." Neridah and Tahlia went into the kitchen, leaving the three men together in the living room. Ben joined Jonathan on the couch.

Kyle found the football game, scowled at it, and muted the volume. "Main game hasn't started yet," he grumbled to no one in particular. "Hey, where's the beer, boy?"

Jonathan breathed slowly and deeply for three heartbeats. "My name is Jonathan. Please call me that. I don't have any beer. I don't drink."

"Oh, I'm sorry, *Jonathan.*" Kyle scowled as he sat up and clicked the footrest back in place. "Jeez, and no beer. You one o' them alcoholics? I thought it was just the abos that were born that way."

In the horrified silence that followed, Jonathan glanced at Tahlia as she mixed something at the kitchen counter. Her head was down and her face bright red. He shook his head. She seemed so nice too. Ben shifted beside him.

"Kyle, I don't know what sort of life you've had up until now, but generally people try to be polite to their hosts and don't insult the original owners of the land. If you have a problem with me being black or gay or anything else, then you'd probably be better off in your own place." Jonathan kept his voice very quiet even though he wanted to stand, loom over his dickhead neighbor, and tell him to get out.

"Oh jeez, all right. I'm going to get some beer from my place, if that's all right with you." He strode out, closing the door firmly and not quite politely behind him as he left.

Ben leaned close to Jonathan. "With any luck, he'll start drinking there and forget to come back."

Jonathan slouched against the back of the couch, his head close to Ben's shoulder. "Did we invite any of these people over? Why do they all want to be here?" He held his breath when the "we" registered. He'd said "we" like he and Ben were a couple who invited people—together.

Ben sighed. "Technically I'm one of those people too. I want to be here because I like you. The more I get to know you, the more I want to know." Ben turned to Jonathan with a self-deprecating laugh, his fingers curling into his palm, warm and comforting. "That doesn't make any sense at all, does it?"

"No, it doesn't, but I know what you mean."

"Yeah?" The word *hopeful* must have been defined by the look on Ben's face.

Jonathan smiled at him.

"Here you are. Hummus with toast and a dried apricot and poppy seed cheese ball with crackers."

"Tahlia, why do you do this?" Jonathan asked as he sat up, moving away from Ben just enough so it didn't look like they were lying all over each other.

"Do what?" Tahlia placed the plates of hummus and toast on the coffee table, then gently pushed them into the right position relative to each other. Beside her, Neridah did the same with the cheese ball and crackers.

"I've been here a week and have yet to cook a meal for myself. You and Neridah are always here, being nice and doing things for me, and you don't know me at all."

Neridah rushed around to the couch and sat beside Jonathan. "Oh, sweetheart." She patted his forearm like she had Ben's at the uni refectory. "Tahlia and me, well, I'm just a lonely old lady looking for someone to care for, and Tahlia loves to cook for someone who appreciates it. And here you are, all sad and moving like you should be wearing a full-body cast." Jonathan frowned at her, and she grinned. "And it doesn't hurt at all that you're gorgeous and your skin is so shiny and smooth it just begs to be touched." She leaned closer, and Jonathan leaned back in horror.

Tahlia laughed. "Back off, Neridah. You're so naughty that you don't even realize you've got just as much chance with him as you have with Ben."

Neridah sat back in surprise. "What do you mean? I get lots of young men interested in me."

"I know you do, but these young men are interested in each other, not you."

Neridah gasped. "No! Not two big lads like you, surely."

"I think you have the wrong idea about us, Tahlia," Jonathan said tentatively.

"You're gay, aren't you?"

Where did this forceful woman come from? Up to now, Tahlia had been the Stepford neighbor. Now she was almost accusing.

"Yes. I am." He glanced at Ben. "We are. But—"

"You're interested in each other too." Tahlia dragged a chair over from the dining area and sat. "Both of you have beard burn that wasn't there earlier."

"There's a lot... a lot...." Jonathan had no idea how to explain.

"Jonathan's just coming out of a bad relationship. We're not going to get involved or anything because he needs to sort all that out first."

Ben looked like he was accepting of it all, but he sounded resigned. Unhappy. Jonathan shuffled away from him a little, even though every atom in his body screamed for him to wrap Ben in his arms and comfort him.

Neridah leaned forward as if she was going to hug Jonathan. He twisted and leaned back, only stopping when he felt Ben's solid presence behind him. "You poor thing. That's why you're hurt, isn't it? Did he do that to you?"

Jonathan stood, his mouth gaping, his breathing harsh in his throat. He stumbled back a few steps and jumped when he bumped into Tahlia, who'd been sitting silently to the side. Her face showed the shock he felt. They could tell that easily? They saw it so readily when he'd been so sure he'd hidden it. He'd had nearly ten years of practice at hiding it. Did that mean everyone knew? Did everyone know how weak he was?

And Ben, who was now on his feet and coming for Jonathan—he knew too. Jonathan's eyes burned, and he gasped against the tears itching to fall. "I think you all need to leave." He turned away so they couldn't see his face. "Close the door on your way out, please," he said as he walked down the hall.

He closed his bedroom door behind him and leaned against it, his head back, damp eyes staring at the dark ceiling.

"Jonathan?"

Ben. Jonathan scrubbed his hands over his face. He'd thought they could…. He would…. God, he'd been looking forward to having sex, but he didn't want a pity fuck. He wanted to be wanted for him.

"Go away, Ben." Nothing. Silence. "I'll… I'll call you." It was a lie, and the silence on the other side of the door told him Ben knew it too. Twin tears rolled down his cheeks. One kiss. That was all he got. One kiss and it was over before it even began.

"Tahlia! What the fuck are you still doing here? Why haven't you brought me some food?"

Bloody Kyle. Jonathan huffed a small laugh, but the tears kept falling.

Murmured voices followed, but Jonathan didn't bother to listen. It didn't make any difference what anyone said or did as long as they left. Jonathan lay on the bed and closed his eyes.

"We're all going now, Jonathan." Ben's soft voice was muffled through the door. "Tahlia put your dinner in the fridge for you." The silence that followed lasted so long Jonathan thought he'd gone. "Call me, will you?"

Tears ran down the side of Jonathan's face and dripped into his ears. Ben sounded like he wanted to cry too. There were more voices, then the solid click of the front door closing. He could get up now. He could go out and eat his meal and read a book or watch TV or anything else he wanted to do.

He stayed where he was and listened to the emptiness of his life.

Chapter ELEVEN

THE PHONE rang just as Jonathan finally got his breathing under control. He lurched to his feet, stumbled to the bedroom door, and wrenched it open. His apartment was empty except for the hurriedly tidied kitchen and the phone vibrating its way across the coffee table. He snatched it up and answered.

"Is everything okay?"

Liam.

"Of course it is. Why wouldn't it be?" Jonathan slumped into the couch cushions and checked that the curtains were pulled tightly across the windows.

"Anthony was released from hospital two days ago. I'm sorry, I didn't know. I'd have warned you if I did."

If Jonathan told Liam that he thought Anthony had been there, Liam would come around. He loved his cousin, and if he felt comfortable with anyone it would be him, but he really needed to be on his own for a while, and he'd only just got the apartment to himself. He had to work out how to live his life without someone else around all the time, demanding he do something or be something. He couldn't even pretend he was living a normal life just like everyone else, because he didn't know what normal was anymore.

"It's fine, Liam. I'll deal with Anthony if I have to." He could have just asked Liam who told Anthony where he'd moved to, but Liam probably didn't know, and it would only worry him. "What's happening with you and Mark?" That should divert him. Liam had been hung up on the handsome jeweler for weeks now.

"Mark's fine." With that tone of voice, Jonathan was sure Mark was very "fine." "We're going out to dinner tonight."

"Ooh, a date," Jonathan teased. He leaned over so he could see his reflection in the face of the television and smiled so the cheerfulness would come through in his voice. "I thought you'd moved past that and into the bedroom."

"Just because we're... um...." Liam cleared his throat. "It doesn't mean we can't still date. It takes time to get to know someone properly."

Jonathan's smile disappeared. He knew Liam didn't mean it as a criticism, but it was. Jonathan had moved in with Anthony after just three dates. They'd had sex after the third date—Jonathan's first time—and he moved his clothes in the next day.

"Well, you go and enjoy yourself, cousin. You don't need to worry about me, and you know I'll call you if I need help."

Liam cleared his throat. "Yes, about that. I forgot to tell you about a conference I'm going to tomorrow. It's in Melbourne, so I'll be away all week."

A chill raced down Jonathan's spine. While he wanted, desperately needed, to manage on his own, he always counted on Liam being there for him. He wouldn't have that for a whole week. He'd truly be on his own. His reflection in the television had slouched, and Jonathan forced himself to sit up straight and lift his chin. "You love those things. You'll have a ball." He nodded at his reflection. He sounded appropriately supportive, not the whiny loser he felt inside.

"Yeah, I'm looking forward to it, but I'm not sure about...."

"About what?"

Liam sighed. "Mark."

"What? You think he's going to dump you because you go to a conference for a week?"

"No, you're right. It sounds stupid when you say it aloud."

"Because it is stupid. Talk to him."

"I did."

"And?"

"He said the same thing you said."

Jonathan laughed. "You're an idiot, Liam."

Liam huffed. "Mark said that too."

"Smart man."

Liam laughed as Jonathan intended but sobered quickly. "You could come with me."

"No." He took a deep breath to calm the panic. If he let them, his family would wrap him in cotton wool and never let him out of their sight again. "I've just moved here. I want some time to settle in. I went to the uni today and submitted an application to study. There'll be loads of things I need to do to get ready for that."

"That's great, Jon. You've been talking about studying again for a long time. What course are you doing?"

"I was thinking about a Master of Museum Studies."

"Museums? Where did that come from? I thought you wanted to extend the business degree you did years ago."

"No, I think I've lost interest in that area. Anyway, I'm not doing the museum thing. I changed my mind."

Liam laughed. "Yep, that sounds like the Jonathan I know. What did you finally decide on?"

"Physiotherapy."

He was silent for several seconds. "It's good to have you back."

Jonathan pressed trembling fingers against his quivering lips. Until that moment, he hadn't realized just how absent he'd been in his own life. *Ten years.* Ten bloody years he'd given to that selfish whore. When he was sure he could speak without breaking down, he whispered, "It's good to be back."

BEN STOOD on the footpath outside Jonathan's building for a long time, trying to decide what to do. Yes, the man was gorgeous and sweet, and his body was so hot Ben felt singed whenever he was in the same room, but he had more baggage than an airport conveyer belt during peak season.

As he stood leaning against the building, he desultorily surveyed the neighborhood. There was a mix of elderly houses in various stages of renovation and three- and four-story apartment buildings. It wasn't a great area, but it was safe enough that people parked their cars along the street and didn't always have their garage doors closed. One car parked just a few houses down had its windows open.

Ben noticed the Jeep because it didn't fit with all the other Ford Lasers, Hyundais, or ten-year-old utes. A shadow moved behind the heavy tinting, and he realized there was someone in the 4WD vehicle. The hair on Ben's neck quivered and he was suddenly sure whoever was in the car was watching him. Why him? He was nothing special. He might have lived here a few years, but he didn't really know anyone outside uni or the removal company. Realization came to him in a rush, and he turned to get into Jonathan's building. The door was locked.

He pulled out his phone and dialed.

"Ben, I don't think it's a good idea—"

"There's someone here. In a Jeep. And he's watching you." It didn't seem like such a leap from the man in the Jeep watching Ben to him watching Jonathan.

There was a long pause before Jonathan answered. "Ben, go home. Now."

"Let me in, Jonathan. Call the police. You have to—" A chill washed over Ben. "You're waiting for him, aren't you? That's why you wanted me to leave. You're not interested in me at all. He's the one."

"Ben—"

"No, no, it's fine. Really. We barely know each other. I was just worried, you know. It's okay." He ran his hand through his hair. He was rambling. *Stop. Just stop. Get off the phone.* "I'll go now." *What now? Have a good life? Could I get more pathetic?* He pressed the phone to his ear, reluctant to disconnect the call before Jonathan did. That's how pathetic he was. Waiting on a silent phone for his—what? Boyfriend? Love interest?—to hang up on him because nothing else would make him realize he wasn't wanted.

"Ben! Wait."

He released his breath on a sigh.

"Get the number of the car."

His shoulders slumped. Of course. He looked over to the Jeep again only to find it moving, coming down the street toward him. Surprised, he forgot to look at the license plate. When his brain finally kicked into gear again, the car was past him and picking up speed. He stepped to the edge of the footpath and squinted to see the plate. "It's dirty. I think the letters are A—something." The Jeep turned the corner. "Sorry, I couldn't see it clearly."

"How did he find me? He has my new phone number too. That's not supposed to happen." Even though Jonathan was asking questions, Ben knew he wasn't really talking to him.

"Jonathan?"

"Thanks, Ben." The call disconnected, leaving Ben standing in the street holding a silent phone to his ear.

He started walking. "Bloody idiot. You've done it again." Ben increased his pace until he was striding toward his truck, halfway down the block. "He's not that into you, no matter what you might think about him. The message couldn't be any clearer than that." He unlocked his door and got into the cab. "The guy in the Jeep is obviously someone special. You're way out of your league here, boyo." His mum was right. He always did this. He met someone he liked and followed them around like a lost puppy, hoping his big sad eyes would make them love him. "Idiot. Pathetic idiot," he muttered as he drove down the street and turned the same corner the Jeep had.

He'd driven a couple of blocks before he realized he'd driven past the Jeep when he turned the corner. He checked his rearview mirror. Directly behind him there was a small red car, but behind that was a big black 4WD. The Jeep. They were following him. His heart rate picked up.

"Why is he following me?"

He turned another corner, then a few blocks down, another going in a different direction. The Jeep stayed behind him. He tapped the button on his Bluetooth. "Call Jonathan." The phone rang so many times Ben was sure Jonathan wasn't going to pick up.

"Ben, I don't think you—"

"He's following me. Why is he following me? Who is he?"

"Oh God. Go somewhere with stairs but no lifts. You have to get off the road because he drives like a demon, but he can't follow you up stairs. Don't go anywhere with a lift, though."

"What?" What the hell kind of person was this? "You know that sounds crazy, don't you? Why can he drive and use lifts but not stairs?"

"He's in a wheelchair, so he can't follow you up stairs."

Ben checked his mirror again. "What about his mate?"

"What?"

"The man with him. What about him? Is he in a wheelchair too? Because if he's not, he'll surely be able to go anywhere I can."

"Oh shit." Jonathan was silent for so long, Ben checked his phone to make sure they were still connected. "I'll call you back." The connection died. Ben planted his foot on the accelerator and sped down the street. He barely slowed enough to check oncoming traffic before he took the corner. Jonathan had better still be there when he got back to his apartment, or Ben was going to be royally pissed.

BEN SCREECHED to a halt at the curb outside Jonathan's building. He didn't take the time to parallel park properly but dove into the space nose first. After quickly checking the side mirror for oncoming traffic, he opened his door, but before he could put a foot out, a revving engine sounded behind him. The impact jolted him forward into his steering wheel and metal screeched against metal as the black Jeep hit the side of his car, taking his driver's door with it as it swerved back onto the road. It sped down the street, gray smoke and noise wafting away on the still air.

Ben gripped his steering wheel, breathing hard as he stared at what was left of his door spinning lazily on the pavement several meters away.

"Fuck." He slapped the steering wheel. "Fuck!" He jumped out of his car, his hands tugging at his hair. He strode to his door and kicked it. "Fuck!"

"Ben? Are you all right?" called Jonathan from just outside the door of his building. He checked carefully before he ran to where Ben still stood in the middle of the street. "He didn't hit you, did he?"

"What the fuck are you involved in?" Ben rounded on Jonathan, too angry to feel any remorse at the way the man backed away from him, fear blooming in his dark eyes. "The bastard came after me and ran into my car." He turned and kicked the twisted door again. "He took the bloody door right off." He ran out of steam and stood there, arms hanging at his sides, and panted through the rush of adrenaline.

Beside him, Jonathan had his phone out. "Hello, I'm not sure if I should be calling emergency but don't have any other number. Police. There's been a hit-and-run, but no one's been hurt." His quiet voice continued, giving information to the operator, and Ben stood, breathing hard, letting Jonathan's calm voice soothe him. When Jonathan's warm brown hand grasped Ben's bicep, he walked beside him to stand on the footpath outside the building. He stared directly across the street, avoiding the still rocking door and his ute.

"I want to know exactly who he is. I want contact details. That bastard is going to pay for the repairs."

Jonathan patted Ben's arm. "That would be good, but I'm not sure we can actually prove it was him."

Ben swung to glare and Jonathan. "What the fuck do you mean? I saw him. I was in the fucking car when he hit my door."

"Did you see his face? Did you get the registration number?"

"You know who it is."

Jonathan nodded. "I think I do, but proving it is another thing altogether." He stepped off the curb. "I'm going to get your door, then we can wait upstairs for the police to arrive."

JONATHAN TRUDGED up the stairs behind Ben. He'd managed to hold it together when Ben lost his shit, but he wasn't sure how long that would last. Anger and fear were battling to take over his body like alien beings. Ben kept walking up the stairs, his buttocks directly in front of Jonathan. It occurred to him he should be enjoying the view more than he was, but he couldn't drag his thoughts away from Ben's door being torn from his car. He was sure it was Anthony, but how would he prove it? How had Anthony found him? He'd only given his new address and phone number to his aunt and uncle, and Liam. And the hospital physio. And Ben.

Ben stepped back when they reached Jonathan's door, then followed him inside. They sat in awkward silence for ten minutes until Jonathan couldn't stand it anymore. He jumped up, wincing at the tug in his chest, then strode into the kitchen.

"I'm going to make tea. Do you want some?"

"Tea? Sure. My mum says tea is always the best thing in stressful situations."

Jonathan turned to stare at Ben, flabbergasted at the blasé response. "Stressful? That bastard ran into your car. He tried to hurt you. I don't know how the hell he's doing it. He should be still writhing around in pain. He shouldn't be driving." He squeezed his eyes shut, shoved his fingers through his tightly curled hair, and pulled. He jumped when Ben's fingers trailed along his forearms before gently clasping over his skin and tugging his arms down.

"Take it easy. The police will be here soon, and they can tell us what to do. We don't need to do anything but sit and wait."

"I can't wait. Every minute I sit here and wait for the police, he's planning something or doing something. He'll—"

"He won't do anything. You said he was in a wheelchair. There's no lift. He can't get up here." Ben maneuvered Jonathan out of the way and walked into the kitchen. "Where's your teapot?"

"Teapot?"

"You're not telling me you offered me tea and you don't have a teapot. I'm a country boy. There's no such thing as tea bags in the country." Ben winked at Jonathan, so he knew the other man was joking, but he still strode into the kitchen and pushed Ben out of the way.

"I'll give you a teapot," he said as he flung open the cupboard door above the kettle. Inside sat three teapots. Ben looked closely, then burst out laughing.

"Okay, you win. Do I get to choose?" He reached around Jonathan, his arm brushing his shoulder, and pulled down one of the teapots. "I've always loved Daffy Duck."

Jonathan took down another teapot. "This is my favorite." He cradled the Sylvester and Tweety pot gently in his long brown fingers.

"Sure," said Ben, replacing Daffy where he came from. "I could go for the puddy tat."

They smiled at each other, and Jonathan was surprised to realize his terror had dissipated. With nothing more than an inane conversation about teapots, he was calm and more relaxed than he'd felt since… in a long time. "Go sit down. I'll bring it out when it's ready."

"What made you choose this place? It's a bit different to where you were living before."

Jonathan was aware of Ben watching him from the living room as he pottered in the kitchen, measuring tea, arranging mugs, taking milk and a plate of Tahlia's lemon slice from the fridge. "It's cheap, it's clean, it has stairs and no lift, it can't easily be seen from the street, and the emergency exit is nearby." Jonathan looked up. Ben didn't look as stressed as he had before, but he was still a long way from relaxed.

"Sure, I get it," Ben said as he sat on the couch and leaned back.

The buzzer sounded just as Jonathan was lowering the teapot to the coffee table, and he fumbled it, spilling tea and clanking china against glass. He took a quick breath and went to find out who it was. "Okay. I'll come down and let you in. Can you have your ID handy, please?"

"I'll come down with you." Ben followed Jonathan out of the apartment, ignoring his querying glance and annoyed frown.

When they returned with the two uniformed cops, Neridah and Tahlia were standing outside Jonathan's apartment. Neridah held a plate of chocolate brownies; Tahlia's plate was piled high with blueberry muffins.

"Hello, dears," said Neridah. "We thought you'd like something to offer these wonderful men in blue."

"I don't think—"

"That's not necessary, ma'am."

"We saw it all, you know," said Neridah. "You'll want to talk to us anyway." She nodded at Jonathan, then at his door. He got the hint, opened the door, and ushered everyone in.

In the end there was nothing they could do. Jonathan hadn't seen the Jeep, even though he knew it must be Anthony. It couldn't have been anyone else. Ben hadn't seen details of the people in the car, other than there were two of them and they were men. Neridah and Tahlia gave their account, which threw even more doubt on the situation. They couldn't be sure the Jeep had been chasing Ben, just that it came around the corner too fast, fish-tailed down the street, and collected his door when he opened it.

Jonathan restrained himself from slamming the door once the police had left. "Fuck." All that baring-his-soul, telling them what his life had been like for the last ten years, and all he'd achieved was to come across as a neurotic, paranoid time-waster, especially when he'd told them Anthony was a quadriplegic. As soon as the police had heard that, they'd assumed Anthony couldn't possibly be a threat, the accident was just an accident, and Jonathan was imagining everything. They went away with a promise to follow up, gave Ben a police report number to give to his insurance company, and that was all.

"Don't you worry, dear. You're safe here now. Tahlia and me, we'll keep an eye out for you." Neridah crossed her arms, plumping her breasts.

Way to make me feel like a whinging child. He returned to the living room to find Ben on his feet, also ready to leave.

"I'm going to head out too, see if I can get my door fixed before the weekend."

"You're going to drive with it like that?"

"Of course. It's just a door. I'll have my seatbelt on."

Jonathan smiled at the image Ben painted of him driving around without the door, exposed to all who cared to look. "You'll get some looks, that's for sure."

"Where I come from, it's not that unusual." Ben grinned at him as he stood in front of him.

The day faded from Jonathan's mind, and he was left with the warm air circling around and between them, the slightly acrid scent of old adrenaline clinging to their heated skin. He swayed, no thought intruding except that he wanted to know if Ben's pink lips tasted as good as they looked. Then Ben moved closer and Jonathan cringed, the response automatic. He sighed and stepped away. It didn't matter if he was attracted to Ben or if Ben was attracted to him. Nothing was going to happen because Jonathan responded to every sigh, every move, as if it was a threat. He opened the door.

"I'm sorry you got involved in this," he said. If there was one thing he could do, it was make sure Ben didn't become any more involved than he was already. He had to make sure Anthony had no reason to go after Ben and make his life the hell he'd made Jonathan's. Logically, Jonathan knew Anthony should be no threat. He was in a wheelchair, for God's sake, but that didn't matter. The bastard had managed to stab himself, Liam, and Jonathan and create absolute havoc in the hospital without the use of his legs. It stood to reason he could do worse if he put his mind to it. Especially if he had an accomplice.

"It's fine," said Ben. He glanced down the hallway, probably making sure Jonathan's nosy neighbors were nowhere to be seen. "If you'd like, we could get together again, maybe go out to dinner or something."

Jonathan was tempted. In the few short seconds it took him to respond, myriad images flashed through his mind. Him and Ben laughing over a meal, walking in the park, going dancing. No sooner had he thought all those things, though, than the wonderful fantasies were overlaid with something that was closer to what the reality would be. Anthony turning up at the restaurant, phoning Jonathan while he was in the park, rolling up to him on the crowded dance floor and stabbing Ben in the stomach. It was the last image, no matter how unlikely it was that Anthony could get his wheelchair in a club and through the crowds, that stopped Jonathan.

"I don't think so," he said and steeled himself against the disappointment on Ben's face.

"Oh, sure. Whatever," said Ben. "I guess I'll…." He huffed a cynical laugh. "I probably won't see you around at all, will I?"

Jonathan shook his head. Ben nodded, turned, and jogged down the stairs as if he couldn't wait to get away. Jonathan closed his door quietly and rested his forehead against it. Bloody Anthony was still ruling his life.

"Just a little longer," he whispered. "I'll get rid of you from my head soon, you bastard. Then I'll build a life you would never recognize and have friends you haven't approved of, and I'll find a lover who really cares for me and not just what I can do for him or how young I can make him look." He sighed and pushed himself upright. "Step one: uni—already applied for. Step two…." He sighed again. "Hell if I know."

He wandered through his small apartment three times, each circuit increasing the claustrophobic tension in his stomach. "This is never going to work here," he muttered as he shoved his wallet and keys in his pockets. He looked out his window, twisting his body to see as much of the small sliver of footpath and road as he could. "There's one disadvantage of not being able to see the street from here," he muttered as he closed his door behind him and headed down the stairs.

JONATHAN RETURNED from his leisurely stroll—he snorted—furtive jog—around the block to find Col, the older removalist from the other day, standing on his doorstep.

"Col? It's Col, isn't it?"

"'Bout time you got here. Haven't got all day, y'know. Let us in and we'll get you moved right enough." Col shifted from foot to foot and peered over his shoulder every time he moved.

Jonathan looked back to the street, but there was no truck and no Ben. "Um, sure, okay. Where's Ben?"

"Ben?" Confusion flooded Col's features, and he shifted uncomfortably.

"Never mind. Let's go up and we can get started." He couldn't let the man wander around the neighborhood. He unlocked the door and waited until Col entered before pulling out his phone and dialing Ben as they walked up the stairs. *What does it say about you that he's already on speed dial?*

"Jonathan? Is everything all right?"

"Yeah, hi, Ben. Everything's fine. Sort of."

"Sort of?"

"Yeah." Jonathan let them both into his apartment and watched Col wander around the furniture in the living room before disappearing into the bedroom. "Col is here, sorting out what needs to be moved."

"Col? Fuck."

"Yeah."

"Okay. I'm on my way back now. I'll ring his wife on the way."

"What the fuck is wrong with you?" Col demanded from the bedroom door. "There's nothing packed."

"Ben will be here soon, Col. He'll explain it all to you."

"If you aren't fucking ready to move, you shouldn't have booked us in." Col shifted on his feet and darted uncomfortable glances around the room. His fingers twitched and tugged on his threadbare shorts. Jonathan stepped across to plant himself in front of the door. He needed to hold Col here until Ben arrived.

"What?" Col fidgeted and darted panicked glances around. "I need—fuck—you black bastard!" He rushed at Jonathan, screaming. "Get out! Get out! Help, police. Thief!"

Jonathan fell back. Mostly it was shock, but part of it was surprise.

"Get out of my house!" Col shoved Jonathan against the wall and fumbled with the door. "Help! Help!" he screamed as he ran into the corridor. Neridah and Tahlia threw open their doors and tumbled into the hallway with them. A scant second later, Kyle rushed out too.

"What the fuck? What sort of queer-arsed fuckwit have you brought home this time?"

Jonathan's jaw dropped at Kyle's exclamation. In his shock, he let Col get past him. "No, Col. Wait," he called as he ran down the stairs after the fleeing man.

"Help! Help!" screamed Col. "I've been kidnapped."

"Col! Wait for Ben," called Jonathan as he swung around the landing to the next level. How the hell could the old man move so fast? *Shit.* He hoped he didn't hurt himself. Jonathan slowed, then picked up speed again. Col was still running, slipping down every second step, landing heavily on his feet, his white hair billowing around his head. Filth and fear tumbled from his mouth in concert.

Jonathan reached the lobby to find Col at the front door, fisted hands thumping rhythmically on the wood and glass. Tears streamed down the old man's face and drool dripped from his chin.

"Col," he said quietly. "It's all right, Col. Ben will be here soon, and he'll take you home."

Col froze. "Home?"

"Yes, Col, home. Ben will take you home to your wife." Silence. "What's your wife's name, Col? Is it Lorraine?"

"Lorraine?" Col looked around the lobby. "Where's Lorraine?"

"Not here, Col, but Ben will take you to her."

"Who's Ben?"

"Ben works with you, Col. He helps you move things."

"Move. Yes." Col turned washed-out blue eyes to Jonathan. There was no recognition in them. No humanity. Col was a breathing, speaking, empty vessel. He looked around the lobby vacantly and jumped when a knock sounded at the door.

"Jonathan?"

Neridah and Tahlia burst from the stairwell. Kyle didn't follow them.

"Hey there, Col. Whatcha doing?"

Col jumped and swung frightened eyes to Ben. He stepped back and cried out when he bumped into Jonathan. Jonathan could see another panic coming on but didn't know what to do about it. Were they going to have to drag a screaming, frightened Col out to Ben's ute? What then? Tie him down?

"Here, Col." Ben held his phone out to the old man. "Lorraine wants to talk to you."

"Lorraine?" Col looked around, bewildered.

"Yeah, that's right, Col." Ben jiggled his phone in front of Col. "Lorraine is on the phone, and she wants to talk to you."

Col didn't move, so Ben lifted the phone close to Col's ear. Jonathan swallowed as Col's expression changed.

"Lorraine?" Col whispered as tears streamed down his face.

Jonathan caught Ben's devastated gaze and swallowed heavily.

"Oh, the poor dear," whispered Neridah from behind him.

"Lorraine is bringing his meds," Ben said quietly. "She had to go out and took longer than she thought, so he's missed a dose."

"You want a cup of tea, Treasure?" Col looked around the lobby. "Where—"

Neridah stepped up and took his elbow. "You tell your Lorraine you'll be up in 1C with Neridah. I'll have a nice cup of tea ready for her when she gets here."

"Tea? She wants a cup of tea." Col nodded repeatedly as he walked along between Tahlia and Neridah. Neridah handed Ben's phone back to him.

"Of course she does, dear. I'll bet your Lorraine has had a busy day, and she'll be looking forward to sitting with you and having a cup of tea when she's done." Tall, thin Neridah, and short, slim Tahlia bracketed Col with his dandelion hair as they disappeared up the stairs.

Ben sighed heavily and brought his phone to his ear. "You there, Lorraine? Yeah, a couple of neighbors have just taken him upstairs to make tea. How far away are you?" He reached a hand out to grasp Jonathan's fingers and drew him toward the stairwell.

Jonathan glanced at their joined hands, then at Ben who was still speaking to Lorraine on the phone. He could tug his hand free—it wasn't as if Ben had him in a death-grip—but he didn't. He hadn't held hands with anyone in a long time and had forgotten how comforting it was. He let Ben's voice drone on as they entered the stairwell and started up as he tried to work out exactly when the last time was. The closest he could figure, he'd been in high school with his first boyfriend. Sort-of boyfriend. They'd held hands that one afternoon while Disney cartoons played, then the boy's mother had come home and suddenly Jonathan was being shoved out the door while the boy told him he "wasn't like that."

Jonathan settled his hand more firmly in Ben's grip and curled his fingers around Ben's hand. Ben squeezed Jonathan's hand and winked at him. Jonathan smiled.

They stopped at the first landing. "Oh, you're here? Okay. I'll come down and let you in." Ben turned to Jonathan. "You go on up. I'll bring Lorraine and we can get Col sorted."

Jonathan curled his fingers around the cool emptiness left behind as Ben trotted down the stairs. *Fool. What do you think you're doing? You only left Anthony a few weeks ago and now you think... what? That you have a new boyfriend just because Ben held your hand? And with all the forwards and backwards steps you're taking, he's probably going to end up with whiplash before you make up your mind what you want. If he stays around that long.* He scoffed and jogged a couple of stairs in his impatience to be done with it, but quickly slowed to plodding one step at a time when his chest let him know he shouldn't be moving so quickly. At least all this going up and down stairs would make his physiotherapist happy.

LORRAINE WAS a tall, thin woman with dyed black hair cut into a severe bob. Her hands fluttered in time with the wattled skin on her neck, and her soft voice held what Jonathan could only assume was habitual apology. She didn't stay long after hurrying into Neridah's apartment and giving Col his medication.

"He'll get drowsy now, so I should get him down to the car before he falls asleep on me."

"How are you going to get him out of the car afterwards?" asked Jonathan.

"Oh, I'll—"

"I'll follow you home and give you a hand. It'll be better for Col if he wakes up in his own bed and not the car." Ben stepped forward and placed his hand on Lorraine's shoulder.

When they had retrieved a stumbling Col and driven away, Jonathan trudged back upstairs to his apartment. "It's nothing but foolish imaginings." He scowled. "I'm not a basket case and don't need anyone holding my hand to go up the stairs." He opened his door, slipped inside, and closed it. He leaned his forehead on the door as he clicked the locks into place.

He'd been there all of three days and had barely had a moment to himself. Why, then, did he feel so lonely?

Chapter TWELVE

SWEAT POURED off Anthony and everything ached, but he knew that Vaughn and the physiotherapist who'd come in had gone easy on him because of his stomach wound. Mostly they'd made him do arm and hand exercises. Anthony watched Vaughn put things away after their session.

Vaughn handed Anthony a bottle of water with the lid already off. It was the first concession the nurse had made all morning. Anthony sighed in relief and guzzled the water. When the physiotherapist left and Vaughn returned to the room, Anthony put the bottle down.

"Why are you doing this?"

Vaughn stopped what he was doing and turned to Anthony. "Doing what?"

"You make me exercise and do things for myself, and you drive me around, but you never make any comment about Jonathan."

Vaughn was silent for so long Anthony wondered if he intended to respond at all. Perhaps he was going to say something about the way Anthony had got him to agree to work for him. It had been surprisingly easy. As soon as Anthony had mentioned drug shortages, Vaughn had capitulated. Had Vaughn really been shorting him on the drugs? And other patients too? Anthony had been bluffing, but that might give him some serious leverage if he could prove it.

"I agreed to drive you around, and Jonathan isn't any of my business." Vaughn's voice was soft and reluctant, and he kept his face averted so Anthony couldn't tell what his mood was.

Anthony wanted to yell at Vaughn and tell him to look at him when he spoke, but he didn't. Most of the time, Vaughn was exactly the way Anthony thought a nurse should be—quiet and caring but still making sure things happened on time. Sometimes, though, there was a look in his eyes that…. Anthony wasn't sure. No, that wasn't true. He was certain. Vaughn was the first person Anthony had met since his father died that Anthony didn't know if he could control. And Anthony had invited him into his house and had put his life into Vaughn's hands. For the first time since Anthony had made sure his father would never hurt him again, he was afraid.

He sat straighter in his chair. His imagination was running away with him. He was the one in control, just like he always was. Vaughn just hadn't worked it out yet. He was still trying to tell Anthony what to do. That was fine with the physio, because Anthony wanted to get out of the bloody chair, but Vaughn would get a very different response from Anthony to anything else. Maybe he didn't even need to prove anything with the drugs. Just the threat of exposure should be enough to keep him in line.

Chapter THIRTEEN

BEN SAT on the grass and watched the ducks dive and wiggle in the pond. Swamp hens herded their chicks through the shallows, and a frilled-neck lizard sunned itself on the paved edging. He ran his thumb over the smooth screen of his phone, over and over. He wanted to call Jonathan but wasn't sure what his reception would be. Part of him still felt like the stalker-extraordinaire, but Jonathan had called him—a number of times. It had been two days since the disaster that wrecked his car, and then the fiasco with Col.

Ben sighed, woke his phone, and flipped through to Jonathan's number. His thumb hovered over the Connect button, but the phone vibrated before he could touch it. A relieved laugh burst from him. *Jonathan.*

"Hey, babe," he said, then cringed. No way would Jonathan want to be called that. That was an endearment for people in settled, stable relationships. They hardly knew each other. He cleared his throat and started again. "Hi Jonathan. What can I do for you?" He smashed his face into his palm. That was worse.

There was silence for several seconds, then Jonathan sighed. "I'm sorry," he whispered.

Ben sat straighter. "What for?"

"I told you to leave. I held your hand and then didn't want you around. I let you nearly get run over. You could have been hurt. I keep doing that."

"Whoa, hang on a minute. You know you're not making a lot of sense, don't you?"

"Sorry, I'll go—"

"No! Wait." Ben sighed. "What is it you want, Jonathan? What's wrong?"

"See? That's it. That's exactly it."

"What is?"

"I ring and you immediately think I want something or something's wrong. Probably both. I'm… I'm a bad risk."

Ben frowned at the lizard in front of him. "Jonathan, what's happened? Why are you—why did you call me?"

"I'm pathetic. I shouldn't have called you. I need to do this on my own."

"Do what?"

"Get my life together."

"Why do you have to do that on your own? Can't you have help from family and friends?"

"I don't have any friends left and my family… my family will do anything for me except believe I can do this on my own." After a short pause, he continued. "They're all out of town this week anyway."

Ben laughed. He knew he probably shouldn't, but he thought it hilarious that Jonathan didn't want help until he couldn't get any. "Like I said, you don't have to do it on your own. Hell, I don't know where I'd be right now without my family. They've pulled me out of more scrapes than you can imagine. Where are you now?"

"I'm at home. I'm always at home."

"Yeah, that's probably half your problem. You've got cabin fever." He looked at his watch. "I've got an hour before my next lecture. Why don't I come and pick you up so you can get out and reconnect with the world again."

"That's crazy. By the time you get here, you'll have just enough time to get back there for your lecture, and I have an appointment at the hospital later, to get my stitches out."

"Come to my lecture with me, then. No one will mind another body in the room, and I can take you to the hospital after."

After a pause, Jonathan asked, "What's the lecture?"

"Textile preservation. After what you said the other day about wanting to get into museums, you'd probably find it interesting."

"Yes, I would."

Ben grinned. Jonathan had gone from hesitant and dejected to interested, almost excited. "Okay, grab your wallet and keys. I'll be there in about twenty." He disconnected the call and jumped to his feet. His grin stayed in place through the jog to the car park and widened as he pulled up outside Jonathan's building to see Jonathan pacing impatiently along the footpath.

He waited just long enough for Jonathan to open the door and climb in before he put the ute in gear. The click of Jonathan's seatbelt coincided with a break in the traffic, and they were on their way. "You must really be interested in this lecture," Ben joked.

"Not really. I mean, I am, yes, but I'm more interested in getting out of the apartment for a while. I can't even go for a drive for a change of scenery."

"What did you do before? You know, before you were injured, before you moved here."

The silence stretched for so long Ben didn't think Jonathan intended to answer. He was just about to apologize for asking too many questions when Jonathan responded.

"I looked after Anthony."

"Anthony's your ex, right?"

"Yes. He's in a wheelchair and needed a lot of care."

"You don't sound so sure about that."

"Oh he's definitely in a wheelchair, but I don't think he needed the level of care he insisted on. I mean, I did at the time, but now I'm not so sure."

"Did he… I mean, is he the one…?" Ben sighed. "Forget it." It was none of his business how Jonathan was injured. It might not have been a deliberately inflicted injury. It could easily have been from an accident of some sort.

"Yeah. I told him I was leaving him. I mean, I'd told him before, but every time… well, then he was injured and it was my fault so I had to stay, but then I couldn't anymore, so I was going to leave, but he didn't like that and he… he…."

Ben pulled the car to the side of the road, turned the engine off, and turned to Jonathan. He gathered Jonathan into his arms, not sure how to comfort a man so much taller than he was. He knew Jonathan was older than he was too, but none of that mattered. He was hurting, and Ben knew something about that.

"Why was it your fault?"

"I was driving. Liam keeps telling me it was the drunk driver in the other car and the rain, and Anthony hit me, but I was driving. I was responsible. And now Anthony can't walk anymore, and he can't even draw. That was the worst of it, you know, that he couldn't draw. But then I found out he hadn't been anyway, even when he could. He'd stolen them all."

"Hon, I know that all made sense in your head, but you need to remember that I'm out here and have no idea what you're talking about."

Jonathan laughed. It was a small, watery one, but a laugh nonetheless. "Sorry. Anthony's a jeweler. That's why drawing was so important to him. He's won awards for years, but then I found out the designs he won with weren't his; they were Mark's. Anthony had stolen them all from him years ago."

"Choice."

Another laugh huffed out. "Yeah. He fooled a lot of people." Jonathan sat back, dislodging Ben's hold on him. "But it was worse than that." He twisted his fingers together in his lap, then looked at Ben defiantly. "He hit me, and I let him. For years." He looked away. "I kept staying because I believed him when he said I'd never find anyone else to love me. I believed him when he said I was worthless and only good for picking up after him, and I owed him because it was my fault that he was like that." He glared at Ben. "But it wasn't my fault. He was like that before me. He was with Mark and beat him too, so it wasn't my fault."

"Of course it wasn't your fault. No one asks to be treated like that." He grinned at the look Jonathan gave him. "You're thinking of the BDSM scene? It's not the same. What Anthony did to you was about taking power without permission. He showed you a total lack of respect. From the little I know of the scene, that sort of thing has no place there."

"I was driving, though."

"You said he hit you? While you were driving? And there was a drunk driver as well?"

Jonathan nodded. "It was raining. When I tried to correct, the car went into a skid."

"Sounds to me like there were a whole lot of things against you, and you still managed to get both of you through the accident alive."

Jonathan stared at him, wide-eyed hope shining on his face. Ben put the car in gear, and they continued their journey in silence.

"Here we are," Ben said as he pulled into the car park and began the usual frustrating search for a vacant spot. "You can come to this lecture and think about something totally different for a while."

"WHY DID you take me to that lecture?" Jonathan asked accusingly. He rubbed his chest where the new dressing sat over his newly stitch-free skin.

"Didn't you enjoy it?"

"Of course I did, but now I want to find some fabrics and practice. Who knew how many things you had to think about with fabrics? I'll never throw my old sheets out again. I'm never buying polyester-blend sheets again, either."

Ben laughed. "Are you serious about practicing?"

"Absolutely, but I don't have any fabrics at all, let alone old ones. I don't even have any old sheets anymore."

"I think I can find a few things for you, if you're really interested."

Jonathan twisted in his seat to face Ben. "Are you serious?"

Ben grinned. "You just wait and see, my friend." He signaled, changed lanes, and headed toward his apartment.

"So you live out in the 'burbs."

"It's not as far out as you'd think. It's right on the freeway, and buses run directly into the city. Even in peak hour, a bus will take less than twenty minutes." He pulled up outside the modest house where he lived.

"Nice place."

"It is. The family that owns it is really nice. They have a couple of dogs and a couple of kids. I live downstairs. It's small, but I don't really need anything big." He got out and waited on the footpath for Jonathan to join him. "It's just one big room, really. I have one end set up for my bedroom and another part for a living room." He opened the gate and slipped through before gesturing to Jonathan to join him.

The clanking of the closing gate was followed by scuffling noises. Jonathan turned and squeaked. "Holy fuck," he breathed as he leaned against the fence while two huge, silent dogs sniffed at his crotch.

Ben pushed the dogs to the side. "Stop it, you two. This is Jonathan. He's a friend and doesn't need your special crotch treatment. Leave him be."

After one more painful nudging sniff each, the dogs backed off, and Jonathan began to breathe again. "When you said there were dogs, I thought you meant *dogs,* not miniature horses."

"They look scary, but they're pussycats."

"What sort are they?" Jonathan asked as he hesitantly followed Ben while the dogs wove themselves between them, bumping against knees and hips as they sniffed shoes and any crevice Jonathan or Ben allowed them near.

Ben ruffled the neck of the black dog. "Traynor here is a Doberman-Rottweiler cross. He looks fierce and has a bark that'll make you piss your pants when he starts at two in the morning, but he's a sweetheart. Delilah is part ridgeback and part blue cattle dog. She's really smart and absolutely obsessed with balls. She'll play fetch all day without a break if she can find someone willing to throw for her." He pulled a key from his pocket and unlocked the glass door, pushing the dogs aside with his hip. "No, you're not coming in today. Go find something else to do."

Both dogs flicked their ears at him and whined a little. "Go on. You're not coming in today." Traynor huffed an exasperated breath, then turned and trotted away. Delilah stared at Ben for several seconds before she also walked away. Ben opened the door and gestured to Jonathan. "In you go, before they change their minds and come back."

Jonathan quickly slipped into the room and looked around as Ben slid the door closed behind them. The small apartment was just as Ben described. It was one big L-shaped room. The narrow end was screened off, but Jonathan could see a bed and side tables behind the screen. There was another door down that end, too, that led to what looked like a small kitchen. The wide end where Jonathan stood held a couch and TV setup and a huge rectangular table. The near end of the table was almost bare, with just a few pieces of paper patterns. The middle of the table was piled high with fabric, some folded into squares, some on long rolls. At the far end, almost hidden behind the fabric, sat a sewing machine and an overlocker similar to his Aunty Faye's.

"You made those cargo shorts, didn't you?"

Ben ducked his head in a show of shyness Jonathan hadn't seen before. "Well," he said, "I found this fabric at a garage sale and thought it would be good in shorts." He looked up and grinned. "And custom-made clothes make my butt look great."

Jonathan walked closer to the table and touched a roll of white fabric. It was crisp and almost sheer.

"That's muslin. That's what they recommend we wrap aged fabrics in."

"We'd have to use cotton gloves, wouldn't we?" The fabric between Jonathan's fingers was fine and would absorb oil and moisture from his hands.

"Here, try these." Ben handed him a pair of white cotton gloves.

"You just happen to have some?"

Ben shrugged. "Sometimes I work with delicate fabrics, and I don't want to pull threads or leave marks."

Jonathan looked at the table again and the neat tallboy next to it. "Exactly how much fabric are we talking about?"

"Ah, well. Um. Do you want a coffee or anything? It won't take me a minute."

A laugh burst from Jonathan before he registered he found any of it amusing. "That means there's lots, doesn't it? I'll bet if I open any of those drawers there, they'll be packed to the gills with all sorts of different fabrics." He narrowed his eyes. "It's probably even sorted into types and color coded too." At Ben's offended, indignant look, Jonathan backtracked. "Why don't you pull out some silk and some wool and, if you have it, some embroidered things, and we'll practice folding and rolling or whatever the hell we're supposed to do with it."

"You have no respect," Ben said in a huff as he pulled open the top drawer of the tallboy. As Jonathan had suspected, the fabric inside was neatly folded and stacked according to color. The entire drawer held soft, silky bundles. Ben dug down and pulled out a piece of folded fabric from near the bottom of the drawer. "This stuff is brilliant. Just you wait until you feel some of this. You'll never dismiss fabric again. And you'll be much more particular about what you buy."

The afternoon passed in comfortable conversation and sharing. Ben's desire to be a textile conservator was clear in every touch of each piece of fabric he owned, and Jonathan couldn't help thinking how complementary their interests were. Jonathan was just beginning to think about dinner when his phone rang. He frowned at the screen.

"What's up? Someone you don't want to talk to?" Ben asked.

"Someone I don't know," Jonathan replied. He tapped the button to connect the call.

"Mr. Watson? This is Senior Constable Ridgeway from Logan Police. Could you confirm your address please?"

"What's going on?"

"There's been an explosion."

Chapter FOURTEEN

JONATHAN HAD his seatbelt undone and the door open before Ben had finished parking down the street. There was one fireman and two policemen standing at the front of the building and a fire truck pulled up across the alley beside them.

"Jonathan! Wait up. Running around like this isn't going to get things sorted any quicker." Ben grabbed Jonathan's elbow and slowed him down. "You're supposed to be taking it easy with your injury."

"He blew up my apartment." Jonathan tugged against Ben's hold. He couldn't get free, but Ben increased his pace to keep up with Jonathan.

"They don't know it was him."

"Who else would it be?" His breathing rasped in his throat. Jonathan pressed his hand over his frantically beating heart. It had been pounding since the phone call, and he was sure he was about to have a heart attack.

"He can't get up the stairs, remember."

"Who else could it be? There's no one else. I don't know...." Jonathan clamped his mouth closed. It was way too pathetic to say he didn't know anyone else, that he no longer had any friends because Anthony had scared them all away a long time ago. He continued in silence.

"There he is!" Neridah stepped from behind the two police officers and strode toward them. "I'm so glad you weren't home." She grabbed Jonathan above his elbows and pulled him toward her. He froze, mouth agape, as her face came closer.

"Careful, Neridah. He's only just had his stitches taken out." Ben stepped smoothly between them, and Jonathan breathed a sigh of relief as Neridah moved back.

"Mr. Watson?"

Jonathan walked over to the two police officers. "What happened? You said there was an explosion?"

"That's what it looks like, sir." The officer moved to block the entrance. "Most of the damage is in the bedroom. The firemen are still working up there. They'll check the rest of the building, but it looks like everyone will be able to return before too long. That is, except for you. I'm afraid there's too much fire and water damage in your apartment. Is there somewhere we can go to talk?"

"You can use my apartment, officers." Neridah stepped to Jonathan's side, her arms crossed beneath her globular breasts. Both policemen glanced down reflexively before returning their stoic gazes to her face and then to Jonathan. Behind him, Ben snorted, then turned it into a cough.

"Thank you, Ms. Ryder," the officer murmured, "but the building is still off-limits."

"What about a coffee shop?" asked Jonathan. As he turned to Neridah, he noticed Tahlia peeping out from the other side of the building and decided to ask her instead. "Tahlia," he called. "Where's your favorite café?"

She beamed at him. "I'll do better than that." She disappeared to return almost immediately with a large Tupperware container in her arms and a flask dangling from her fingers.

The bark of laughter that escaped surprised Jonathan, but he was glad he hadn't completely lost his sense of humor. "Don't tell me; part of your evacuation plan is to grab food."

"Of course it is. With all the standing around we're going to be doing, we'd starve without something to eat and drink." Tahlia walked over to the police car sitting at the curb and began setting out her wares on the bonnet.

"Mr. Watson, I'm not sure—" began one of the policemen.

"Believe me, Constable, it's easier to give in now, and I'll bet you anything you like at least one of these ladies saw something that might be of interest to you."

The interview began with the policemen asking Jonathan where he'd been at the time the fire started. He suppressed his automatic scoffing. As if he'd want to burn his own apartment when he'd only just moved in. Everything he owned was in there. He knew they had to ask, though, so he answered as calmly as he could.

Finally, finally, they consented to tell him what had happened.

"It appears a Molotov cocktail was tossed in from the fire escape after someone broke your bedroom window with a brick." Someone with terrible aim, luckily for him and his landlord. The bottle had struck at the juncture between wall and window and exploded. Fiery fuel had cascaded inside but also down the outside wall and arced out to land on the wheelie bins lined up, waiting for the garbage collection day. The back of the building was scorched; the stucco facing from the third floor outside Jonathan's bedroom lay in blackened, crumbled pieces on the ground. Half his bedroom was destroyed, but the mandatory sprinkler system had stopped it from spreading. The wheelie bins were completely melted.

"The fire escape was slightly damaged, so it's likely whoever threw the bottle was also injured."

"They were burned?"

"There's no indication of major injury, so probably just some scorch marks, or perhaps some burned clothing. We've alerted the hospitals in case someone comes in for treatment."

The police took thorough notes as Jonathan told them about Anthony, but stopped when he mentioned Anthony was in a wheelchair.

"I know it seems unlikely, but it's just as unlikely that he could have stabbed both me and my cousin, but he did. I don't know of anyone else it could be. Perhaps he has someone helping him. Ben said there was someone else in the car yesterday." Even to his own ears, it sounded unlikely, but Jonathan didn't know who else it could be.

"We'll look into it, Mr. Watson. You'll need to ring your insurer and book an assessor. I believe your landlord has already contacted his insurer. You won't be able to have access to your apartment before tomorrow. Do you have somewhere to stay tonight?"

Tonight? Jonathan turned to peer down the street as if that would give him an idea. Liam and his aunt and uncle were out of town for the week. It had been a long time since he'd had a key to any of their houses. It hadn't been safe with Anthony.

Ben's soft voice, directly behind him, made Jonathan jump. He'd had no idea the other man was so close.

"You can stay with me."

Chapter FIFTEEN

ANTHONY DREW to a stop outside the door when he heard the angry tone of the voices in the kitchen. One was Vaughn. He didn't recognize the woman's voice.

"It is the right place. He gave us the address last week, remember?"

"It might have been the right place last week, but he's not there now."

"Bullshit. I saw him."

"He's not there now, you moron. I was there yesterday. Someone else is living there now."

"They can't be. The place was full of his shit."

"Hold still. I need to get this dressing on properly or you'll scar."

"Fuck, that hurts. There were clothes and shit all over the place."

"The new guy's just moved in. He's gone."

There was a long pause punctuated by water running.

"There. Leave that in place for at least two days. Don't get it wet."

"How the hell are we going to get our money now?"

The anger had dried up. They spoke quietly now. Anthony leaned forward to try to hear better.

"How bad is the damage?"

"The bloody bottle bounced off and back at me. I only stayed around long enough to see there were flames inside. You know the cops and firemen always look for someone hanging around a scene. I got out of there quick smart."

"We'll have to go back and see if he left anything behind, but that's not going to be easy with the new guy there."

"There won't be anyone there for a day or two. Once the firemen and cops are finished, they'll mask it off for the insurance people."

The pause was so long, Anthony thought they'd left the room. He wheeled forward a few inches, wincing as the rubber on his tires squeaked on the tiled floor. He continued to roll. They might have heard him and stopping now would be suspicious. He bumped his footrest into the swinging kitchen door and rolled through. There'd be time later to find out what his new nurse was up to.

"Anthony!" Vaughn jumped to his feet and rushed to the kettle. "Did you want a cup of coffee?"

"Yes," Anthony said as he eyed the strange woman in his kitchen.

"This is Rebecca. Her shower has sprung a leak, and she can't use it for the next week while they fix it. I told her you wouldn't mind if she stayed here. There's plenty of room."

Rebecca's surprised expression would have told Anthony they hadn't discussed anything of the sort, even if he hadn't overheard their conversation. He took a cautious sip of his coffee as he regarded her. She was tall and buxom, with broad curves that emphasized her femininity. Her long blonde hair showed dark roots and freckles were strewn across her skin, making her arms look like shade-dappled saplings. Her large breasts ballooned from the neck and sleeves of her tank top. The jeans she wore barely contained her wide thighs. She was gorgeous, except for her eyes. They were hard and calculating. He smiled. "Of course there's room. You're welcome to stay as long as you need to, Rebecca." *Keep your enemies closer.* He waved at the white dressing on Rebecca's arm. "What happened to your arm?"

"Oh... um...." She looked frantically at Vaughn.

"The leak in her shower is the hot water," Vaughn said smoothly. "She was scalded."

"Must be some leak," said Anthony.

Rebecca nodded vigorously, finally getting with the program. Anthony almost laughed at how long it had taken her. "Yes, it was awful. I've never been burned before."

"You mean scalded."

"Of course," she replied tersely.

Anthony put his coffee cup on the table and pushed away. "I think I'll go and read for a while." He smiled at Rebecca, then stared at Vaughn long enough for him to squirm in his seat. "Call me when lunch is ready."

The silence in the kitchen followed him down the hall and into the elevator. He wondered if he needed to start carrying his knives with him again. He rolled into his bedroom and pulled his phone out. Jonathan had to come home so Anthony would have someone he trusted looking after him. Vaughn obviously had other priorities.

He dialed Jonathan's new number, smirking as he thought about the look on Jonathan's face when he realized Anthony could find him anywhere.

"Hello?"

Not Jonathan. He recognized that voice. "Mark?" Why was Mark answering Jonathan's phone?

"Anthony. What do you want? How did you get this number?"

"Why are you answering Jonathan's phone?" Anthony countered. He grinned. He'd always enjoyed bantering with Mark. He'd missed it.

"What do you want?"

"I want to talk to Jonathan."

"He's not available right now. You need to stop ringing him. Leave him alone, Anthony."

"Do you miss me, Mark?" Of course. That's what this was about. That's why Mark answered Jonathan's phone, so Jonathan couldn't talk to Anthony. Mark wanted him back. He grinned at the ceiling. He always knew this day would come.

"I repeat, what do you want, Anthony? You're not getting any more of my designs."

Was that a sneer? Of course not. Mark was a kitten. He always gave Anthony exactly what he wanted. All Anthony had to do was get him into bed. He heard another voice in the background. Jonathan. He'd almost forgotten he'd rung Jonathan in the first place. He'd have to do something about Jonathan before Mark could come back to him. "Everything will be fine, Mark. I'll fix everything, then we can be together again, just like it was always meant to be."

"What!"

Anthony disconnected the call, not needing to hear how much Mark was looking forward to being with him again. But what to do about Jonathan? Up until now, he'd been insisting Jonathan come home, but that couldn't happen now. Mark had never been one for sharing him. He'd become very upset whenever Anthony hooked up when they were together. Jonathan said he wasn't coming back, but Anthony knew that was only temporary. Eventually, Jonathan would realize he couldn't live without Anthony, and he'd come home.

The only way that wouldn't happen was if Jonathan was dead.

Chapter SIXTEEN

"THAT MAN is stark raving mad." Mark tossed Jonathan's phone back onto the coffee table as Jonathan came out of the bathroom.

"Who is?" Jonathan asked as he flopped—began to flop, then slowed and sat carefully when his chest hurt—onto the couch. Dampness quickly seeped through his clothing, and he shot to his feet. "Fuck." Not only were his pants wet, they were covered in sticky soot. One second, that's all it took for him to forget his apartment was a fire zone and he'd got covered in muck. He pressed his hand to his chest, the pain there significantly more uncomfortable than his wet bum. He'd be glad when it stopped hurting and he could move normally. The pain was better, only sharp when he moved too swiftly or in the wrong way, but it was a reminder he didn't want of his past life.

Mark held out a hand to help if Jonathan needed it but otherwise let him find his own equilibrium—a sure sign he wasn't part of Jonathan's family. Jonathan took a deep breath and waved Mark's hand away.

"Sorry. Your phone rang when you were in the bathroom, so I answered it for you. It was bloody Anthony again."

Jonathan tensed, his racing heart and spiking fear making it impossible to even *appear* relaxed. "What did he want this time?"

"I don't know. He seemed surprised I answered the phone. Hopefully, he got the message you don't want to talk to him."

"God, I hope so too, but I'd really like to know what he wanted." Jonathan held his hand up as Mark began to protest. "You know as well as I do, it's always a good idea to know what Anthony's up to. If we don't, we'll get blindsided again." It was weird to talk to someone who actually knew what Anthony was like.

"You're right, but I don't know what to do about that now. I guess we just have to hope he'll eventually get the message and leave you alone." Mark looked around. "Is there anything you can do here now, or are you going back to Ben's?"

"No, there's nothing I can do until the insurance assessor has been. The door has a new lock after the firemen smashed it in. I've grabbed some clothes for the next few days. They'll all need washing, but hopefully the smoke smell will come out quickly." As he spoke, Ben arrived at the front door laden with Tupperware containers. Jonathan laughed. "That looks like there's enough food to feed most of the people in your street."

Ben grinned and nodded. "I hope you don't mind, but I tucked a few dollars into Tahlia's cutlery drawer. She shouldn't have to pay for all this food she's not even eating."

"I think that's a great idea. I should have thought of it myself."

Ben shrugged. "You would eventually, but you've been dealing with a lot of shit." He looked at Mark curiously.

"I'm just here because Liam's in Melbourne, and he was ready to fly back and miss his conference until I said I'd check on Jonathan for him."

Jonathan rolled his eyes. "I'm an adult, you know."

"I know, but your ex-boyfriend tried to kill you, your new boyfriend was a victim of a hit-and-run, and now your apartment was set on fire. Your family, and by extension, me, are all going to want to check you're okay."

"That's right, babe, so you'll just have to deal with it." Ben hefted the Tupperware containers in his hands. "So are you ready to leave now?"

Jonathan grabbed the plastic bag with his clothes and followed them out of the apartment. He locked up and walked away. He wondered if it was normal to feel like he'd never come back. He'd only been there a couple of weeks, but it felt less like his place than it had the first night.

IT WAS strange being back in Ben's apartment, a bag of hastily purchased toiletries and cheap underwear dangling from his fingers. The sound of the washing machine running reverberated through the small space. Ben had detoured to the laundry room as soon as they arrived so they didn't bring the rancid smell of smoky clothing into his apartment.

Jonathan stood just inside the door, surveying the room with new eyes. Last time his focus had been on fabrics. This time he wondered where he was going to sleep. He darted a frantic look at Ben.

"Don't worry," Ben said with a laugh. "The couch is big enough for me."

Jonathan knew he should be relieved, but... actually he wasn't sure how he felt. He hadn't shared bedroom space since before the accident that crippled Anthony, so part of what he was feeling was something akin to claustrophobia. That wasn't everything, though. There was an ache low in his belly, a tingle that shivered across his skin whenever he envisaged sleeping close to Ben. He strode to the couch and dropped his shopping bag on the end. He didn't want to dive into another relationship.

"Are you sure this isn't a problem? I can get a room somewhere."

"You don't need a room. It's probably better for you to be with someone tonight anyway." At Jonathan's curious glance, he continued. "Your apartment was blown up. If you aren't already experiencing some shock, you will be. You shouldn't be alone right now."

Right. That's what this was: Ben being a Good Samaritan. It was probably something everybody who lived out in the country did. It wasn't because Jonathan was anything special. They'd only known each other a couple of weeks. Jonathan was being silly—juvenile and romantic—if he thought it was anything else.

"Shock," he mused. He'd gone so far past shock, he was numb.

"So," Ben said into the growing silence. "The police are checking on the previous tenants. They might have been into something dodgy."

"It was Anthony. I don't care if no one else thinks it could have been him. It's exactly the kind of thing he would do to get me to call him." He ran his hands over his closely-cropped hair. "To get me to go back to him."

"Will you?"

Jonathan studied Ben's face. His question held something tentative and fearful in it, but Jonathan couldn't work out what Ben could be frightened of. Regardless of how comfortable Jonathan felt with the other man, how much he wanted to be around him, they hadn't known each other long enough for that kind of connection to grow. He couldn't tell him the truth; couldn't expose himself as the coward he was. He rubbed absently at his chest, pressed his palm against the wound, and allowed the pain to remind himself he was out now. He was alive and safe, and he wanted to stay that way.

"I won't ever go back to Anthony. It doesn't matter what he says or does. I'm out and I'm staying out."

"Hey, it's okay now. You're out. You're safe." Ben continued to murmur soothingly into Jonathan's ear. When his large hands rubbed Jonathan's back rhythmically, Jonathan realized he was crying. He tried to pull away, pull himself together. He tried to breathe, but the ache in his chest grew and grew until it felt like it would crush him and he would explode, or implode, every heavy, lonely, injured atom of him collapsing on top of itself until the only thing left of him was the tears soaking into Ben's shirt.

The room grew still and quiet, and Ben still held Jonathan in his arms, not moving, not seeming to expect anything from him but to be there. That lack of expectation was as alien to Jonathan as the idea that he could one day have the life he'd dreamed of as a child—way back when his parents and cousin were still alive. Even his family expected something of him: his love, his continued striving for happiness. Not Ben. Jonathan didn't have to do anything or be anything for Ben. Jonathan shuffled closer into the hug, leaned more heavily on Ben's strong, solid form. He breathed in slow, shuddering breaths, the scent of mingled fabric spray starch and faint car exhaust screaming "home" in a way nothing else ever had.

And that was something he couldn't have. He'd tried finding his home with someone else before. That's how the whole debacle with Anthony began: Jonathan searching for his home, a place and a person he belonged with. This time he had to do it on his own. He had to build a life that was his alone, that no one else could claim or destroy. He stepped out of Ben's embrace, stumbling a little at the loss of support and comfort. He shivered with the lost warmth of Ben's body pressed against his.

In that first instance of aloneness, he realized what else he'd missed. The heated pressure of an erect penis. He glanced at Ben's crotch, his breath catching in his throat. *Dear God, I thought he'd be a shower, but he's not. That's definitely a grower there.* A whimper of desire escaped before he could stop it. Ben's hands covered his very impressive package as he turned away and cleared his throat.

"Okay, then, um, well, I have some study I need to do. At the library. So I'll go and do that." Ben walked over to his large table, then around it, his hands fluttering over the fabric, touching one, flipping a trailing corner back over the rest. He moved his sewing shears two centimeters to the right, pushed a chair in, then shoved his hand into his pocket and retrieved his keys. He kept his head down as he worked a key off the ring and placed it on the corner of the table. "This is for the apartment. I'll have to get another one cut for you tomorrow." He sidled by Jonathan and picked his backpack up. "Can you let me know if you go out? I can't get back in unless you're here."

"Ben?" Jonathan didn't go any closer, sure if he did, Ben would spook like a startled horse and take off. "We've touched before. We...." He gestured at Ben's crotch but aborted the movement halfway through. "I don't understand the problem."

Ben ran his hands over his head and linked his fingers behind his neck. "You've had a hell of a day. The last thing you need is me or anyone else hitting on you. I'll let you get settled and have some quiet time. I'll be home in a few hours and we can have dinner. Okay?"

Jonathan didn't have the heart to argue in the face of the plea in Ben's eyes. He nodded and watched as Ben walked out, got into his truck, and drove away.

The silence of the empty apartment tugged at the atoms holding him together. It took all his effort not to fly apart and disappear, unnoticed and unmissed.

Chapter SEVENTEEN

ANTHONY WHEELED into the kitchen and came to an abrupt stop. "Why are you still here?" The strange woman from yesterday was in his kitchen, standing close to Vaughn. Her lips were painted a crisp new red, totally unlike the faded color of fear she'd worn yesterday. Today her laughing eyes gleamed green in the light and her hands were steady, without the nervous fluttering of the day before. Today she was comfortable in her skin. She was real. She was the most beautiful woman Anthony had ever seen.

None of that changed the fact that he didn't know her and hadn't invited her into his home. He glared at Vaughn.

"I'm Rebecca, Vaughn's friend, Mr. Porter. We met yesterday." The woman walked over to Anthony and held her hand out. He responded automatically, absently noting the calluses across the base of her fingers, a sharp contrast to the softness of the rest of her skin. "I really appreciate this opportunity." She spoke quickly and confidently, not giving him an opportunity to respond. "I know you have cleaners come in twice a week but, really, there's only so much they do. I'm going to make sure your home is exactly the way you want it." She laughed, a light, giddy sound. "Once you taste my cooking, you'll never want to get rid of me."

Anthony dragged his eyes from her and turned to Vaughn. "Vaughn?"

"I asked Rebecca to stay and act as your housekeeper." He shifted uncomfortably, and Anthony sat straighter in his seat. At least the man knew he shouldn't have employed someone without asking him first. "I've been here over a week now and, to be honest, you need more help than you've got."

"I've never needed more help. Jonathan does it all." But Jonathan was gone and Mark wanted to come back. He'd have to do something about Jonathan before he could invite Mark to move back in.

There was a long pause before Vaughn spoke again. "Yeah, well, Jonathan isn't here right now, and you don't pay me anywhere near enough to do everything that has to be done. I wouldn't be able to anyway. The cleaners keep the place clean enough, and I can look after your needs, but that's it. That's why I asked Rebecca to come here. She can do everything else."

"What everything else?"

Rebecca stepped forward. "I'll be doing all the cooking and the washing, and I'll run errands, like to the dry cleaners and stuff."

And stuff? "How old are you?"

"I'm twenty-two. I have a lot of experience managing homes. I've been doing it for a long time." She glanced at Vaughn, then reached for an envelope on the kitchen counter. "This is my résumé and copies of references from previous employers."

Anthony took the envelope and regarded the two people in front of him. He was missing something but couldn't work out exactly what it was. He emptied the envelope onto his lap. The sheets were crisp and new. They looked like originals. *What sort of person hands over originals in a job interview?*

"Jonathan hasn't called yet," said Vaughn. "But I'm sure it's just a matter of time."

Anthony scowled. That made him sound like a last resort, like he was manipulating Jonathan's actions. He spun around and wheeled himself out of the room. If Jonathan were here where he was supposed to be, Anthony wouldn't have to do anything like this. He wouldn't have to have Jonathan watched, or have to plan something elaborate so Jonathan would just be gone and Mark could come back. He glared at the door to the kitchen. And he wouldn't have a house full of strangers. He had to find a way to make Jonathan come home. Then he could deal with him, and Mark could come back to him. Then his life would return to normal. With Mark here, he'd win awards again.

Chapter EIGHTEEN

JONATHAN COULDN'T sleep. The couch was hard and too short. He punched the pillow and folded it in half, but that just made it too high and bent his neck so much that his chin nearly rested on his chest. He pulled the pillow out and tossed it to the floor.

"Jonathan, what's wrong?"

He jumped at Ben's quiet words from his bed. He shouldn't have been surprised. It wasn't as if he'd forgotten there was another man in the room with him. He'd spent a significant amount of time listening for any movement Ben made, but then became restless and impatient with his own inability to sleep. He stood up and walked to where Ben lay in his bed.

"I can't sleep."

"I gathered that." Ben lifted the covers, silently inviting Jonathan to join him. "I told you to take the bed."

Jonathan hesitated. "If I get into bed with you, I'm going to want more than sleep."

"From where I am, that could only be a good thing. I can take the couch if you want." Narrow stripes of light streaked from the curtains and across his abdomen, making the shadows deeper around Ben's face, but Jonathan knew he was smiling. The covers remained lifted and Ben stayed where he was.

Jonathan pushed his briefs down and off, then crawled into the bed. "I'm not looking for another relationship. I've just come out of one."

"Sure. I'm your rebound guy. It's just sex. Right?" Ben sounded relaxed and carefree. Perhaps Jonathan imagined the disappointment he thought he heard underlying the cheerful tone.

The sadness that ate at his stomach was simply because he was alone, not because he couldn't have Ben in a more permanent way.

THE HEAT from Ben's body radiated from him, warming Jonathan immediately as he slid into the bed. He shivered as he settled on his back but then, feeling too vulnerable, rolled to his side, facing Ben.

Ben closed his eyes and nodded slightly, as if he'd made a decision. "You don't have to do this, Jonathan." He reached his hand out and laid it over Jonathan's hand where it rested between them. "You're just coming out of a bad relationship. You probably need a friend more than anything right now."

Jonathan leaned forward and stopped Ben's words with his lips. The chiseled edge of Ben's lips softened, then disappeared as Ben stopped trying to talk and relaxed into the kiss, opening for him. The scent of warm, sleepy body and rampant desire bombarded his senses. Jonathan entered the warmth of Ben's mouth and lowered his body onto Ben's hair-roughened chest. He groaned and squeezed his eyes closed, not daring to open them for fear this would disappear. This heat. This thrill. This—

Ben tore his mouth from Jonathan's. "Christ, you're perfect. This is too good." He moaned as he grabbed at Jonathan's body, pulling them closer together, pressing them skin to skin from chest to Jonathan's ankles, which was as far as Ben's feet reached. Then the difference in their heights didn't matter because Ben lifted his leg and slid it around Jonathan's hip, drawing him in so tight they fit together like a complex two-piece jigsaw puzzle.

Jonathan searched for and found Ben's lips again. He needed more of the taste of this man. He shoved his arm under Ben's neck, wrapped it around his shoulder, and shuffled closer still, his free hand maneuvering Ben until he achieved the exact right connection between their cocks.

Ben tore away from the kiss again. "Yes. That's it. Harder. I want to feel you." Ben's fingers dug into Jonathan's buttock in a rhythm he couldn't mistake. "You feel so good. So hot." Ben rambled, words pouring from him in a thunderstorm of need.

Jonathan gasped his response, the heat between them enough to sear conscious thought, destroy sensibilities. He rutted against Ben, his cock rubbing against Ben's and digging into the divot inside his hipbone. Ben's cock pressed, hot and urgent, against his stomach. Every muscle strained to increase the contact and pressure between them. His fingers dug into Ben's pale skin. He knew his grasp would bruise but in this moment didn't care. He needed more. He needed everything this man could give him. He needed to give all he could to wipe out everything that had come before.

The small pain he heard in Ben's heavy breathing ramped his need higher. He rolled more firmly onto Ben and shifted his hold to Ben's head so he could kiss deeply, consumingly. It wasn't enough. He needed more. A whimper escaped, and Ben pulled out of the kiss.

"Sshh. It's okay. Ease up a bit."

Jonathan lurched back, mortified. He was hurting Ben. It wasn't just need—he'd seriously been hurting him, and he hadn't cared. Just like Anthony. He kicked his feet to untangle his legs from Ben's, his breath cutting sharply through his body, the blood pounding frantically in his effort to give Ben some space, to stop hurting him. The mattress beneath him bounced and dipped, then disappeared completely, and Jonathan dropped with a thump to the floor. He bumped the edge of the bedside table on his way down, and the few objects on top of it rattled and shifted. He came to rest with his head twisted uncomfortably to one side and his legs, still on the bed, wrapped securely in a tangle of sheets.

As he stopped struggling, his body settled, buttocks thudding to the floor, the sheet twisting his right ankle a little. He moved his head to a more comfortable position, and the radio on the bedside table toppled and fell. The corner jabbed painfully into his chest before the whole rattling casing slid off his shoulder to lean drunkenly against him.

Absurdly, what mortified him most was his now flaccid dick, resting limply in the crease between his abdomen and thigh.

With a groan, he opened his eyes to find Ben leaning over the side of the bed, laughter in his eyes.

"Are you all right? I didn't mean for you to back off that much."

Jonathan pulled his feet free, rolled, and pushed himself to his feet, stumbling as he overbalanced and nearly fell again.

Ben laughed. "Come back to bed."

Jonathan took a couple of stumbling steps back, then turned away. His face burned with humiliation and shame. After all the time he'd spent with Anthony, he'd become just like him.

"Jonathan? What the hell is going on in your head this time?" Bedclothes rustled behind Jonathan. The bedside lamp came on, flooding the small area with muted gold. Ben was coming for him. He needed to leave. He had to find somewhere else to stay; somewhere away from Ben so he'd be safe.

Ben grasped Jonathan's shoulder and tugged. He turned to find confusion and sparking anger in Ben's expression, but no fear.

"I'm sorry," Jonathan murmured. "I'll go."

"What the hell are you talking about? Why would you want to go anywhere? I thought we were finally going to… well, fuck."

He still wanted to do it? "I hurt you."

"You didn't hurt me." Ben grinned at him. "I loved the way you wanted me, like you couldn't resist, like you were on the edge and just one kiss away from jumping over and taking me with you. Hell, what's not to like about being wanted that much?" Ben stepped closer and grabbed Jonathan by his shoulders. "At no time did you hurt me or scare me. I just thought you'd want to slow down a bit. Savor it."

Jonathan's breathing finally eased, and Ben's words penetrated his panicked brain. *Savor it.* Like Ben was the meal and Jonathan was going to devour him. Was that really what Ben wanted? Ben stepped closer to him and nuzzled his neck, the soft skin under his jaw. Jonathan automatically lifted his head to give the other man better access. Ben's teeth latched onto the sensitive skin over Jonathan's Adam's apple and sucked gently. Jonathan shivered and brought his arms up to enclose Ben and draw him closer.

"Shall we try this again?" Ben asked. "I'd really like to find out what you feel like inside me."

Jonathan groaned his acquiescence and shuffled them both back toward the bed.

Neither of them was willing to let the other go, so they tumbled to the bed with a bounce and a soft "oomph" from Ben when Jonathan landed on him. Jonathan lifted off Ben but was dragged back down.

"Oh no, you don't. You're staying right here and fucking me. Now stop thinking so bloody hard and get on with it."

A surprised bark of laughter burst from Jonathan, and he gave in. Ben had made it clear he wanted Jonathan here, and there was nothing in the world right then that Jonathan wanted more, so he switched his thoughts off and rolled with whatever was happening between him and Ben. Well, sort of.

He lifted back far enough to focus on Ben's face. "Are you absolutely sure this is what you want? I mean, I haven't—" He sighed. "I'm not very good."

"Stop." Ben placed two fingers over Jonathan's lips. "Everything is fine. I like you just the way you are."

Hell. Jonathan's breath caught in his throat. His eyes stung. He was going to cry, but he couldn't stop smiling. What an idiot, what a— he leaned down and kissed Ben again and stopped thinking. The heat between them grew, and Jonathan surrendered to it. He rolled them and settled against Ben, snuggling between Ben's thighs as his legs fell open. The heat of their groins, when Jonathan's cock slid between Ben's thighs as if seeking its true north, seared every conscious thought from Jonathan's head. All he could do was feel.

Jonathan released Ben's lips and trailed kisses down his neck, licking and nipping as the graveled stubble gave way to soft, smooth skin. At the juncture of neck and shoulder, Jonathan paused, testing the texture of the skin to see if he could taste the change from tanned skin to pale, milky white. He wanted to stop and lift away from Ben so he could look at the contrast between his own dark skin and Ben's creaminess. He could be fascinated with that difference alone forever.

He nuzzled lower, his tongue trailing a damp path to Ben's tight nipple. He flicked the nubbin, then laved it with the flat of his tongue before sucking strongly, drawing it into his mouth.

Ben groaned and tunneled his fingers through Jonathan's hair, holding him tightly against his chest. His other hand fumbled under his pillow before emerging. He slapped a cold packet against Jonathan's shoulder blade. "Here. I want you in me, Jonathan. If you keep doing this, I'll blow, and I still won't get to feel your cock sink into me and burn me good."

Jonathan released his hold on Ben's nipple, gasping at the images planted in his head. He pressed his hips firmly to the mattress, hoping the pressure would stop him shooting his load right then—from just Ben's words, his need. He breathed through the urgency, then lifted up from Ben's chest and held his hand out. Ben slapped the condom into his palm.

"Lube?"

"It's lubricated. Now get it on and get in me."

"I don't want to hurt you."

"If you don't get your cock inside me within the next five seconds, you're the one who's going to be hurt." Ben arched up, rubbing his abdomen and cock against Jonathan. "Christ, I need you in me now. I don't want to come before you're inside me."

Jonathan sat back on his haunches and ripped open the condom packet. Ben used the freedom to bring his legs up and hook his hands behind his knees, opening himself for Jonathan with shameless urgency. Jonathan gripped the base of his cock tightly as he rolled the condom down. Just looking at Ben like that was enough to make him come, but he couldn't, not yet.

Once the condom was in place, Jonathan scooped out the remaining lube from the pack and rubbed Ben's hole.

"Jonathan," Ben ground out.

"I'm not going to hurt you. If you want me to keep going, then shut up and take this." He pushed his lubed finger past the tightness and into Ben's heat.

Ben stopped complaining.

Jonathan added more lube and another finger. Ben moaned.

Jonathan shuffled forward and replaced his fingers with his dick. He'd done nowhere near enough prep, but he couldn't wait. Ben's heat below him, the needy sounds he was making, begging Jonathan to fuck him, blew away the rest of Jonathan's control. "Don't let me hurt you," he murmured as he breached Ben's hole.

Ben groaned. "Oh yes. Burn me good. Fuck me." He continued to babble as Jonathan pushed slowly forward. Jonathan pressed a hand behind Ben's knee, opening him farther. The thin sheen of sweat on Ben's leg made his fingers slip, so he gripped tighter.

The sound of Ben's hand frantically rubbing his dick filled the room. "Move, Jon. Slam it into me. I want to feel you in my throat."

"Oh God," Jonathan groaned. He leaned over Ben, gripping him tightly as he slowly drew back. Just as his cock was about to slip free, Jonathan changed direction and slammed back into Ben.

Ben grunted. "Yes! Like that. More." His right hand sped up on his dick, the sound of skin slapping against skin almost as loud as their harsh breathing.

Jonathan plunged again. And again. The rhythm and the heat consumed him, burning away every conscious thought and emotion except for need. The air around them thickened with heated skin, sweaty musk, and incoherent cries of need.

Ben's ramblings reduced to explosions of "Ugh, ugh, ugh."

Electric tracers skittered down to the base of Jonathan's spine and over his skin, numbing his extremities with explosive pleasure. "Ben." His voice, hot and dark, warned of his impending orgasm.

"Yes! Now, now, now," Ben screamed. His whole body froze, then tightened and jerked in an explosive ripple. The force of it dragged Jonathan over the edge as well.

He threw his head back, the tendons in his neck straining against the searing pleasure that ripped up his spine and down his legs, centered in his groin as his balls squeezed tight against his body and pumped his life into the condom. Into Ben.

After an interminable, frozen moment, Jonathan's muscles liquefied, and he collapsed forward. His fall dragged a grunt from Ben, and Jonathan used the last of his energy to slide to the side enough so Ben would be able to breathe.

Gradually his senses returned, and Jonathan reveled in the slick slide of their sweat-soaked skin. He forced his rubbery arm down to where they were joined and gripped the condom as he slid free, smiling at Ben's resultant fart.

"I'll get something to clean up in a minute," Ben whispered in a hoarse, uneven voice.

Jonathan slid off Ben's leg so he could straighten it and nuzzled him beneath his ear. A huffed breath of agreement escaped as he flopped his arm over Ben's sweaty, sticky stomach, then dropped into a dreamless sleep.

Chapter NINETEEN

JONATHAN OPENED his eyes to find the coffee he'd smelled at the end of his dream was in a mug in Ben's hand. Ben stood beside the bed, staring at him.

He could have said "Is that for me?" or "Why aren't you still in bed with me?" or "So I guess that means no morning sex," or pretty much anything at all, but he didn't. The silence lengthened until it became uncomfortable, and Jonathan began to wonder if he should be creeped out by Ben watching him while he slept, or if he should have woken earlier and left.

Ben turned away and walked into the small kitchenette.

Jonathan threw the covers back and scrambled for his clothes, tugging his underwear out from under the bed. His jeans from the day before were over the couch. He stepped around the screen into the living area and pulled his clothes on. The rasp of his zipper was loud in the silence of the small flat. He looked up to find Ben a few paces away, holding out a second gently steaming mug.

Ben nodded at Jonathan as he took the mug and tested the heat of the coffee. Jonathan lowered the cup, resigned to wait until the liquid wouldn't scald his mouth. "Thank you," he said.

"There's toast or cereal too, if you want it. Or I could cook some eggs." Ben stood still as a statue, regarding Jonathan solemnly.

"No, I'm fine. Thank you." The only morning after Jonathan had experienced before was with Anthony, and that was very different to this one with Ben. He couldn't get a read on Ben at all. "Do you want me to leave?" he blurted.

"Why would I want you to leave? You haven't had breakfast yet." Ben stepped forward and gently grasped Jonathan's arm. He led him to the sofa. "Sit here. I'll get you something to eat." As he wandered toward the kitchenette, he continued. "You need to eat more regularly, Jonathan. You'll waste away to nothing if you don't."

Jonathan bounced back to his feet and stared after Ben. "What is wrong with you? You wake me up, staring at me like, like, I don't know, and then you want to feed me. You always want to feed me."

"Of course I do. You're skinny."

"I'm not skinny!"

Ben returned with a small white bowl, a spoon sticking out of it. "Here, eat this. Then you can shower, and we'll see what we need to do today to get your apartment operational." He jiggled the bowl in front of Jonathan like he'd done with the sandwiches when Jonathan first moved.

Jonathan took the bowl with a sigh and started eating the cereal. "What *we* need to do?" he asked around a mouthful of cornflakes.

Ben tilted his head as he looked at Jonathan. Jonathan swallowed swiftly so he wouldn't spurt milk and half-chewed cereal everywhere. "You look like a cat I had when I was a kid."

Ben grinned, and suddenly all the awkwardness of the morning was gone, dissipated into the air like smoke from a snuffed candle.

Phoning the police and the insurance company took all morning, and Ben dropped Jonathan at his apartment after making a salad sandwich so big Jonathan had to cut it into four to eat it.

"I have a lecture, then a tute, so I won't be back until about six. Message me if you need anything."

Jonathan slapped his pocket with his phone in it and gasped. "Shit! I've had it turned off all this time and didn't ring Liam or anyone. They'll kill me."

"I don't think so." He nodded down the street, where two men ran toward them. Liam—tall, dark, and scowling—easily out-paced the shorter, silver-haired Mark.

"Damn," Jonathan whispered.

"Good luck. I've got to book it or I'll be late." Ben tapped his hand against the outside of his new door, then pulled away from the curb.

"Jonathan! Where the hell have you been? Turn your fucking phone on, will you?" Liam stormed up to Jonathan and grabbed him by the shoulders.

Jonathan tugged free. "Aren't you supposed to be in Melbourne for another couple of days?"

"Fuck Melbourne. Mark said your apartment was burned down."

"Jonathan! Yoo-hoo, Jonathan."

Jonathan closed his eyes and breathed deeply for three breaths before looking up to the windows on the third floor. Neridah's stringy blonde hair waved in the breeze, Tahlia's dark cloud of curls beside her.

"Come on up. Tahlia's got morning tea ready."

He solemnly regarded his cousin and Mark. "Come on. We can talk up there."

White chocolate macadamia slice, melting moments cookies, and apple cinnamon muffins greeted them when they arrived at Neridah's apartment. They were set out on two small round tables that were covered with lace tablecloths and hand-embroidered doilies. Vases of pink and white roses were dotted around the room, complementing the pink and cream floral upholstery, fluttering lace curtains, and soft pink walls. Jonathan froze just inside the door, immediately feeling far too large and too dark for this delicate room.

"Come in, dear." Neridah bustled over and gently cradled Jonathan's elbow. "You come and sit down here, and I'll get you a nice cup of tea. It's just what you need after the shock you had yesterday."

Shock? Jonathan stared at her for several seconds before he realized she was talking about the fire, not what he and Ben had done last night.

"My Brian-who-is-Brianna now always swears by a cup of tea. She says there's nothing quite like it to begin a day or to end one." Neridah tittered in her smoke-damaged way. "Of course our days *always* began and ended with wall-shaking sex, but the tea always came after—or before, as the case may be." She sidled up to Mark. "I told Brianna tea was one of them afro-diziacks, but she always said it was me." She tittered again, but it quickly turned into one of her hacking liquid coughs. Neridah waved her cigarette-holding hand in front of her face, and the cough subsided.

She had her claws dug deeply into the flesh above Mark's elbow. He pointed to Liam as he lowered himself into one of Neridah's dinky chairs. "I'm with him," he squeaked.

"Well, lucky you, darl." Neridah dragged Mark to a two-seater couch. "Now you sit here with me and tell me all about yourself and how you came to be with that tall streak of smooth coffee over there."

"Here you are, Jonathan." Tahlia handed Jonathan a plate piled high with sweet treats and a small pink cup on a saucer. Jonathan took them both, then sat there wondering how he was expected to either eat or drink his tea with both his hands occupied. "Just put it down on the side table."

The side table was another small round table, about a foot in diameter and smothered in lace and pink. He carefully placed the plates on the embroidered cloth.

"So what can we do to help set things to rights, Jonathan?" Neridah, at last leaving Mark alone, leaned toward Jonathan, her breasts bulging from her low-cut dress.

"We can pack everything that's not damaged and throw out the rest," said Liam.

"What? Why would I pack everything up? I just moved in."

"It's clearly not safe here. You can move in with me—like I suggested when you were in hospital."

"And I told you in hospital, I wasn't going to live with you. That hasn't changed." Jonathan stood, too agitated to sit and pretend everything was all pink and pretty. The smoke smell was too strong and rancid to mistake it for Neridah's ever-present halo. He could only imagine his apartment would be worse.

Liam stood too, his fists jammed on his hips. "Jonathan—"

"No! This is my life and, for the first time in ten years, I get to choose how I live it. No one else—not even you."

Mark stood close to Liam, his hand rubbing soothing circles on Liam's back. Liam's shoulders slumped.

"Okay. I don't like it, but I'll help."

Jonathan nodded, the fight suddenly draining from him. That small show of independence and defiance was about all he could muster at the moment. "I... I...."

Liam came over and drew him into a hug. "Finish your tea, then we can check out your apartment and see exactly what we're working with. If it's just a cleanup, we'll do it. If it's worse than that, we'll decide what's next then. That sound okay to you?"

Chapter TWENTY

"IT LOOKS worse than it is," Mark said into the silence that had consumed them since they'd walked in the door.

Jonathan coughed at the stench of melted carpet and plastic. He flicked the light switch. "Power's off."

Liam strode to the window, his steps sloshing through the large area rug, but the boards over the broken window were secure.

Their movements created clear swirls of active air in the dingy haze of the room. A layer of soot covered every surface. Jonathan ran his finger along the back of a dining chair, but all that did was spread the soot in a greasy smear. He turned at the sound of water dripping, only to find a small puddle forming under his new flat-screen television.

"We'll have to call the insurance company and get an assessor out here," said Liam.

"I called them on the way over here. I have to call again this afternoon, but they said it was fine to go ahead with a cleanup. I also spoke to the landlord. The windows and other repairs will be done tomorrow, and the electricity will go back on then too. If we can throw out anything not salvageable, he'll get cleaners in." Jonathan wasn't sure if he should be pleased or annoyed at the look of surprise on Liam's face. Did his cousin think so little of him that he didn't think Jonathan was capable of making a few phone calls?

"He dropped in this morning," said Tahlia. "He brought some contractors with him to look at the damage to the bedroom. They said they'd be back tomorrow."

"Looks like all that's left for us to do," said Neridah, "is grab some garbage bags and throw out everything that can't be saved. Tahlia, do you want to man the kitchen and clean anything that's not damaged?"

Tahlia bustled to the kitchen. "Lucky the hot water is gas." She ran a finger over the kitchen counter and grimaced. "Nothing but hot, soapy water and elbow grease will shift this lot." Neridah followed her and rummaged under the kitchen sink for large black bags.

Jonathan stood in the middle of his living room and let their busyness wash over him like white noise. He'd barely been here a fortnight, and it was already destroyed. There hadn't been time for him to work out how he wanted to live his life or what sort of person he was now, and he had to start over.

"Jonathan, why don't we take a look at the bedroom and see what that's like?" Mark stood by his side, a quiet, steady presence. Jonathan could see how he would be good for Liam. "If it looks like too big a job for us, my friends Jeremy and Daron said they could help."

"Thank them for me, but we'll manage." He strode down the short hallway.

The smell was worse in the bedroom, thicker and greasier. Jonathan gagged, then swallowed against it and resolutely walked into the room. In the middle of the bed, a pile of charred bedding sat in a pool of black water. One side of the wooden headboard was burned so badly it was nothing but coals and twisted metal. The other side was cracked and streaked with black. The wall behind the bed showed the same dark pattern, the worst burns at the burnt side of the bed, fanning out to gray streaks on the other side of the room. The plaster in that section was burned through and crumbling. It would all have to come down and be replaced. The joists in the wall were black but didn't look badly damaged. Jonathan turned slowly, looking around the room as cold realization settled in his stomach.

"He aimed for the bed," he whispered.

After a shocked silence while Liam and Mark investigated Jonathan's claim, Liam said, "Fuck. The bastard's crazy as a magpie in October."

Involuntarily, Jonathan chuckled. "Christ, imagine what he'd be like with a thousand times the testosterone."

"I have bags," said Neridah from behind them.

Jonathan sighed and grabbed a few from her. "Okay, let's do this. The sooner we get the place empty, the sooner I can get back to my life."

Whatever that was.

BEN ARRIVED a couple of hours after they'd sorted out the perfect cleaning routine, and he fitted seamlessly into it. He bumped his hip into Jonathan's a couple of times but stopped when Jonathan started stepping around him to avoid it. The frown on his face made Jonathan's face heat uncomfortably, but Jonathan didn't want to field the questions Liam would ask if he noticed.

The conversations echoing through the apartment centered on whether something was salvageable or not. The rote movement of picking up wet, burned objects and shoving them into a garbage bag, tying them, then gathering them to walk down to the new, unburned bins, soothed Jonathan. He stopped thinking about what had happened and what he still had to do. He just bagged and wrapped. Over and over.

"Come on. Grab those two and I'll walk down with you." Ben tapped Jonathan on the shoulder to draw his attention to the bags beside him.

Jonathan dropped what he was holding, picked the bags up, and followed Ben downstairs. When they dropped everything in the wheelie bins, Jonathan turned to listlessly trudge back upstairs and begin again.

"Jonathan. Wait."

He turned to see Ben frowning at him but couldn't work out why. He stood there, shoulders slumped, breathing in and out, and waited for Ben to say what he wanted to. Ben stepped close, lifting his shirt as he walked. With one hand on Jonathan's shoulder to bring him closer, Ben used the inside of his shirt to wipe Jonathan's face. "It'll be okay, babe. I promise. There's no need to cry anymore."

Oh. That's what that was. The burning eyes, the tightness in his chest, the ache in his stomach. He'd been with Anthony so long he'd forgotten how to be himself, and he knew that nothing he did would ever make a difference. He was lost. Disappeared in the void of Anthony's madness. Never to be seen again.

Ben held him as he sobbed. He sat with Jonathan as Jonathan collapsed to the gritty concrete and totally lost his shit. The whole time Jonathan was clinging to him, tearing his life into small pieces with his tears, Ben held him and spoke to him. Jonathan heard the words but couldn't tell what they meant. Gradually the tears stopped, and Ben's gentle hands stroked life back into Jonathan, first through his back, then his face.

Jonathan whimpered when Ben lifted his hands away. Without those hands on him, he'd shatter again. He couldn't find all the pieces by himself.

"You're going to be okay, Jonathan. You've come this far, and we're not going to let the bastard win. You're not battling this alone."

Eventually Jonathan's breathing calmed, and Ben used his shirt again to dry Jonathan's face. Jonathan rose to his feet, feeling like ninety-two instead of twenty-nine.

Back on the third floor, outside his apartment where he could hear the sounds of love and support and caring, Jonathan turned back to Ben.

"We're good," Ben said with a smile.

Jonathan nodded and got back to work.

FOUR HOURS later, Jonathan had made so many trips to the bins at the back of the building, he'd lost count. His legs ached from traipsing up and down three flights of stairs and his chest burned from the strain on his wound. It took him a full hour to realize they could open the fire escape door at the end of the hall near his apartment and use those stairs instead of having to walk around the building. He'd tossed one bag down, but it bounced against the fire escape and exploded, spraying the back yard with the charred remnants of his life. After chasing scorched papers over the concrete yard and down the alley beside the building, Jonathan decided to walk the bags down two at a time.

Tahlia had supplied tea and sandwiches-on-the-go for lunch. Jonathan had managed to ignore her most of the day, but now his stomach cramped from hunger.

"It's getting too dark to keep working. We'll have to finish up tomorrow," Tahlia said authoritatively as the sunset cast deep shadows around the room. "You all wash your hands, then come back to my place. I, for one, will be glad to breathe clean air again." She wiped her hands on a dish towel, dropped it on the bench, and walked to the door. "Dinner will be in twenty minutes, cold drinks available in two."

"Jonathan, you and Ben use the bathroom here to clean up. Liam, you and Mark can use mine. It'll be quicker. I'll go and help Tahlia."

Neridah dragged off the rubber gloves she'd been wearing and draped them over the sink. Guilt tugged at Jonathan as he watched her walk slowly down the hallway to Tahlia's door, fatigue dragging her shoulders down and pasting a gray mask over her face.

Jonathan turned to Ben. "I'm going to pull the bed apart and take it down to the bins before we stop. It'll be easier for the contractors to see how much damage the wall sustained if it's not in the way."

Ben wordlessly accompanied him to the bedroom, and they began dismantling what was left of the bed. The mattress was tossed from the fire escape landing with a yell to "look out below." Jonathan dragged pieces of the bed frame through the living room, while Ben ripped some of the plasterboard from the wall to see how far the damage to the joists went.

They finished just as Neridah called everyone for dinner. Jonathan trudged down the hallway, the weight of never getting his life right weighing on him. It didn't seem to matter what he did, everything fell apart. In the middle of all the chaos, he was surrounded, pulled and pushed in different directions by everyone he knew, and even people he didn't know. If he didn't get some quiet, calm time soon, he'd start screaming.

Ben gulped the water he'd grabbed from Neridah's fridge before turning back to Jonathan. "What's wrong?"

Jonathan shook his head, ready to say "nothing." It wasn't *nothing,* but there was no way he could say what he really thought without sounding like an ungrateful, selfish bastard.

"Don't tell me it's nothing. You've been antsy since I got here. Sure, your place has been destroyed, but you've got all this help—" Ben's forehead creased as he looked at Jonathan. "Is that what's wrong? You don't want me here?"

"No!" Jonathan burst out. He ran his fingers through his hair, tugging as they tangled in the tight curls. "It sounds stupid."

"Tell me anyway."

Jonathan stepped back into the hall and flapped his arms as if the action would somehow help him find the words he wanted to say. "I've been with Anthony a long time—ten years." He paced while he walked, frustrated that the hallway was only two steps wide. He couldn't pace along it without leaving Ben behind and alerting the others that something was wrong. "I lived in a big house with just the two of us and weekly housekeeping. After a while, except for Liam, my family stopped visiting. It was just me with all this space. Now....” He sighed and walked back to Ben. “Now I'm in a tiny apartment, and I haven't even had time to get used to the small space and it's been burned down, and everywhere I turn I run into someone. Everyone's here. *All the time*. I don't even know how... who....”

He flopped onto the couch that had been dragged into the hall, ready to haul down to the alley, but jumped up immediately as it squelched beneath him and cold water soaked into his pants. “Fuck!” He grabbed the offending cushion and tossed it at the wall. The corner of it splatted and crumpled before the cushion bounced back and landed with a sloshing thud at Jonathan's feet. At impact with the wall and with the floor, dirty water sprayed out, decorating the wall, the floor, and Jonathan with sooty starbursts.

To his horror, tears burned Jonathan's eyes. Again. His chest heaved with his breaths, getting tighter and tighter until he couldn't breathe at all and the tears filled his eyes and, like a flooded stream, burst the banks and fell in rivulets down his cheeks. “I'm such an idiot. A fool. A—a bloody cry-baby,” he wailed.

Warm comfort burned Jonathan's face as Ben mashed him against his chest, the silky skin of his neck somehow reducing his need to scream and throw things or punch his fist through the dirty, stained walls. He hiccupped through his tears. “I can't... I can't....”

“Sshh, you don't have to do anything. It's okay.” Ben's hand delved into Jonathan's pocket but before he could think what it might mean, the other man held his phone up. “Unlock this and I'll let Liam know we're leaving.”

He punched in the numbers automatically, then dropped his head back on Ben's shoulder. Breathing in the warmth of Ben's skin through the sweat and soot and grime helped him even out his breathing. The tears slowed, then stopped as Ben spoke quietly above him.

“Okay, it's all square. Let's go.”

Jonathan straightened up, lifting his head off Ben's shoulder and standing tall, but he didn't move away. “Go where?”

“We're going home. You're going to have a long, hot shower and something to eat, and then you're going to sleep. There's nothing else you need to worry about tonight.”

“But—”

"You've done everything you can here for the moment, Jonathan. The apartment should be clear for the contractors to come in tomorrow to repair everything, the cleaners will come in the day after that, then we'll see what needs to be done. Until then, you're going to rest."

Feeling numb, Jonathan allowed himself to be led away. It wasn't until they arrived at Ben's place that he realized he'd done it again. He'd completely handed over control of his life to another person. Tears welled again. He'd never be free.

Chapter TWENTY-ONE

"WHERE IS he? His family is out of town. There's nowhere for him to go except here—home with me." Anthony wheeled to the kitchen table, where Vaughn sat catty-corner with Rebecca. Between them was a sheaf of papers. Rebecca casually folded her hands on top of the papers so Anthony couldn't see what they were about.

Vaughn stood and moved to the sink, making Anthony turn away from the table to keep him in view. Before he answered Anthony, he nodded to Rebecca, who gathered up the papers and left the room.

"Anthony, we need to talk."

"You're damned right we need to talk. You said you'd help me with Jonathan, but you haven't. I have to deal with him before Mark can come home."

"Anthony, stop it." Vaughn's voice was harsher and more strident than Anthony had heard it before. "Jonathan doesn't need to come back here for us to deal with him. Understand?"

Anthony nodded sullenly.

"We've followed Jonathan. We've followed that friend of his in the old ute. We've practically destroyed that guy's ute. You've rung Jonathan and demanded he come home. We've helped you do all these things, and still you want more." Vaughn scrubbed his hands over his face. "I saw on the news that Jonathan's apartment was burned down the other night. He wasn't injured, but he has nowhere to live. If he was going to come back to you, he would have then. It's time you let this go."

Vaughn leaned forward, gripping the arms of Anthony's chair, forcing Anthony to lean back away from him. Anthony's breathing increased in tempo and sweat coated his palms and underarms. For the first time, it hit him. Really hit him. He was a sitting duck with a grudge, stuck in a wheelchair with no way to escape or protect himself. He glanced at the kitchen benches. The magnetic strips that usually held his knives were starkly empty. *Hell*. He opened his mouth to breathe so it wouldn't be so obvious to Vaughn that he was panting.

"You need to accept that Jonathan doesn't want you anymore, Anthony." Vaughn smiled at him, and sweat trickled down his back. Vaughn looked up as Rebecca returned to the room and grinned as she nodded to him. "But that's okay, because Rebecca and I are here, and we're going to look after you."

"That's right, Anthony," Rebecca said as she leaned over his shoulder. "You won't have to worry about a thing. We'll do it all."

It should have been reassuring but for the first time in his adult life, Anthony was deathly scared.

Chapter TWENTY-TWO

"YEAH, HE'S sleeping now." The words were soft, but they were enough to interrupt Jonathan's dream. "I know. ... Yeah, I gathered that. ... No, it's fine. I don't have any classes today and I'm not needed at work until Monday. He can stay with me until the cleaners finish with his place. If he's up to it, we'll take all his clothes to the dry cleaner and start looking at beds."

Jonathan cracked his eyes open, surprised the room wasn't brighter. It felt late. Ben was a purple shadow passing on the other side of the screens that separated the bedroom space from the living area.

"It's fine, Liam. ... No, he just needs some space without all the neighbors and everyone around." The shadow crossed in front of the screen again. "Yeah, they're great, but they're a bit much, you know. I swear if Neridah thought she could get any of us naked by doing it, she'd dance on the coffee table." He chuckled. "I know, right. And Tahlia is going to give me a heart attack with all the food. I've only eaten there a couple of times, and my pants are already getting tight."

Jonathan sat and pushed the bedding away. He was wearing a pair of Ben's sweats and hoped he didn't need to go out in them. He was sure he looked like an emaciated refugee with the fabric hanging in folds at his groin and the hems not reaching his ankles.

"It's fine, Liam. Why don't you and Mark come over this evening? I can order a pizza. ... Sure, no, you gotta do what you gotta do. ... Yeah, that's fine. I'll keep you posted."

Before Jonathan could let Ben know he was awake, Ben came around the screen. "There's cereal for breakfast, or I could scramble some eggs. Which would you prefer?"

"You don't have to—"

"You have to eat, Jonathan. Skipping meals because everything seems to have turned to shit won't help anything." As Ben spoke, he walked into the little kitchenette and rummaged in the cupboards and fridge. When he turned, he held a bowl of cereal with milk and a spoon. "Here." He held the bowl out.

Jonathan stood. "I just need to…." He nodded at the doorway to the bathroom, then ducked around Ben and left the room.

BEN MADE some sandwiches and took Jonathan to the park for lunch. They ate in silence as they watched the ducks and swamp hens herd their chicks. The heat sank into Jonathan's shoulders and head, making the scene in front of him swim in a drowsy haze. He slid down in his seat by increments as each muscle relaxed a little more. A large water dragon sunned itself on the concrete verge of the artificial lake, staying perfectly still while Ben snapped photos with his phone.

"My mum loves these things. She'll get a kick out of how close it is to us." As Ben spoke, he tapped steadily on his phone until a soft *whoosh* indicated the message had been sent.

The hum of traffic behind the trees faded as Jonathan settled farther into his seat and began to listen to the sounds of nature around him. There wasn't a lot of movement at this time of day, but the gentle slosh of water as a duck dove for food, the creak and rustle of a willow swaying in the breeze, finally gave him the quiet and peace he needed to be able to think. "I have to get Anthony to stop."

The non sequitur caused Ben to start, but he recovered quickly. "We don't have any proof that it's been him the whole time. The police can't even prove it was his car that hit mine, although I thought there'd be a dent in his car from my door at the very least." He shrugged his shoulders as though none of it mattered to him anymore. "If it was him or someone working for him that set the fire in your place, then we have to find a way to stop him, or prove it was him so the police can stop him. They don't seem to think it was him, though."

Jonathan's shoulders slumped, the impossibility of it all slithering through him like a ravenous tapeworm, consuming every possibility of a future for himself just like the fire had consumed his apartment. Ten years with Anthony had shown Jonathan how manipulative and cruel the man could be. That last horrible day when he'd told Anthony he was leaving had shown how far Anthony would go in his desperation to keep control. Even with all of that, Jonathan had never really believed Anthony was capable of this type of concerted effort to destroy another person. "It doesn't make any sense. Why would he be doing this? And how?"

Ben gently rubbed Jonathan's back. "Everything will be fine, okay? We'll work out what we need to do, and then we'll do it."

"We're probably never going to be able to prove it was him. He's in a wheelchair. No one will believe he was capable of any of that stuff. They don't even think he's dangerous enough to keep in a psych ward or anything. They sent him home on bail." Jonathan rubbed the almost healed wound on his chest, despair eating at him. "I didn't think he would do this."

He was trying to cut all his ties with Anthony. He was trying to build a new life for himself, but everywhere he turned Anthony was there, calling him, demanding he do things, come home. Jonathan had been followed and threatened and his home had been burned. He was just lucky he hadn't been home at the time. He could have been injured or killed.

Jonathan shot to his feet. "They could have died," he burst out. Neridah and Tahlia had been home. They could have been killed. Sure, they were intrusive and irritating, but they meant well, and they had nothing to do with Jonathan's problems with Anthony. His chest ached, his breathing increased, and black dots danced at the edges of his vision. "I have to fix this," he panted. He spun in a circle but couldn't see a way out. Everything spun around, out of his control.

Ben gripped his arms, anchored him to the ground, and stopped the spinning. "It's okay, hon. Take a deep breath…. That's good. Now another." He put his arm around Jonathan's waist and turned him in the direction of the car park. "Let's head home. You can relax for a while, and then we can work out what we can do."

"Relax! I can't relax. I need to stop Anthony. He's going to seriously hurt someone."

"He's been charged with what he did to you, hasn't he?"

"Of course."

"Then I'm guessing he won't be a problem too much longer. He's out on bail right now, but when his case comes up, you probably won't have to worry about him for a long while. Attempted murder is a serious thing."

"How did you know?" Jonathan stumbled along beside Ben, his gaze glued to the other man.

Ben shrugged as he opened the car door for Jonathan. "I didn't, but I recognize a knife wound when I see it, and I'm smart enough to join the dots." He gave Jonathan a gentle shove to get him into the ute, then walked around to the driver's side. As he closed the door and started the engine, he continued. "We'll work out a plan of attack for Anthony, but you're not going to make the best decisions while you're still so worked up and stressed out. You're going to spend the afternoon in bed relaxing, and then we'll work something out tonight."

Jonathan started shaking his head as soon as Ben said the word "not." "There's no way I'm going to be able to relax when I know I have to—"

Ben chuckled—the insensitive bastard actually chuckled. Jonathan rounded on him to tell him this was serious, and Ben winked at him.

"I'm sure we can find something to do that will relax you."

All the air in Jonathan's lungs left him in a rush, and the blood in his head charged through his body to settle heavily in his groin. That suddenly, there was only one thing on Jonathan's mind. He gasped. "How do you do that?"

BEN FUMBLED his keys as he unlocked his door, cursed the fumble, cheered the save, and breathed a sigh of relief when the door finally slid open under his hand and he tumbled into his flat. Jonathan followed close behind. He slammed the door closed and flicked the lock before he grabbed Ben by the back of his neck and dragged him in for a kiss.

"I want you in me." Jonathan's voice came out as a low growl.

Ben groaned against his lips.

Jonathan raised his leg and hooked it around Ben's thigh, but the difference in their heights pulled Ben off balance, and they stumbled into the wall with a thud.

"Bed," whispered Ben.

Jonathan tried to nod agreement but wouldn't break the kiss to make the movement. Ben pushed his leg down and crab-walked them around the screen.

They fell in a tangle of limbs and screeching wood against the tiles. Something thudded against the wall, something fell and rattled, there was a crack of breaking glass. Neither paused to see what had broken.

Jonathan dragged Ben's shirt up his back and ran his hands over the smooth skin. Muscles rippled beneath his fingers, and he gasped into the sensation.

Ben's hips jolted, grinding to Jonathan as he grabbed Jonathan's face. "No. You fuck me," he whispered. "Deep and hard."

Jonathan moaned and pushed Ben's shoulders. "Up." He tugged Ben's shirt up with one hand as his other fumbled with the button on Ben's jeans. "Off."

Ben chuckled. "If I ever think you're talking too much, I'll just ask you to fuck me." He groaned as Jonathan shoved his fingers into his jeans and rubbed against his cock.

"Enough talking. Strip." Jonathan pushed at Ben's jeans until Ben sat back and finished the job. Ben's frantic fingers joined his as he started removing his own clothes. "Hurry," Jonathan groaned as Ben stood to remove his jeans. "I'm going to get you some stripper's pants. That way I can just rip them off you without all this bother." As he complained, Jonathan lifted his hips and slid his own jeans down his legs, thankful Ben was no longer straddling him. His legs were too long to do this gracefully. He kicked his underwear off and reached for Ben again.

Ben slid open the bedside table drawer, retrieved what he needed, then climbed over Jonathan again. Jonathan gasped as skin met skin and arched into the scalding heat of Ben's crotch. Ben shuddered as Jonathan's cock dug in behind Ben's balls, but he didn't lift off. Jonathan reached for Ben, grabbed him behind his neck, and drew him down for a wet open-mouthed kiss.

"I don't know what I want more," he whispered. "Kissing you is like—" Instead of finishing the sentence and exposing all his raw emotions like nerves stripped bare, Jonathan thrust his tongue into Ben's mouth. *Coming home.* That's what it was like, but he couldn't tell Ben that. He could barely even think it.

Ben lowered himself over Jonathan, covering him from knees to lips. Jonathan broke the kiss to haul in essential air, then sought Ben's lips again as his hips punched up, rubbing his cock alongside Ben's. *Smooth. Hot.* Christ, he was going to come.

"Wait." Ben tore himself away and sat back. "Wait." His heavy breath scalded Jonathan's neck as he fumbled beside them. "Here. Suit up while I get ready." He slapped the condom onto Jonathan's chest as he sat upright. There was a click and a soft *phht* as lube squirted from the tube, then Ben sat back farther and reached a hand behind him.

Jonathan fumbled the condom but eventually tore the package open and put it on. He ran his hands up Ben's stomach and pinched his nipples.

Ben jerked. "Oh yes. Harder." He brought his hand around from behind and shifted position as he grabbed Jonathan's cock and held it up.

"Are you sure you're stretched enough?" Jonathan asked. He didn't want to stop or even slow down, but hurting Ben wasn't on his agenda. Ben didn't reply, just lowered himself, hissing as Jonathan breached him. Jonathan grabbed Ben's hips to hold him still. "Wait," he panted. He gritted his teeth and closed his eyes to ward off impending orgasm. It had been far too long since this had been part of his life. Anthony had never allowed him to top after the first year.

Okay, stop thinking about Anthony right now. If he thought about his bastard ex too much, he'd lose his erection completely. At least he was down from the edge now. He eased his hold on Ben's hips and only then became aware of the man above him and the sweat-slicked skin under his fingers. "Easy, Ben. There's no rush."

"Bullshit." Ben's strained whisper flowed over Jonathan in anguished need. "I want to feel—" Ben panted and *whoosh*ed, his lips pursed, his cheeks puffed out, as he lowered himself a scant inch before raising up and lowering again, farther. "Oh God, that feels good." He groaned and huffed again. "Shit. Hard but good."

It was barely seconds later, or perhaps an hour, that Ben was fully seated and Jonathan was in as far as he could go. The urge to move rushed through him like hot oil racing through his veins. "Ben." Jonathan arched his neck, holding onto his control by a thread as he waited for Ben to give the go-ahead.

"Move," said Ben at the same time he lifted until Jonathan's cock hovered barely inside him. He dropped his hips, grinding onto Jonathan. Their simultaneous shouts echoed in the room. The harsh sounds sweated out of their pores in barely-there grunts and groans and slick skin, grasping fingers, and sloppy kisses.

"Jon." Ben's gasping whine skittered over Jonathan's skin, and he shifted his legs for better leverage, pounding up with every downstroke from Ben. Above him, Ben's breathing rose, a high-pitched whine escaping on every exhale, increasing as he slammed himself down.

"Now. Now. Now." Jonathan huffed the word out with every thrust. His fingers dug into the soft skin at Ben's hips and held on as scalding heat rushed through him and he froze, arched and pulsing.

Ben's whine stopped. Through the pounding of his heart and rasping breath, Ben's ass squeezed Jonathan in an age-old rhythm. He opened his eyes to watch Ben, eyes closed, cheeks flushed, come arcing between them.

"Christ, you're beautiful," Jonathan gasped.

JONATHAN PUSHED at Ben's shoulders, lungs too compressed for a deep breath. "Move," he gasped. Ben lifted off him to the squelch of sticky come between them.

Ben grimaced. "Wait," he said as he reached between them and grabbed the condom, still thankfully holding position on Jonathan's spent cock. That taken care of, Ben fell to the side and groaned as he stretched his legs out. Then he laughed.

Jonathan turned his head to watch Ben's face as it lit up, but the movement took all his energy. He sighed when Ben curled into him and rested his head on Jonathan's shoulder. He turned his head and inhaled; the earthy scent of their loving washed away the lingering memory-scent of his smoke-damaged apartment and his failed life. With Ben, it all seemed, if not yet right and good, at least achievable.

Chapter TWENTY-THREE

"HE'S NEVER coming back," Anthony whispered to himself. He looked around his opulent home and, for the first time, it was nothing but ashes and dust. "Not Jonathan." The bitterness of loss squeezed at him, restricting his breathing and screwing his face into a rictus of failure. "Not Mark either." He spun his chair, grabbed a vase of flowers from a side table, and smashed it to the floor.

"I think it's time you had a rest." Vaughn came into the room and grabbed the handles on Anthony's chair.

"I'm not a bloody child to be put down for a nap."

"You're behaving like one, so I'll treat you like one."

"You work for me, you bastard. You do what I say." He grabbed at the wheels on his chair but released almost immediately when his hands burned from the friction.

Vaughn leaned down to whisper in Anthony's ear. "You haven't realized it yet, Anthony, but you don't have much say in anything anymore."

"What the hell are you talking about?"

"You're on bail. You've been charged with two counts of attempted murder. Surely you don't think you'll be getting out of that."

"I have a lawyer. He'll do what I tell him to do."

"I wonder how much he'll do when he realizes you can't afford to pay him."

"What the hell are you talking about?" Anthony had plenty of money, even after that bastard Jonathan had taken nearly half of what was in their joint account.

"Your bank accounts are empty."

Anthony froze and twisted to look at Vaughn. "What the fuck? I cancelled Jonathan's access. You did that for me last week!"

"I remember you giving me access to your accounts." Vaughn pushed Anthony toward the lift. "Remind me again. Did you change your passwords after I cancelled Jonathan's access for you?"

Chapter TWENTY-FOUR

"I DON'T know what to do."

Liam sat next to Jonathan on the new couch that had been delivered that morning. "You do the same thing you've been doing. Decide what has to be done next and do it. Before you know it, the apartment will be looking great again, and you can get on with your life."

"That's just it. This—" Jonathan waved his hand around, indicating the apartment. "This is easy. It's cleaning and buying furniture and clothes and decorating." Jonathan scrubbed his hands over his head and sighed. "It's the rest that's hard. I don't know what my life is."

"It's whatever you want to make it."

"You're not helping, Liam." He stood and paced to the window and back. "It's been ten years since I've made a decision by myself. Not one single decision. I'm like those long-term prisoners released from jail. *I don't know what to do.* How do I start making a life for myself if I can't even do the basics?"

After a long pause, Liam said, "I'm hungry. What's to eat?"

"There's quiche—" He grimaced at the thought of the quiche. Hopefully Liam would take it off his hands. "—and salad that Tahlia brought over this morning. I need to get some steak to have with the roast vegetable salad she said she'd bring over at dinner time, or maybe chicken would be better." His heart rate increased as he tried to weigh the relative benefits of beef and chicken.

Liam grinned at him. "And there you have your first decision. It might not look like it right now, but what you were doing was working." He stood in front of Jonathan and drew him into a hug. "You'll know what to do again, Jon. You don't have to make every decision today. Start small and take them one at a time and you'll be fine."

"Are you sure?" Jonathan grasped his cousin to him. Liam had been there since Jonathan's parents died, talking him down from whatever emotional cliff he'd managed to climb onto. "I don't know what I'd do without you."

"Lucky you don't have to find out." A final squeeze and Liam stepped back. "Even if you did, you'd be fine. I know that."

Jonathan held Liam's gaze until the warmth of his love and support seeped in and strengthened him. Liam was right. He'd be okay, and if he wasn't, he could always call Liam to talk him down from the edge. There was just one more thing….

"What about Ben?"

Liam slapped Jonathan on his shoulder and returned to his seat on the couch. "You don't do things by halves, do you?"

"Liam." Jonathan clamped his mouth closed on the whine.

"What is it you want from Ben? Is it just a fling?"

"Shut up. When have I ever been into flings?"

"I know you were always convinced your first would be your ever-after, just like Cinderella, but that didn't work. I don't know what you want now. Are you still expecting your ever-after?"

"I don't know." Jonathan paced around the small room, his steps getting faster and faster as his agitation grew. Liam stepped in front of him to stop him.

"Okay, here's what you're going to do."

Thank God. Liam would tell him what to do, and Jonathan could do it and that would be that. The relief was intense, but underneath that there was a twinge of irritation. That's what he'd thought with Anthony, at first. He'd gone through all of the shit with Anthony, taken everything he could dish out. He'd nearly died to get out of it, and here he was, giving Liam permission to take over his life. After everything he'd gone through, he still wasn't going to be able to choose his own life.

"Jonathan, pay attention. This is important." When Jonathan stopped moving and looked at Liam, he continued. "The first thing you're going to do is stop freaking out every time you think you have to make another decision. You don't have to decide everything at once. You only have to make one decision at a time. You can dive right into a serious relationship with Ben, or you can back off and date for a while. Whatever you decide will be fine."

Silence filled the room along with Jonathan's confusion.

"I can see you thinking from here," said Liam. "What is it?"

"You're not going to tell me what to do?"

"It's not my life, Jon. It's yours. You get to decide, right or wrong, every step of the way."

"What if I make the wrong decision?"

"Then you live with the consequences or you fix it, just like what the rest of us do."

Jonathan imagined being with Ben every day, building a life with him. It was a fairy tale, but Jonathan was a cardboard cutout. He wasn't really there. Next he imagined dating Ben, but the idea seemed silly in the face of what they'd done the night before. And the night before that. How could you go back from that? He lowered his head into his hands and scrubbed his fingers through the tight curls. It was too hard. He couldn't decide.

"Remember that deciding not to make a decision is also a decision. Setting yourself up to fail because risking success is too scary is also a decision. You can't get out of it, Jon. You'll decide something, and that decision will impact your life. That's the way it works. You know that."

Liam was right. That's what Jonathan had done ten years ago with Anthony. He'd decided not to decide, and his life had spiraled out of his control. If he did the same thing with Ben, he'd end up right back where he was before. That's the last thing he wanted. He stared at Liam, who smiled gently.

"I know you're scared. That doesn't make you weak. I'm scared too—about Mark—but I'm not going to let that stop me getting what I know will be the best thing that has ever happened to me. Whatever obstacles Mark and I stumble across, I'll work through them with him." He held his hand up to forestall Jonathan's reply. "I know it's not the same thing. I don't have the horror of Anthony living inside my head. What I'm saying is, it doesn't matter where you've come from. Starting something new is bloody terrifying, but if you take control right from the beginning and know where you want to be by the end, I think you'll have a better chance of getting it."

Nope. Not helping. It was still as scary as hell. Jonathan's head was whirling. Deciding between beef and chicken for dinner was too much for him. No way would he be able to decide anything about Ben. Would Ben be expecting a decision from him? Could Jonathan put him off? Just for a while. And there he had his answer. He could barely cope with making day-to-day decisions for himself. Trying to make a potentially life-changing decision about Ben would send him to the loony bin.

Liam checked his watch and stood. "I have to get going. My shift starts in a little while, and I want to see Mark before I go in. It's a double."

Jonathan closed the door behind Liam and leaned against it. The silence of the apartment soaked into his pores. It was a different silence to what he'd had in the house with Anthony. There Anthony had always been expecting something of him. Here no one expected anything. He truly was master of his own destiny. If only he could work out what that destiny was supposed to be and how he was supposed to achieve it.

And why it felt so lonely.

EVEN AFTER all the cleaning, the apartment still smelled of smoke. The cleaning crew had sprayed something around that was supposed to mask it and left small tubs of blue powder that was supposed to absorb it, but that just made the apartment smell like a cheap perfumery that had been burned. Jonathan opened all the windows and the door and sprinkled bicarb soda over the floor.

"Oh," said Neridah from the doorway, three large boxes of bicarb soda cradled in her arms. "I suppose you won't be wanting these, then."

Jonathan smiled what felt like his first genuine smile since the fire. "I'll be vacuuming this up in the morning, but I think it'll still smell. We might need to do it a few times." He took the boxes from Neridah and put them on the kitchen bench. "Thank you for thinking of this."

"Tahlia mentioned the odor. I didn't think it was that bad, but she was really bothered by it."

"Is she okay? Does she get asthma or anything?"

"No, she just doesn't like smells. It irritates Kyle."

Jonathan squashed the uncharitable thought that everything seemed to irritate Kyle. "Well, I hope this works. The cleaners left some tubs of stuff around, but I couldn't stand the stench."

"I know that stuff. It's awful, isn't it? I don't know how anyone could think making places smell like burned plastic Juicy Fruit is an improvement over just the burned plastic." Neridah waved her hand in front of her face. The action was already familiar, but something was missing.

"You're not smoking?"

Neridah dropped her hand away from her face and looked away. *Shit, she's embarrassed.*

"No. Well, I've been thinking about it for a while and...." She straightened her shoulders and lifted her chin to look Jonathan in the eye. "I'm giving up."

"Good for you."

"It probably won't work. You know how it is. You've got this habit going on for years, and then suddenly you try to change. You know it's the best thing to do, but there's that habit."

Jonathan knew all about how hard it was to give up a habit. He'd stayed with Anthony for ten years, eight years too long. "Yeah, it's hard, but at some point you realize it's do-or-die time, and you have to move forward or...."

"Yeah. I don't want the 'or' either," said Neridah with a small smile. "I'd better get out of your hair before the crazy bitch I become when I'm quitting surfaces. I'll never get into your pants if you see that version of me."

Jonathan stepped back, out of reach. "Uh, Neridah—"

Neridah cackled. "Oh, that's precious." Her laugh turned into one of those hacking liquid coughs, and she waved her hand in front of her face as she usually did. The coughing didn't stop immediately but eventually she recovered, still smiling. "You're safe, baby boy. I'm just teasing." She turned to her apartment, waving a hand over her head as if there was still a cigarette between her fingers.

As Neridah's door closed, the door to apartment 4C opened. Two suitcases slid out into the hallway, then Tahlia stepped out, a backpack and handbag over her shoulders. She froze when she saw Jonathan.

Into the frightened silence, he asked, "Do you need a hand with those?" He nodded at the suitcases.

She nodded, so Jonathan picked up the cases and walked down the stairs with her. The silence to the front door and the waiting taxi was heavy with fear, secrecy, and promise. Jonathan loaded the cases into the back of the taxi as Tahlia dropped her backpack beside them.

He pulled a piece of paper from his pocket, borrowed a pen from the driver, and jotted down his number.

"If you get stuck and need some help, call me."

She shook her head before he'd finished speaking. "You don't know—"

"I've been there myself. Just got out of hospital from the last round, actually. It took me too damn long to learn this, but it's okay to need help, and it's okay to ask for it." He slipped the paper into the zip opening of her backpack.

"Thank you," she whispered.

He watched her drive away. *Good God, Jonathan. You're acting like a grown-up. You might actually survive this.* His grin stretched his cheeks all the way up three flights of stairs and into his stinking apartment. Even the twinging pain in his chest from carrying Tahlia's suitcases downstairs didn't dim it.

BEN RANG that evening.

"You're lucky you're not here right now."

Ben laughed. "I think I'd be lucky to be there." His voice was a cat-tongue rasp over Jonathan's skin.

Jonathan cleared his throat and pushed on his dick, hoping it would behave. "Neridah's stopped smoking."

"Good for her."

"You don't get it. She's chewing gum all the time with her jaw rolling in sideways circles like a cow. She's wearing patches too, and when she takes them off, they take her tan with them, so she has these white squares marching up and down her streaky brown arms. The worst of it is, none of it's working."

"What do you mean, it's not working? Those things are loaded with nicotine."

"I know, but I think she must be addicted to one of the *other* chemicals in cigarettes. She threw one of her side tables down the stairs yesterday because she bumped it and the tablecloth twisted off center."

"Holy…."

"I know." Jonathan leaned over, shielding the phone just in case Neridah could hear him through his door. "I'm scared to open the door when she knocks."

Silence greeted him, and Jonathan heard his words echo in his mind. Warmth flooded him as he realized what Ben must be thinking. In the same confidential tone, he whispered, "Do you think an exorcism would work?"

Ben laughed, relief and joy lifting his voice. "I could come over and protect you."

Silence hung in the air, thick and heavy like Neridah's smoke haze.

"Forget I asked. You said you needed—"

"I'm sorry."

"You have nothing to be sorry about. I just miss being with you."

Jonathan didn't sleep well that night.

BEN RANG the next night too. "You should have seen this house we moved today. I don't know why they didn't get a skip and be done with it. The couch was an old vinyl futon that had more cracks than vinyl. I don't think any of the things from the kitchen were actually clean, and none of it was packed properly. It clanked with every step I took. Who knows how much of it actually arrived unbroken?"

"Not everyone can afford new things, Ben."

"I know. I think what bothered me most was that the number of boxes of booze they moved outnumbered the toys their three kids had."

"That sucks."

"Yeah, and it took forever because the new guy kept stuffing up."

"So Col's not working anymore?"

"No. Lorraine's taken extended leave from her job to care for him."

Jonathan's throat locked. That sucked blue bananas. Ben cleared his throat.

"I could do with a hug right now," said Ben quietly.

Jonathan wanted nothing more and opened his mouth to say so but couldn't. If he gave in now, he'd keep giving in. He'd bury himself in his need and when it didn't work, he'd be lost again—even more than he was now.

"Sorry."

"No, I'm sorry. I want to but—"

"Jonathan. It's fine. I understand. Can we talk again tomorrow?"

Jonathan sighed in relief. "Yeah, I'd like that."

It was hard to keep refusing, because he could hear Ben's disappointment each time Jonathan said no, but it was the right thing to do. For the first time ever, Jonathan was setting the pace for a new relationship. He was in control of his life, even if it didn't feel like it most of the time.

Choosing what to eat was still difficult. He'd always just made what Anthony wanted. The only thing easy was deciding not to have quiche every Sunday like Anthony insisted—or ever. Filling his days was also difficult. Anthony's needs had kept him more than busy for the last two years, and until the new semester at uni started, Jonathan would have to find ways to keep busy.

Liam called every day before his shift. Bruce and Faye called every day too, at odd hours because of the time difference. It was in turns nice that his family loved him so much, and frustrating that he never seemed to have time alone to be inside his own head.

Jonathan met Ben for lunch the next day. They sat in a busy food court in a nearby shopping center and ate toasted sandwiches. Ben tapped the table beside Jonathan's plate whenever Jonathan stopped eating.

"Why do you do that?" Jonathan asked.

Pink flooded Ben's cheeks. "Sorry. My younger brother had leukemia when he was little. He was skinny as, just like you, and he was so sick he wasn't hungry at all."

"So do you do it to me because I look like I'm dying or because you think of me as another brother?" Jonathan burst out laughing at the disgusted look on Ben's face. When he realized he was being teased, Ben laughed too.

When the laughter faded, Ben asked, "So why won't you see me?"

"I am seeing you."

Ben shrugged and played with his scrunched-up napkin. "You won't let me come round to your place. You won't come round to mine." His large, wounded eyes implored Jonathan not to hurt him.

Jonathan knew he'd have to tell Ben everything at some time. He'd hoped they could spend more time getting to know each other first, but that wasn't to be.

"I was with Anthony for ten years. I moved in with him after the first time I slept with him. That was our third date." Jonathan stared at the table, tracing his finger around and around the wet ring left by his glass. "I don't want to make the same mistake again."

When Ben didn't respond, Jonathan looked up. Ben was grinning.

"So what you're saying is, you don't want to move in together after the third date." Ben grinned as he spoke.

Jonathan wasn't sure why that made Ben smile, but he nodded.

"You want to date a while and get to know each other properly before we live together."

"Yes—no—wait." He hadn't promised they'd live together.

"We can stay in our own places and when we're ready, we can get a place that's just for us."

"Ben—" He was going too fast, and it was making Jonathan—he scrunched his napkin in his fist and pushed his seat back.

"Hey, Jon. What's wrong?" Ben leaned over the table but didn't touch Jonathan. "Shit, what did I say? Am I going too fast again?"

Jonathan nodded. Every cell in his body screamed at him to escape, to run away and not let Ben trap him, but he forced himself to stop and listen. He was through with running away, just as much as he was through with being pressured into things he wasn't ready for.

"Okay. We'll date. I'd really like to fuck again, but if you don't want that for a while, I'll live with it." Ben leaned over the table again, his face earnest. "I get excited about things I want, Jon, and I push for them like some bloody bull in a china shop. That's what my mum says, anyway. I can't see the point of sitting and thinking about stuff when I already know what I want, but that doesn't mean everyone else thinks the same thing. I want you more than I've ever wanted anyone, but that doesn't mean what I want is more important than what you want. It just means you have to tell me to back the fuck off if I get too much for you, okay?"

"Back the fuck off," said Jonathan. Ben jolted back in his seat, and Jonathan laughed at the mixture of horror and humor in his expression. "Are you sure you want me to say that?"

Ben laughed. "As long as you don't tell me to fuck off and never come back, I'll deal."

Chapter TWENTY-FIVE

"WELL, THAT bastard won't fuck us over again, that's for sure." Rebecca dropped her handbag on the kitchen table and sank gracelessly into a chair.

"Fuck. What exactly did you do?" Vaughn turned the burners on the stove off so he could focus completely on her. He needed his wits about him with her on a good day, and judging by the smile on Rebecca's face, this was not going to be a good day. Not for him, anyway.

"Stop panicking, will you? I didn't do anything bad." She grinned at him, and his stomach turned over.

"How bad?"

"Let's just say he's going to find it difficult to run away next time. In fact, he won't be walking anywhere for a long while."

"Shit. He's going to talk." Vaughn paced between the stove and the table, trying to think what links there were between him and her that the police would find. He watched as Rebecca pulled a cigarette from a pack in her bag and lit it.

"He won't talk," she said confidently. "He knows exactly what will happen to him if he does."

He had to get her out of here. He had to make her go away and not come back. She was going to get him killed, or worse, arrested. He opened his mouth to suggest… something but didn't get a chance to say anything.

"I think it would be best if we went our separate ways for a while. I think I'll go away and lay low"—she squinted at him through the cigarette smoke—"just in case he does talk." She drew on the cigarette, then blew a stream of smoke into the air above her head. "You're set here for a while—at least until the lame guy gets put away—and no one but me knows you're here, so you could just stay here."

Shit. She's going to kill me too. Vaughn froze, but then forced himself to breathe evenly and nod, as if he accepted what she said.

"Where will you go?" he asked, although he didn't want to know. "What will you use for money?"

"Don't worry about me. Jimmy told me where he stashed our cut. I'll go and collect it and keep your half for you until it's safe again."

The bitch was going to stiff him out of his dough. Heat flooded Vaughn's face as the anger overtook him. He glared at her face, placid and expectant. *Fuck*. She wanted him to react. She was looking for a reason to kill him, or whatever she'd done to Jimmy. He took a deep breath, then another, until he'd calmed enough to speak. Even then, the only thing that stopped him grabbing her and smashing her head in was the knowledge that he had the money from Porter. Rebecca didn't know about that.

"How will I collect it if I don't know where you are?"

"I'll contact you. I know your number." She was cool, blasé, as she stood and picked up her handbag. "Stay safe, Vaughn."

From her, those words sounded like a threat.

Chapter TWENTY-SIX

A WEEK later Jonathan was surprised his dick hadn't developed calluses that matched the ones on his right hand. He'd seen Ben nearly every day and had begun to wonder why he was holding back. Ben was everything Jonathan wanted in a man. He was strong and confident and made no excuses or apologies for who he was, but he was also kind and sensitive. Jonathan wanted to give in. He wanted to sleep with Ben, and he wanted them to move in together and spend every spare moment together, but after Anthony he had to be really sure it was the right thing for him to do, and he couldn't allow good sex to cloud his judgment.

It was all happening so quickly. Jonathan had only just moved out of Anthony's house and got a place of his own. While he hadn't heard from Anthony or seen him since before the fire, Jonathan didn't assume that meant his ex had given up. No, Anthony was just regrouping, making plans for the next thing he could do to destroy the life Jonathan was building for himself. Jonathan knew Anthony and knew how he worked. He certainly didn't underestimate the man just because he was in a wheelchair.

What he had with Anthony wasn't over. He'd made a start with moving out and refusing to speak to him, but that didn't mean it was done and dusted and Jonathan could move on to the next man. There'd been too much time, too many years in between where Jonathan was a husk, a shell of a person that Anthony filled up with what he wanted Jonathan to be. Jonathan had to work out what he wanted that husk to be filled with, and he couldn't allow another person to do it for him. Not his family and certainly not Ben.

AS HE arrived home after having lunch with Ben, the door to Kyle and Tahlia's apartment flew open and slammed against the inside wall. Kyle lurched out.

"You! You did it, didn't you?" He stumbled down the hallway toward Jonathan. "Where is she? She's not with any of her family. No one's seen her. I know you helped her. Are you fucking her? Are you the one? I'll smash you in two, you black bastard."

As Kyle came level with the stairwell, Neridah stepped up into the hallway. Jonathan moved forward to intercept, to stop Kyle's forward momentum from toppling Neridah down the stairs but he needn't have worried. Neridah dropped her bag of groceries and swung her handbag squarely into Kyle's groin.

Kyle went down with a howl.

"Oh dear, did I do that?" said Neridah with a wink at Jonathan. She picked up her shopping and stepped over a writhing Kyle. "I'd get that seen to, Kyle. Blows like that can cause lasting damage, you know."

Neridah laughed and went into her apartment with another wink at Jonathan, leaving him standing in his doorway, his mouth hanging open as wide as his door. Kyle continued to writhe on the floor. "Dear God, I'm surrounded by idiot felons and ninja grannies." He stepped back into his apartment, slammed the door, and threw the dead bolt against the possibility of Kyle recovering and coming after him.

He smiled as he dialed his phone. He couldn't wait to tell Ben about this.

"How on earth do you manage it?" asked Ben once he'd recounted the story.

"What do you mean?"

"I thought you were just a guy who'd left his violent rat-bastard ex, but you're more than that, aren't you? You're like this supermagnet for all the arsehole troublemakers in the city. You not only have your ex on your trail, but you've got violent boyfriends wanting a piece of you and a really slutty cougar after you too—although she's more funny than scary."

For a second Jonathan wondered if he was unconsciously looking for people like that—people who would hurt him.

"Do you think I ask for this stuff to happen?" Jonathan shut his mouth with a snap. He sounded like a whining child, and he knew it wasn't true. He didn't believe that. He was worth more than the type of mistreatment Anthony had dished out. Anthony *was* his problem, and he'd have to fix that once and for all but the other things weren't his responsibility. He was just in the wrong place at the wrong time. Why, oh why, did it all land on him, though? And cue the whining child again. "Fuck."

"You don't really think that, do you?" The smile was gone from Ben's voice. Until that moment, Jonathan hadn't realized how often Ben sounded happy. Now that he didn't, the lack of it pricked like pins jabbing his fingertips. He rubbed his hand across his face.

"Sorry. I'm still learning all this stuff, Ben. Shit. I don't know." He paced between his couch and the kitchen bench. "I think I need therapy." He'd meant it as a joke, but as he heard the words coming out of his mouth, he realized he probably did need to talk to someone who actually knew how to help him.

Ben spoke into the silence that filled the seconds after Jonathan's revelation. "I'm sorry. I didn't mean to make you think... I don't think... I'm sorry."

"Ben? This is me. I've never lived my own life. Decisions have always been made for me, and I've allowed it to happen, but I'm trying to stop that. But I didn't encourage Kyle to attack me. That wasn't me."

"I know." Ben sounded like he was near tears.

"Can you...." Jonathan tugged on his hair, not sure he knew how to ask for what he wanted. "I'm going to stuff it up, Ben. I'm going to say the wrong thing, do the wrong thing. Hell, I'm even going to do nothing and that'll end up being the wrong thing, and I'll get angry, and I'll probably yell at you, and then you'll... you'll...." He stopped. He really didn't know what Ben would do if he did all those things, but he... feared. And the fear ruled him.

"Then I'll shut up and listen to what you're saying, and I'll wait until you sort it out and tell me what you need." Ben's voice was quiet and more serious than Jonathan had ever heard before. "How does that sound? Would that work?"

"I like the sound of that. Can we try that?" He grinned. It wasn't much of a decision, but asking Ben to be patient with him felt like the largest adult decision he'd ever made.

"Yeah," breathed Ben. "I think we can try that." The grinning silence between them strained Jonathan's cheeks, so he laughed. Ben laughed with him.

Finally they were quiet again, and that's when Jonathan felt it—a warm burbling deep within him. *Hope*. That would be a nice thing to be able to hold on to and not have it smashed every time Jonathan turned around.

"So what ended up happening with Kyle the bastard?"

"I don't know. He was gone by the time I gathered the courage to check outside, and I haven't seen or heard him since.

The silence stretched between them, not uncomfortable, but heavy with expectation. "I could come over for a while, if you'd like some company," said Ben quietly.

Jonathan's breath rushed from him, and he slumped into the couch. "I thought you'd never ask," he said.

"I'll be there in twenty." The line went dead before Jonathan could respond. Laughter burst from him as he pulled out clean sheets from the linen cupboard and erupted sporadically as he made his bed and cleaned his teeth.

JONATHAN WAITED at the downstairs door for Ben to pull up outside. His laughter had deserted him and worry had settled back in like a comfortable cushion. Jonathan knew where they were going to end up within minutes of getting inside his apartment. Pretending otherwise would be foolish. Ready or not, Jonathan was in a relationship again. He hoped to God Ben wasn't more like Anthony than he seemed.

Neither of them spoke as Jonathan unlocked the downstairs door. A man Jonathan didn't know came in behind Ben before Jonathan could lock the door again. He was medium height and wore a beanie. If Jonathan had passed him in the street, he wouldn't have noticed him at all, but his eyes were so pale a blue they looked silver, and they were rimmed with white eyelashes. Coupled with his pale skin, the man looked like he could fade into sunlight or glow in the dark. He asked him, "Are you visiting someone here?"

The man said, "I'm on the second floor."

Jonathan shared a glance with Ben but said nothing. He'd met none of the tenants on the other floors, so he wouldn't know who belonged and who didn't. The stranger went ahead of them, taking the stairs two at a time. His footsteps stopped at the second floor, and Jonathan heard a door close as they continued to the third. He didn't see which door the man had gone into.

He leaned closer to Ben. "I'm glad he went where he said he was going to go."

The silence filled the stairwell as they climbed the stairs to Jonathan's floor. For once both Neridah's and Tahlia's—Kyle's—doors were closed. Jonathan hoped Tahlia stayed away. She'd be better off out of it, but Jonathan knew exactly how hard it was to leave once you'd become ensconced in a relationship like that. So far he hadn't found *staying out* particularly difficult, probably because Anthony was still in the picture and trying to influence him, even if he'd been quiet lately. Jonathan felt he was still trying to leave, new apartment and new bank accounts notwithstanding.

"I could stay with you for a while," said Ben as Jonathan unlocked his door. He put his hands up as if surrendering. "Just until things settle down and you stop jumping at shadows."

"Is that what you think I'm doing?"

Ben shrugged. "I don't know. I've never lived with anyone who tried to kill me. I've never trusted someone who meant me harm. My experience tells me everything's okay, but my experience isn't yours. You're the only one who can decide what feels safe and what doesn't for you."

As Jonathan pushed open his door, he asked, "How did you get so wise?"

Ben laughed as he followed Jonathan across the threshold. "My mother would beat me bloody if I didn't consider how other people felt." At Jonathan's horrified look, he backtracked. "No, no, I don't mean that literally. She just has a way of standing with one hand on her hip and the other in front of my face, pointed finger practically jabbing me in the nose. And she's angry and scared when she does it, so her voice vibrates with the terror she feels at what I've done." He shuddered. "I try to avoid that if I can."

Jonathan laughed as he turned to close the door behind them and cried out when it was pushed open with a force that knocked him back several steps, stumbling into Ben and forcing him against the wall.

"Get down, now!"

"What? Who?" The words burst from Jonathan in uncontrolled exclamations. Beside him, Ben moved sideways, putting space between them.

The intruder lashed out at Ben, hitting him on the shoulder with a short black truncheon. "Get the fuck down, now! On your faces. Porter wants his money back."

With a glance at Ben, who crouched slightly, Jonathan began lowering himself too. Ben was farther away again and Jonathan finally got the message, so he stepped to his left, even as he bent his knees more to make it look like he was following the man's instructions. He looked up into the pale eyes glaring at him.

"I already told Anthony he wasn't getting that money back. I took my share from the ten years we were together, and that's all I took. You can tell him if he contacts me again, I'll take out a domestic violence order. He can talk to his solicitor about it if it's that important to him," he said as he stepped to his left again. Now Ben was almost behind the man, whose full attention was on Jonathan.

"Wha—?"

Ben slammed his joined fists down on the man's forearm, the sick snap making it clear he'd broken a bone. The truncheon fell to the ground as Jonathan pushed the man's chest, causing him to stumble backward and trip over Ben's feet. He landed heavily, his head cracking against the corner of the coffee table.

The silence that followed was punctuated by Ben and Jonathan's rasping breaths and broken as Jonathan pulled his phone out and rang emergency services.

THE POLICEMEN who attended the scene were the same ones Jonathan had spoken to after the fire, and also when the Jeep had run into Ben's car.

"You've been having a pretty exciting time of it here, haven't you, Mr. Watson?"

"I don't want exciting. I moved here because I wanted a quiet life."

They'd gone through the details of what happened. The blond man had roused as the paramedics were loading him onto the stretcher and glared at Jonathan but not said anything before he was wheeled out and carried down the stairs. The police had more questions for Jonathan. It seemed there were always more questions.

"Was this the first time you met Mr. Lindgren?"

Jonathan nodded. "I've never seen him before. I'd have recognized his eyes if I had."

"His eyes?"

"White eyelashes. It's unusual, so I noticed."

"Not many white eyelashes where you're from, I suppose," the second officer said.

Jonathan stared at him until he looked away.

After a pointed look from his colleague, the officer stepped back and said nothing more. The police left soon after with admonishments to keep the downstairs door locked and not allow anyone in who didn't belong. Jonathan wasn't sure how he was supposed to accomplish that when other tenants in the building regularly left the door open. Short of standing guard downstairs twenty-four hours a day, there was no way he could monitor it.

After the police left, the building seemed empty and silent. He didn't see Neridah at all and, with Tahlia gone, felt a pang of loss. Until now they'd been constantly there, on the stairs, at his door, in his kitchen. Regardless of how intrusive his neighbors were, he'd grown to like them. Now all his troubles were proving too much, and they were leaving or withdrawing. He should have expected it. He *had* expected it. It was just....

"You know," said Ben, "most people just put the kettle on when they're expecting company. There really wasn't any need to go to all this trouble to entertain me."

Jonathan ran his hands over his head and down his face, peeping between his fingers to gauge Ben's mood. Ben's words and tone of voice were light and amused, but his eyes were serious. "I'm so sorry," Jonathan said. "I must have some sort of chip inserted that acts as a magnet for all the weirdoes."

"Well, I'll certainly never be bored, that's for sure." As Ben spoke, he wandered into the kitchen, checked there was water in the kettle, and turned it on.

"Oh God, I'm sorry. I can't even do that right." All of a sudden Jonathan was near tears. His throat was tight and his eyes burned. "This isn't the way I thought this evening would go."

Ben stopped fidgeting with the mugs and moved close to Jonathan. "Me neither." He lifted his hand and brushed a featherlight touch across Jonathan's trembling bottom lip. "I think we need a cuppa and some time to calm down before that story's ready to be told again, don't you?"

"I can make it. I'm a big boy, you know."

Ben laughed delightedly as he looked Jonathan up and down, lingering at his groin on both the down sweep and up again. "Yep, I kinda worked that one out, but thanks for reminding me. It gives me all sorts of things to look forward to. Get the cups down, will you? We'll sit and chat, and you can tell me exactly how much of a 'big boy' you are."

Heat rushed through Jonathan at the idea of calmly sitting at the table with Ben and discussing... anything related to how big he was. Suddenly the tea didn't matter, nor did the fact they'd spent over an hour subduing an intruder and then discussing it over and over with the police. Jonathan stepped forward as Ben replaced the kettle on the hob and boldly ran his hands over the firm globes of Ben's ass. Ben started but then leaned back into Jonathan's palms. He tilted his head back until it rested on Jonathan's shoulder.

"I'm suddenly not thirsty anymore," he murmured as he wriggled his ass against Jonathan's hands.

Jonathan slid his fingers around Ben's hip bones and pulled him back, grinding his needy cock against Ben. He licked the lobe of Ben's ear, then trailed soft kisses down his neck. They both groaned as he opened his mouth and drew the sensitive flesh between his teeth.

The doorbell rang, and they froze.

Ben dropped his head forward and braced himself against the counter as Jonathan released his hips and stepped back. "Your place is like Grand fucking Central," he complained.

"Tell me about it. If I hadn't just moved in, I'd leave," Jonathan mumbled as he walked to the door and yanked it open.

Neridah stood outside. She wasn't smiling, her lipstick was smeared, and there was no cigarette.

"What's wrong?" he asked as he looked behind her for any hint of danger. He opened the door wider and ushered her inside. "Are you all right? What's happened?"

"Oh, Jonathan. I'm so sorry," sobbed Neridah. "I didn't mean for this to happen."

"I think you'd better come in and explain what you're talking about." Jonathan stepped back and ushered her inside.

"It's all my fault," sobbed Neridah. "I didn't mean to."

Jonathan led her to the dining table and pulled a chair out for her. Ben brought her a glass of water. "Okay, now tell me what this is about."

"I… this is so stupid," she wailed. Ben brought a box of tissues from the bedroom and put them on the table. Neridah grabbed a few and blew her nose.

"What's stupid?" Jonathan asked.

"It's been so exciting around here since you moved in. I mean, with your family being so nice and you just sweet as pie. I just had to share it with everyone." She sipped her water. "I was at the shops chatting to Ramon at the till, and that man was there—the one the police took away." Neridah looked imploringly at Jonathan. "I didn't know who he was, I promise. It was like I was suddenly the most popular girl in school, so I kept talking and told them all about how you left your ex but brought a lot of nice things with you, and you didn't seem in a hurry to get a job so you must have got money too." She gripped her water glass with two hands and stared into the remaining water. "And the next thing I know, he's here and attacking you." She slapped the water glass onto the table and buried her face in her hands. "And it's all my fault!"

Jonathan patted Neridah's back. "It's okay, Neridah." It wasn't okay at all. She shouldn't be telling everyone and anyone his business. He bit his tongue on his thoughts when he realized what he was doing—looking to blame someone else so he could reduce his own culpability. The man who attacked them had come from Anthony, and Anthony was his problem, and his alone. He dropped into the chair beside her. "It's okay," he repeated. "He knows Anthony and would have come around anyway. At least this way, the police might be able to link Anthony to it." He breathed slowly and organized his thoughts. It didn't matter that he was feeling overwhelmed and persecuted. Neridah's anguish wasn't about him, and couldn't be about him. He'd deal with his own angst later. "So you've probably helped in that way," he finished.

Neridah smiled tremulously at him. "You're a good boy."

Jonathan's breath caught, and he looked away quickly. His mother used to say that to him whenever he was kind to someone. He pressed his lips together and blinked rapidly, feeling stupid to be so affected by a few small words, especially after all this time.

Ben's arm landed softly around Jonathan's shoulders, and another shuddering breath centered him again.

"I think we should all go out for a while," said Ben. "It'll give us time to wind down a bit after all the excitement here."

Jonathan glared at Ben. He'd been looking forward to the most recent bit of excitement. Ben winked at him, and Jonathan found himself inexplicably smiling. Yes, he wanted Ben in his bed, but as long as he was with Ben—anywhere, anytime—he was happy.

Calm and happy.

Who'd have thought Jonathan would be able to apply those two words to his life? They certainly hadn't been true at any time over the last eight years, and probably longer than that.

THEY ALL walked together to Neridah's favorite coffee shop on the next block.

"You'll just love their vegetarian crêpes. It's a basic breakfast crêpe but they've added fresh pineapple and some chili. The sweet and hot explode in your mouth along with the silkiness of the mushroom and the bite of shallots. If Tahlia was here, she could make it for you but this is the best I can do."

Jonathan smiled and nodded, not willing to interrupt Neridah's happy voice now she'd put her guilt behind her and dived back into life.

"Do you think he's gay?" Neridah motioned to the man walking just in front of them. "God, I hope not. Those buns are just begging to be squeezed." Neridah's hands formed claws as she mimed gripping the buttocks of the young man in front of them.

Jonathan grinned at Neridah's antics as the stranger broke into a jog and crossed the road as soon as there was a break in traffic. He remained silent and enjoyed the happiness that bubbled through him like lemonade. His cheeks ached from the grin stretching his mouth, but it only made him smile wider. This was *it*. This was way more important than a stalker ex-boyfriend or not knowing who he was or what he wanted or not being able to make even the simplest decision. It was more important than violent intruders. This, just this, was what life was about. Sunshine and friends—he glanced at Ben—and budding love.

And Ben…. Ben held Jonathan's hand the whole way to the café.

Chapter TWENTY-SEVEN

JONATHAN FOUND a table for them while Neridah went to the counter to order. Ben leaned out the door and called hello to someone before joining Jonathan. He raised his eyebrows at Neridah, but Jonathan shook his head. "Neridah can choose something for me. I trust her," he said in a voice loud enough for her to hear. He smiled at the beaming woman. "Anything but quiche," he cautioned.

"I won't let you down, Jonathan," she replied. He knew she was talking about more than the food, but Jonathan didn't want to talk about it anymore. She felt guilty. They were all still alive and safe. There wasn't anything left to say. Within minutes she joined them, and they sat in comfortable—and unusual—silence.

Then the door burst open and Lorraine rushed in and ran to Ben.

"Have you seen Col? Ben, he's gone again."

Ben stood, his hand immediately resting on Lorraine's shoulder like an anchor. She calmed as Jonathan stood and joined them between the tables. "You were both there when I waved. How far from you was he standing?"

"Right beside me. I waved to you, then turned to see if the bus was coming. When I looked back, he was gone. I thought he might have come in here. He loves the pastries they make, but he's not here, and I thought… I thought…." Lorraine broke down into noisy sobs.

Ben drew Lorraine into a tight hug. "It'll be okay, Lorraine. We'll help you find him, and then you can take him home with you. Did he miss his meds again?"

She nodded against his chest. "He's been hiding them. I can't… oh God, I can't…." She peered up at Ben, a plea for understanding clear on her tortured features. "Today is our last day together. I'm taking him to a nursing home in the morning. Tomorrow will be the first day in forty-eight years we've been apart, except when I had the children." Her knees gave way, and Ben only just managed to save her from dropping right to the floor. Jonathan scooped his arm around her waist and helped her to a chair. "I don't know what I'm going to do without him," she wailed. "He's my husband. He's... he's everything."

"There he is now," exclaimed Neridah. She pushed her seat back and ran for the door. Across the street meandered Col, his dandelion hair glowing white in the sun, his legs and arms even skinnier than they'd been last time Jonathan had seen him. As Neridah ran out calling for Col, he turned, his gaze in turns blank, confused, and alarmed.

"No!" called Lorraine as she pushed away from Ben and Jonathan and ran after Neridah. "Don't frighten him!"

Jonathan and Ben raced after Lorraine.

Col calmed as soon as Lorraine touched his arm. Jonathan stood, mute, as Lorraine spoke quietly to Col. His throat ached with unshed tears as he watched the heartbreak on their faces. Lorraine was losing her husband, the love of her life. Col, unable to remember or function the way he once had, also carried an air of great loss around him. His fingers held tight to Lorraine's hand, his gaze focused solely on her as she led him away.

"Look at the way he watches her," whispered Ben. "Lorraine said he's her everything, but I don't think she's alone in that."

That's what I want, thought Jonathan. *I want a love like that. I want to love and be loved so deeply, so purely, that even when I can't remember my own name, I'll remember who he is to me.*

He drew in a shuddering breath, and another and another. He only calmed when Ben slipped his hand into Jonathan's and held it tightly.

"WELL, THAT just pisses me off," exclaimed Neridah into the silence that hovered over their table. They'd eaten in silence and then continued to sit there, not even looking at each other until Neridah's personality once again thundered over everything.

"Yeah," said Ben. "It's a horrible thing to happen to anyone."

"I'm not talking about that. Sure, Alzheimer's would be awful, but did you see them? Of course you saw them. It's like they're one person. Neither one of them can function without the other there propping them up." She stared out the window as if she could still see Lorraine and Col standing on the other side of the road. "It was beautiful."

"If you think it's so beautiful, why are you pissed?" asked Jonathan.

"I'm pissed because I only had my Neil for one year before he died. We never had the chance for what we had to grow into something like that. I'm pissed off because I thought Brian was another chance at that, but Brian wanted to be Brianna more than he wanted me. And even though I still loved him—her—I married Kevin-the-drunk-manwhore. I'm never going to have that sort of love."

Jonathan stared at her, open-mouthed.

"What? I'm not allowed to be envious that someone else got to be happy and in love for forty years and I didn't? Get real. Even now when I'm with Brianna, I feel like it's possible, but she's a she...." Neridah's voice broke on a husky cough, and her eyes filled with embarrassed tears. "I'll never have that." She covered her mouth with her hand, shoved her seat back, and ran from the café.

Jonathan stood to go after her but stopped when Ben put his hand over his.

"Fuck," said Jonathan as he sat and watched Neridah tear down the street toward their building. "Could this day get any worse?" Before Ben could respond, Jonathan's phone rang. He looked at the screen. "Fuck. Anthony."

"I think you jinxed it with that comment," said Ben with a small smile. He nodded at the phone in Jonathan's hand. "Are you going to answer it or let it go to voice mail?"

Jonathan swiped the screen to take the call. "I need to know what he's up to," he said. "Anthony. What do you want this time?" If it was more bloody garbage about him going back to the abusive bastard, Jonathan would probably throw something.

"Jonathan, you have to help me."

The temptation to disconnect the call was strong. Jonathan never wanted to be subjected to another session of Anthony telling him what to do. The only thing that stopped him was the thickness in his ex-boyfriend's voice. Like he'd been crying or was scared or something.

"I don't *have* to help you, Anthony, but please tell me what you think I have to do now."

"They're saying I paid him to do it, and they're going to arrest me."

"I don't know what you're talking about, and even if I did, it's none of my business. I don't live there anymore. I'm not your boyfriend anymore. You need to accept that and move on." Although how much moving on Anthony would be able to do, considering he had already been charged with two counts of attempted murder among other things, Jonathan didn't know.

"Jonathan, please." Anthony sounded more frightened and uncertain than Jonathan had ever heard before. "I don't know what to do."

Jonathan closed his eyes and tried to make a sensible decision. It was so tempting to just react like he always had and do what Anthony wanted. Not as tempting, but equally compelling, was the thought he could just walk away and pretend he'd never received this phone call. He opened his eyes to see Ben on the other side of the table regarding him steadily, waiting for whatever decision he made. He looked away, out the window, to where Lorraine and Col had stood less than an hour before .

Jonathan had never been loved like that. What he and Anthony had was never anything even close to what Lorraine and Col had, even with the terrible disease destroying them both, but that didn't mean Jonathan didn't care. He'd loved Anthony once, and even after everything that had gone before, he realized he still cared what happened to him—at least enough that he didn't wish him harm. He supposed that made him one of the good guys.

"Where are you now?" he asked. The resignation in his voice must have alerted Ben, because he frowned at Jonathan before stacking their plates and preparing to leave. "Okay. I'll sort something out. Let me know if you get arrested and taken to the police station."

"I knew you'd—"

"You know nothing, Anthony. Don't...." *Don't what? Don't expect me to come back? Don't try to kill me?* He disconnected the call and stood.

"You're going to see him." Ben shoved his hands into his pockets as if to stop himself from shaking Jonathan. Or perhaps to stop himself from holding Jonathan back, to stop him going.

"I couldn't just call someone to go and check on him." He had to get Ben to understand, even if only a little. "I was with him for ten years. You don't just walk away from that as if it never happened. Ignoring him is what he would do to me. I don't want to be like that." He touched Ben's shoulder. "I'm not going back to him, and I'm not going to give him another opportunity to kill me, but I need to make sure he won't come to harm and that someone is there to take care of him."

Ben sighed and stepped back, giving Jonathan room to walk around him and leave the café.

"Would you...? I know...." Jonathan ran his damp hands down his jeans and took a deep breath to try to calm his racing heart. Sure, going to see Anthony again was scary, but he didn't want Ben to think... well, anything except what was real. He took another deep breath and just said what he wanted. "Would you come with me?"

Ben stilled, frozen in the moment.

Jonathan clarified, "I don't want to go there on my own. I'm... I'm scared, but I might also need help with Anthony, if he's fallen or something."

Heat raced across his face as Ben's serious look changed to one of joy. "Let's go see what the bastard's done to himself, but I'll warn you, I have the police on speed dial on my phone, and I'm not afraid to use it."

Chapter TWENTY-EIGHT

THE HOUSE was dark when they pulled into the driveway. Jonathan knew that was a strange way to think of it, because there were still hours till the sun set, but it described it perfectly. The front yard felt abandoned, even though the lawn was recently mowed. The windows were all closed and the curtains drawn. Jonathan sat in the car and watched, not entirely sure what he was waiting for. His hands were clammy again.

"We don't have to go in there. We can call someone and get them to check on him."

Jonathan shook his head. "It's not only for him. I need to go in there to…. It's so I can…. I'm sorry. I'm not explaining it very well." He slumped in his seat.

"Is this where he hurt you?" Ben nodded toward Jonathan's chest.

Jonathan rubbed at the scar, still sensitive enough to feel how deep the knife had plunged. He opened the door. "Let's do this. Then I can start my life." He stood and shut the door behind him, looked over the car at Ben as he also stood, nodded decisively, then walked to the front door.

Almost immediately on pressing the doorbell, Anthony responded. "It's open." Jonathan glanced at Ben. Anthony didn't sound upset now.

"Perhaps things aren't as dire as he said on the phone," said Ben as Jonathan pressed the handle and opened the door.

"We'll soon find out," murmured Jonathan.

Noisy sobbing greeted them as they entered the foyer. Jonathan's breathing ratcheted higher as every nerve in his body screamed *trap*. He paused in the entry, the reassuring heat of Ben's body behind him. He moved his arm back and smiled when his hand connected with Ben's as he moved to Jonathan's side.

Hand in hand they walked to the open-arched doorway to the living room.

Everything in the room was exactly as it was the last time Jonathan had been there. The white leather lounge suite was still arranged artfully in front of the open fireplace that never got used. There were still empty rectangles pressed into the white carpet where the pieces of furniture he'd taken once sat. Faded brown blood stains still marred the stark whiteness in a bizarre abstract painting on the floor. Jonathan swayed.

Ben gripped his hand tighter, his warm body pressed against Jonathan's arm. Jonathan sucked in a deep breath and looked away from the stained carpet to find Anthony sitting on the couch, his face buried in his arms. His wheelchair sat beside the couch. The sobs continued, but Jonathan noticed Anthony peek up from the crook of his elbow when Jonathan didn't immediately run over to him. The sight calmed him, and he sighed.

Usually when Anthony went into one of his crying fits, Jonathan would rush around trying to placate him, to get him to stop. Now, after being away from him and seeing how normal people behaved with each other, it didn't have any impact on him at all.

As soon as Anthony saw Ben, he sat up straight. "Who's he? Why've you brought someone else here?" He glared at their joined hands before his narrowed eyes returned to Jonathan. "You brought the whore you've taken up with?" Deep color flooded Anthony's face.

Jonathan released Ben's hand and walked over to one of the single chairs. Anthony's gaze followed Ben as he went to stand by the window. "Shut up! What do you want, Anthony?" Anthony ignored him and continued to glare at Ben. As he sat, Jonathan said, "It doesn't look like you need help."

Anthony shifted his head and glowered at Jonathan. His eyes were red but dry. He'd probably been rubbing them to make them look like he'd been crying.

"Why did you bring him here?"

"Anthony, if you don't tell me what's wrong with you right now, I'll leave and you can sort it out by yourself." He clasped his trembling hands together and shoved them between his knees. He never spoke to Anthony like that.

"You left, that's what's wrong." Anthony kept darting narrow looks at Ben as he spoke.

Jonathan had no intention of buying into that, but he gestured at Anthony to continue. "And…?"

"You're my husband, but you left me when I needed you most," his ex accused. Jonathan marveled that he was suddenly married, especially when Anthony had always scoffed at the idea. "I was injured and in hospital and you didn't even come and visit me," Anthony continued.

Jonathan sat perched on the edge of his chair and tried to marshal his thoughts. "You tried to kill me. I stayed away from you because I wanted to live. I'm not going to discuss that further. Now, what do you want?"

Ben lowered himself to the arm of Jonathan's chair, not touching, but close enough that Jonathan could lean over and rub his face into his abdomen if he wanted to. The thought made him smile again.

"It's not funny," Anthony screamed, making both Jonathan and Ben jump. "Get away from him. He's mine!"

"Anthony." Jonathan's voice deepened as his own anger grew. Anthony didn't have any right to him anymore, and it was time he realized it. Before he could speak, Anthony continued.

"I need to talk to you." Anthony glared at Ben again. "Alone."

"Forget it, Anthony. We don't have anything to talk about that Ben can't be part of."

An ominous silence stretched between them. Anthony's knuckles whitened as his grip on the arm of the couch tightened. Jonathan flicked a look at the door, gauging the distance to safety. Then Anthony took a deep breath and released his hold on the couch, and Jonathan breathed again.

"I had to get Vaughn to come and look after me, and I thought it would work, but he… he…."

Jonathan leaned forward, for the first time concerned that something had actually happened to Anthony. Had this Vaughn person beaten him? It didn't matter that Anthony had done that to Jonathan for years. No one deserved to be beaten. No one. Not even bloody Anthony.

"What did Vaughn do?"

Anthony looked away, his lips pursed.

"Why don't I make tea or something?" said Ben.

"I don't think we need—" began Jonathan.

"Would you? You'll find everything you need in the kitchen." Anthony waved a nonchalant hand toward the doorway.

Jonathan narrowed his eyes at the sweet-as-pie tone but didn't stop Ben leaving the room.

Anthony smiled once Ben was gone. "I know how much you like Earl Grey tea. There's a quiche as well. It's your favorite. You can heat that up for dinner."

Ten years and he still doesn't know I hate quiche. And *Earl Grey tea.* "We're not staying for dinner, Anthony. Now tell me what happened with Vaughn."

"Why did you bring him?" There was an angry growl in Anthony's voice, but for once it didn't have Jonathan jumping to smooth things over.

"Anthony, if you want me to help you with anything, you have to stay focused. Now tell me what happened with Vaughn."

Ben slipped back into the room and stood just inside the door.

"At first it was good. He was helping me. He found out where you were and gave me your new number so I could get you back, but then Rebecca turned up and everything went to hell."

Who are Vaughn and Rebecca? He glanced at Ben, but he was just as mystified.

"Stop it!" Anthony snarled. "Stop looking at him like that. You came to see me."

Ben pushed away from the wall. "The kettle's probably boiled by now," he said as he left the room.

Anthony smirked at Ben's back, then scowled at Jonathan. "Now I'm broke, and it's because of you."

Jonathan scoffed. "Don't be ridiculous." His heart pounded as he heard his dismissive tone. Just a month ago, that would have earned him an hour-long vitriolic rant or a punch to the stomach. A month ago he wouldn't have dared speak back. He sat straighter in his chair as realization stole over him. He really was out. He was out of this house and out of this relationship with Anthony. He was out of any situation that meant he would blindly do what Anthony said, whether for fear or for peace. None of it mattered anymore. Anthony didn't matter to him any more than any stranger would matter. "You have plenty of money," he continued, his voice stronger than before. "I only took half what was in the joint account. I didn't touch anything else."

"Vaughn took it," Anthony yelled. "He took everything. Then he said Rebecca disappeared with his money. *His* money! It's *my* money, and you stole it and then he stole it but now she's got it." Anthony leaned forward, his feet shifting apart for balance. His voice rose in pitch until Jonathan had trouble making out the words. "And now he's gone and got himself arrested and he's not even here to look after me. It's all your fault!"

Jonathan laughed as he stood up. "You know, Anthony, I came over here thinking there was something I should do to help you. I was with you for ten years, after all. I thought surely that had to mean something. It couldn't have been totally wasted time. It wasn't a waste, I know that now. I learned a lot of things while I was with you, even though I didn't think I did."

Ben came back with a single mug of tea. He bent to place it on the coffee table in front of Anthony. Jonathan walked across the room and stood on the other side of the coffee table, seeing nothing more in Anthony than a mean little man who deserved every bad thing he got in life. "I would have helped you too. I'd make sure you were cared for if that's what you needed. You don't want help, though, do you? You want to have someone around that you can use and manipulate. Someone you can mistreat if you want, with no consequences. You thought you'd found that in me. Naïve nineteen-year-old me who was craving someone to love—but I grew up. I've grown up since I left, and I don't need or want anything that you're vying for here."

He stepped back and nodded to Ben for them to leave. "I'll call someone to make sure you have the care you need while you're waiting for a trial date, but that's all I'm going to do." He turned and walked to the door.

"You bastard," Anthony screamed.

Jonathan ignored him, but Ben cried out. He spun to see his lover on the floor beside Anthony, his bloody hands gripping his thigh.

"Ben!" He rushed back but stopped when Anthony stood, a knife held negligently by his side. One leg dragged a little before lifting and flopping forward in a small step, and Anthony shifted his grip on the knife, preparing to throw.

"You won't walk away from me, you bastard. This is all *your* fault. If it wasn't for you, my life would be exactly the way I wanted it."

Jonathan had tried, really tried to be the grown-up here, but suddenly that didn't matter. The last ten years of lies and abuse bubbled up, and he ran at Anthony, knocking him over onto the couch before he could bring the knife up.

"No way, you bastard. You already tried to kill me once. No way am I going to let you do it a second time." He grabbed Anthony's shirt and dragged him off the couch. He cocked his other arm back, his hand already fisted, then let fly. The crunching impact of his fist with Anthony's cheek tore Anthony from his grip. He dropped, senseless, beside the couch.

"Fuck!" Jonathan cradled his hand to his chest. "That hurts."

Ben groaned, and Jonathan rushed to his side, his hands fluttering over him. He gritted his teeth and carefully looked at Ben's leg. Blood spread in a pool beneath it, seeping between Ben's fingers.

"Ohmygod, ohmygod. There's so much blood. Don't die," he whispered.

Ben groaned again and Jonathan froze. "Jon, call the police."

Jon dug his phone out of his pocket and dialed 000.

"Police and ambulance, please." The operator began asking questions, and he tried to focus on his answers, giving the address and other details, but Ben's pained panting distracted him. "There's so much blood. Please get someone—" Anthony stirred. "No. He's coming around. Fuck, where did the knife go?"

"Sir, can you tell me what's happening?"

"I knocked him out but—shit—" He dropped the phone next to Ben and lunged for Anthony. "No."

"I'm going to kill you!" yelled Anthony. "You're going to pay for what you've done to me."

"Jon! The knife." Ben's voice was low, full of pain-filled urgency.

"Drop it, you bastard." Jonathan grabbed Anthony's wrist and thumped it against the floor. "You had your chance to kill me. I'm not giving you another one."

Sirens sounded in the distance. Even as Jonathan struggled to prevent Anthony from reaching the knife again, the wailing grew closer, then abruptly shut off. Within seconds police had stormed through the front door and pulled Jonathan off Anthony.

"Stop him! Stop him! He's trying to kill me." Anthony skittered away from Jonathan toward a police officer, then pulled himself up onto the couch.

"Don't even try that, you bastard. You're going to jail already, and this lot today will just make it worse for you."

He leaned over to jab Anthony's chest with his finger, but a police offer restrained him. "You lied to me, you bastard. You can walk. Not just a jerk from faulty nerves, like you told me after the accident. Actual walking. You're no more a quadriplegic than I am. It was just another way of manipulating me to do what you wanted. Well, I'm done. Do you understand me? I'm done." Jonathan's voice barely worked anymore. The anger and the tension held his throat so tight it hurt to speak, so he stopped. He closed his mouth and breathed against his pounding heart and fisted his trembling hands. Fear and anger threatened to overwhelm him, but he wasn't just done with Anthony, he was also done with living his life in fear, without control.

He turned his back on Anthony and watched in anguish as the paramedics secured Ben to a stretcher and raised it, ready to wheel out to the waiting ambulance.

"Is he going to be all right?" Shame filled him that he had become so absorbed in his rant at Anthony, he'd forgotten Ben's injury.

"I'm fine. Make sure he can't do this again," said Ben as they wheeled him away.

"And him! You're *cheating* on me too. If it wasn't for you, I'd be rich and famous: the most lauded jeweler in the world. One or two more awards and I'd have had it all, but *you* ruined that."

"You never earned any awards to start with. You stole all those designs from Mark."

"Okay, that's enough," said the police officer with Jonathan. "Let's get you down to the station so we can sort this out."

"I don't need to go to the station. He tried to kill me. Arrest him!" Anthony screamed from the couch.

Jonathan took a step back, physically distancing himself from Anthony so he could think rationally. He wasn't going to get buried in Anthony's dramas again. He needed to make sure Ben was okay, and he needed to make sure Anthony was out of his life for good. "Yes," he said. "Let's go to the station." He turned to the officer. "You can check that he is already facing two charges of attempted murder, and now he'll have another for Ben." He walked toward the front door. "Can I call my cousin so he can make sure Ben isn't at the hospital alone?"

"Jonathan, get back here. You have to help me into my chair."

The police officer paused and looked back at the other police officer with Anthony.

"He can walk. If he wants to use the chair still, he'll get into it himself," said Jonathan.

"You bastard. You're abandoning me again! You just wait. I'll make you pay for everything you've done to me. Do you hear me? Next time I won't miss. Next time I'll kill you!"

Jonathan stepped out of the house and took a shaky breath. Anthony's voice faded the farther away he walked. "Thank you for coming so quickly," he said to the police officer. "I don't have to ride with him, do I? Do you think it'll take a long time? I want to go to the hospital and check on Ben."

Behind them, Anthony continued to scream, this time threatening to sue the police officers for abuse and neglect and for not helping him into his wheelchair. As Jonathan sat in the back seat of the police car and the door closed, he saw Anthony stumble out of the house on unsteady feet.

Anthony had lied to him in the most fundamental way. He could walk. All those times Jonathan had noticed movement, Anthony had dismissed it as uncontrollable nerve twitches.... And that last time, when Jonathan had refused to accept that excuse after walking into the bedroom to find Anthony lifting his foot onto the wheelchair rest—without using his hands to lift his leg.... Jonathan pressed his hand to his chest. His injury wasn't the result of an overwrought, depressed man. Anthony was willing to kill to preserve his secret, to keep Jonathan as his slave.

Chapter TWENTY-NINE

JONATHAN SLUMPED in the uncomfortable plastic chair and tilted his head back. He'd spent altogether too much time in the hospital in the last couple of months. At least this time he was on the right side of the emergency room doors.

"Fuck," he mumbled. *How bloody ungrateful and selfish can you be, Watson?* Ben was in one of those cubicles, in pain. He'd risked his life for Jonathan, and all Jonathan could think about was how much he hated hospitals.

He looked up as brisk footsteps came toward him and stood when he recognized Liam. Without hesitation he walked into Liam's waiting arms and held on tight.

"Are you all right?" Liam grumbled against Jonathan's head. He wrapped his arms wrapped tightly around Jonathan and held him secure and safe. Protected. Jonathan nodded and loosened his grip around Liam's waist. Liam stepped back but kept his hands on Jonathan's shoulders as his dark eyes inspected every part of Jonathan's body he could see. When he seemed satisfied Jonathan wasn't injured, he let go and led them both to the chairs.

"They're treating Ben now, but he's okay. There's some muscle damage but nothing vital was punctured." Jonathan leaned forward, elbows on knees, buried his fingers in his hair, and breathed through the nausea.

"Why the hell did you go there?"

Jonathan sighed and sat up straight. That's what everyone wanted to know. It was the first thing the police had asked him. From their expressions when he told them, they were probably wondering if he shouldn't be under psychiatric care along with Anthony. "Anthony called." He leaned forward again, into his hands, so he wouldn't have to see the disgust and disappointment on Liam's face. "He said he needed help. I couldn't let him...." He sighed and sat up again. If the same circumstances happened again, he'd do the same thing—although he'd leave Ben behind—so he wasn't going to act like he was ashamed of what he did. "I was going to call someone to take care of him, but I needed to know...." This is where it all went arse-over-tit. Liam would either understand, or he wouldn't. "I needed to be sure that I didn't want to go back to him. I don't want to be like him." That didn't make much more sense than the first time he'd said it.

Liam flung his arm around Jonathan's shoulder and brought him close for a kiss on his forehead. "You're nothing like him and never will be." After a pause, he continued, "Are you sure you did the right thing now?"

Jonathan slumped into Liam's side. "I love you, you know that, right?"

"Feeling's mutual. Now tell me."

"I made a lot of mistakes where Anthony is concerned, but leaving him wasn't one of them." He looked earnestly at Liam. "I'm vacillating between being so angry I want to destroy something and wanting to burst into tears if someone smiles at me."

"That's normal after what you've been through."

Jonathan took several deep, slow breaths. This was it. The big moment when he made his life-changing announcement. Liam seemed to sense Jonathan was building to something because he sat quietly, watchful.

"I've made a decision," Jonathan announced.

Liam grinned at him, pride shining in his dark eyes. "Tell me."

Jonathan shook his head. "I need to talk to Ben first, to see if I need to change things."

"Jonathan, you don't need to change anything based on what someone else wants."

"I know that," Jonathan snapped. He wasn't nineteen anymore, and he'd been through enough to know that what he used to do didn't work. He'd have to do something different. "When getting what I want depends on the way someone else responds, then I have to talk to him about it first. Isn't that how relationships work?"

"Relationship? Are you and Ben...?"

"I don't know, but I want to see if we could be. I'm going to see a therapist too." He glared at Liam. "How do you always do that? I told you I wanted to talk to Ben first!"

Liam laughed. "I'm a doctor. It's my job to get people to tell me what's wrong with them and how they want to fix it."

"Rubbish. You're an emergency doctor. Most of your patients are unconscious. You don't give them a choice."

Liam slapped Jonathan's shoulder, just like he used to when Jonathan was a teenager. He hadn't done that since it had become obvious Anthony was abusing him. Jonathan hadn't realized he'd missed it so much. Liam stood. "I'll check to see if you can see Ben yet. The sooner you have your talk with him, the sooner you can make more decisions." He strode away but turned back after a few steps. "I'm really proud of you, Jonathan," he said quietly.

Jonathan nodded, his throat tight with overflowing emotion. He watched Liam stop at the reception desk, then stride through the emergency ward. A few minutes later, a nurse came up to Jonathan. "Mr. Watson? Mr. Urquhart would like to see you."

Jonathan stood and followed the nurse. *He asked for me. He wants to see me. That's a good sign, isn't it?* He slipped through the curtain as the nurse held it, then stopped. Ben sat in the bed, a starched gown stretched across his chest, one leg sticking out from the covers. A stark white bandage wrapped around his thigh. The sight of it stopped Jonathan's forward momentum. Ben's smile faltered, and Jonathan moved again.

"Are you all right?" he asked. Warmth flooded him when he realized it was exactly what Liam had asked him. It was the question you asked someone you... cared about. Jonathan wasn't ready to admit more than that right now.

"Come here, babe." Ben held his arms out, and Jonathan leaned over the bed to hug him. "Now I'm just fine."

"I'm so sorry. I shouldn't have taken you there."

"Jonathan, stop." Ben released him enough that they could look at each other's faces as they talked. "After what Anthony had done to you, there was no way I was going to let you go there without me." Jonathan stepped back, but Ben kept talking. "Don't look at me like that. I wasn't going to tell you what to do, but I *was* going with you. It's a good thing I did too. That man is a serious nutter, babe. How the hell did you survive so long with him?"

Jonathan took another step back and looked away. *I spent ten years with a "nutter." By choice. I must be crazy myself to have done that.* "I'm sorry," he whispered. This wasn't going to work. There was no way Ben would want to be involved with a madman.

"Jonathan, whatever you're thinking right now, stop it." Ben's voice was sharp, bringing Jonathan's attention back to him. "You have no idea just what it is you've accomplished, do you? You lived with that man for ten years and endured abuse I don't want to imagine, much less know about. Yet less than a month out of it, you not only have enough compassion to make sure he gets the care he needs, you stand up to him and refuse to let him continue his abuse. I could see how it was tearing you apart, but that wasn't because you're weak. You were affected because, even after everything you've gone through, you're still capable of feeling compassion. And in the middle of all that, you fucking saved my life." Ben grinned at him. "You're a fucking hero, Jonathan." His grin softened to an intimate smile. "My hero."

Jonathan couldn't breathe. His throat clogged with gulped-in air, his face burned, and his eyes stung. Ben reached for him and he fell forward, burying his face in the crook of Ben's neck. The warm hospital smell of his skin seemed like the only real thing, the only thing that wasn't crazy. It was the only thing he could hold onto to stop him spinning, spinning away into the dead space of despair and loss.

"I'm sorry," he sobbed. "I'm so sorry I took you into that. I'm sorry…." He was sorry for so many things, he no longer knew what they were. He was sorry he went back to see Anthony. He was sorry he hadn't stopped talking to him after he left. He was sorry he'd left Anthony in the first place, because then he wouldn't have put Ben in danger. More than anything, he was sorry he couldn't be what Ben needed him to be. After Anthony, he was… broken. Ben deserved so much more than that. He'd been foolish to think, even for a second, that he and Ben could build a fairy-tale romance.

Ben said nothing, confirming Jonathan's worst fears. Sure, he was still holding Jonathan tight against him, still rubbing his hand soothingly up and down Jonathan's back, but he wasn't saying anything. There was obviously nothing he needed to say. Yet Jonathan couldn't let go. He kept his arms jammed underneath Ben's torso, gripping tight. He kept his face buried in the dark, soothing hollow where his neck met his shoulder, and as his breathing eased, he allowed the warm, earthy smell of Ben to soothe him. There were undertones of hospital and old fear, but it was Ben, and nothing calmed Jonathan more completely than Ben.

Finally, when Jonathan lay limp against him, Ben spoke. "Are you ready to talk now?"

Jonathan sighed. It was inevitable. After seeing Ben in the hospital bed, Jonathan knew any chance of them building something lasting together was impossible. Ben had seen what Jonathan had come from, and Jonathan knew how impossible it would be for Ben to love him now. That didn't mean he could look Ben in the face as he said it, though. He tugged one hand out from under Ben and used it to wipe the moisture from his face, even while he kept his face snuggled into the crook of Ben's neck.

He took a deep, fortifying breath. "What do you want to talk about?"

"So tell me what happened at the police station. I only know what I said to the police who interviewed me here."

"Apparently Anthony attacked one of the police officers when his coffee didn't have froth on it, so he's facing even more charges. That's as well as all the assault and attempted murder charges from this morning. Adding all that together with the previous charges, they don't think he'll be granted bail." Jonathan ran out of steam. He couldn't say the rest right now.

"That's good, right? Now you know he won't be following you around, and he won't be able to call you all the time." Ben's long fingers massaged Jonathan's neck. "What about the guy who attacked us at your place?"

"Apparently, that was the Vaughn Anthony was talking about. From what they said, I think Vaughn was close to being caught by the police for other things he was doing—it sounded like drugs. So he went with Anthony to hide. I don't think they've found Rebecca yet. If she's got all Anthony's money in cash, it could be a while before they find her, especially if she disguises herself."

They sat silently for several seconds, Ben's hand desultorily trailing along the skin at Jonathan's neck.

"What about us?" Ben asked quietly.

Jonathan froze, then pushed himself away. He couldn't take this lying down—literally—regardless of how much he craved Ben's touch. He didn't look at Ben. "I'm sorry," he said. "I know how you must feel." He pushed himself onto his feet, gravity and sorrow fighting him the whole way up off the bed.

"Jonathan."

Jonathan looked up, surprised at the sharpness of Ben's tone.

Ben held his hand out. "Stop whatever is going through your head and come back here and talk to me."

Ben was right. Jonathan was an adult, and regardless of how much he wanted to avoid hearing Ben tell him to go away, he had to face up to things. He'd buried his head in the sand for too long with Anthony, and he wasn't going to do that anymore.

"I'm going to contact a therapist," he blurted, his gaze flitting over Ben's features, looking for any sign that Ben—what?—wanted him, hated him, loved him?

Ben smiled. It was like his usual smile but not quite as bright. "That's great, babe. I think that'll help you work through a heap of stuff." His voice was softer too, more tentative.

"I—I…." Jonathan stopped.

"You what?" Ben said softly.

Jonathan shook his head. Nothing he said now would change anything. He was still a wimp who'd allowed another man to abuse him for ten years. He still didn't know how to make a decision or how to assert himself with anything he wanted. What use would someone like that be for a man like Ben?

"Do you know what I'd like to happen now?" asked Ben.

Jonathan shook his head, mute.

"I'd like you to think about something for me. And I'd like you to tell me what you think—not right now, though. Maybe next week."

"Next week?"

"Yep. They're really only keeping me here now to make sure I don't develop an infection. After that I'll be in physio for a while, so you can tell me what you decide next week."

Physio? Next week? "I don't understand."

Ben grinned at him—his old grin, full of fun and mischief. "Come here and I'll tell you what I want you to think about."

Jonathan moved forward, automatically sitting back on the bed and burrowing his head into the quiet depth of Ben's neck.

"That's better," sighed Ben. "I like snuggling with you. We should do it more often."

"Is that what you want me to think about?" An involuntary smile tugged at Jonathan's lips. He was beginning to get an idea that Ben wasn't going to kick him to the curb. Nobody could call him a slow learner.

Ben chuffed a laugh. "What I want you to think about is the idea of me moving in with you."

Jonathan jumped and would have pulled out of Ben's hold if Ben hadn't tightened his arms and prevented it.

"Not straightaway. Not for a while, actually. But I want you to think about it. That's not what I want you to tell me next week, though. Next week, after you've been thinking about me moving in with you, I want you to tell me if you want to keep seeing me."

Jonathan pushed out of Ben's hold and stared at him. "That doesn't make sense. It's backwards."

"I want you to know that if you and I spend more time together, see each other, and date... and stuff"—he waggled his eyebrows—"then it's going to be leading toward me moving in with you. Or you moving in with me. I'm not in this for a random sex partner, Jonathan, or friends with benefits. I want something more than that with you, and I want you to know that." He raised his hands and cupped Jonathan's cheeks. "But I don't want you to feel pressured into doing anything other than having a good time with me. Just know that if we start this thing, it's going to be heading into something long-term. Something permanent."

"What if...." Jonathan sucked in a panicky breath. He had to ask. He had to make sure this wasn't going to turn into something like what he had with Anthony. "What if I decide to leave?"

"Then we talk about why you want to leave, and if it's still something you want to do, then you do it. No fault, no penalty. Same goes for me."

No! Jonathan wanted to shout it out. He wanted to grab Ben and hold him close so he couldn't leave. In such a short time, Ben had become the eye of the storm, the calm center that Jonathan returned to when the rest of his swirling life became too much for him. He didn't want to lose that. There was another problem, though. "What if, with the therapy and everything, I find out you're just my transitional guy? Not the real thing." Oh, but dear lord, he *felt* like the real thing.

"Do I feel not real to you?"

He'd made Ben sad. "No. You feel real, but I don't... I can't trust my own judgment."

"You trusted your judgment with Anthony. To move in and then to leave. Were both of those decisions bad ones?"

Jonathan remained quiet for several seconds as he really thought about the circumstances around the beginning of his relationship with Anthony. "I didn't really decide to move in with Anthony. It just happened. I just went along with what Anthony wanted." He looked at Ben, noting how his features changed with the news. "I let Anthony rule my life because it was easy. I was still feeling so guilty about being the only one who survived the accident that killed my parents and my cousin, I just wanted someone to take me away from that so I wouldn't have to think about it anymore."

"And now?"

"Now I realize I have to deal with it. All of it." This was it. This was the moment that would make a relationship with Ben possible or destroy it completely. "I'm going to tell you what I want. Do you promise not to laugh?"

Ben smiled. "You know that almost guarantees my laughing, don't you?" He stroked his fingers down Jonathan's cheek. "Tell me what you want, babe."

Jonathan took a deep breath and plunged forward. "I want what Col and Lorraine have. Not the whole Alzheimer's and being put into a home thing. A love like that, that endures everything life throws at it, even through forgetting who I am and who you are. I want to love like that and be loved like that."

Ben had gone very still, and Jonathan faltered. Telling him half of it wouldn't be enough, though.

"I think I could feel that kind of love for you, but I don't want to rush it. I don't want to go through all the stages of building a relationship unless that's what I'm working toward." He sat back a bit and tucked his trembling fingers into his armpits.

Ben rested his head back against his pillow and closed his eyes. The urge to jump up and run away hit Jonathan like a speeding train. It was so shocking it immobilized him completely and he sat, frozen in place, watching Ben's closed-off face. Then he noticed....

He untucked his hands and leaned forward. Yes, it was. A tear slid down the side of Ben's face to his ear. He reached out a finger and wiped it away.

"Ben?"

Ben opened wet eyes and reached for Jonathan. He went willingly, needing to comfort Ben from whatever had upset him.

"What's wrong, Ben? Tell me what's wrong and I'll fix it."

Ben shook his head. "Nothing's wrong, babe. Everything's right."

"I don't understand."

Ben pushed Jonathan back so they could look at each other. "I want that too. Everything you said, I want. I want to hold your hand and feel like I've come home and never want to leave. I want to wake up beside you and know the sun shines inside my house because you're there. I want to grow old with you and have daily troubles wiped from my mind because it's so full of your smiles and the memories we've made together."

"Do you really think we could have that?"

"I really think we can," said Ben as he drew Jonathan down to kiss him.

JONATHAN SAT in the emergency waiting room and waited again. He was still nervous, but not about Ben. He and Ben would work out. Now, he was nervous about telling Liam. Then he'd have to tell his aunt and uncle. The sharp snap of shoes on vinyl brought his eyes open to see Liam striding toward him again, concern on his features.

"You're still here. What's wrong?"

Jonathan stood and hugged his cousin. His best friend. His brother. "We're going to try—" He shook his head and started again. There'd be no *trying* in this relationship. "We're going to do it."

"Do what?" Liam held him at arm's length, still frowning, but seeming less worried now he'd heard the hope in Jonathan's voice.

Jonathan grinned. "We're together. We're going to go out and talk and laugh and… and…." He laughed. "We're not going to move in together until we're sure." He gripped Liam's waist and pulled him into a hug.

"Mark and I are." Liam's voice was a weird combination of joyful and uncertain.

Jonathan stepped back to look at his face. "You and Mark are what?" No way. It had only been a couple of months. Liam never made quick decisions. Never.

Liam grinned at him. "I'm crazy, I know, but it works. We're moving in together. Well, I'm moving in with Mark." He dragged Jonathan into another brief hug. "We're going to live together and get a dog."

"A dog!" *Holy shit*. It was serious.

Liam nodded. "Mark already has a cat." Liam shook his head as if realizing how besotted he sounded. "Anyway, we'll be having a housewarming, even though Mark's not moving house, and we're inviting everyone. It has to be before September because Jeremy has finished his degree and just taken a job with a mining company in South Australia. Rebel's going with him. He said he's finally going to use his pharmacist's degree and do some temp work. Daron said his café will cater, and Peter is flitting around making sure everything is color-matched." He hauled in a deep breath. "God, that feels better." He grinned at Jonathan. "I haven't even told Mum and Dad yet. You're the first to know."

"Wow." Speechless was a definite possibility right now. "I don't think I've heard you talk that fast—ever."

"I know! Mark's a bad influence." Liam laughed. "No, really, I'm just so excited. I've never felt like this. All those stories Mum and Dad tell about when they met in Somalia and fell in love—I never thought it would be possible for me. But Mark is…. Mark is…."

"Perfect for you."

Liam sighed. "I didn't say all that to steal your thunder. It's just bursting from me. When you told me about you and Ben, I knew you'd understand. You've felt it yourself."

Jonathan smiled. He actually had.

Chapter THIRTY

Six months later

"HOW LONG did he get?"

Jonathan dropped down onto the bench beside Ben and stretched his legs out. In front of them, a small family of ducks paddled desultorily in the pond. "Fifteen years. Parole after twelve."

"I'm so glad the mental incapacity claim didn't stick."

"Me too. Mark's testimony helped with that. When they heard what Anthony did to him and how he stole all his designs, I think they realized this wasn't any mental strain caused by the accident."

They sat quietly for several minutes before Ben spoke again. "What's wrong? I thought you'd be happy with this."

"I am, but...." Jonathan shifted on the seat and turned to face Ben. "Anthony isn't the problem." He immediately knew "problem" was the wrong word to use. Ben looked devastated. He grabbed for Ben's hand to stop him leaving, even though he hadn't made any move to do so.

"I'm listening," said Ben quietly.

"I think I've found an apartment for us." *Oh yes*. That's the reaction he wanted. Jonathan shook his head. Ben had it wrong all those months ago in the hospital. The sun didn't shine on them because Jonathan was in the room. It was because of Ben.

"Why would that be a problem?"

"It's Kyle's apartment. His lease is up and he's leaving. It's a two bedroom, like Neridah's. Only less pink."

Ben laughed. "I'm glad he's finally given up on the idea that Tahlia's coming back to him."

"Yeah, he got that message when I told him she'd moved to Perth."

"She moved to Melbourne, not Perth."

Jonathan shrugged. "Perth, Melbourne. It's easy to get those names mixed up." He grinned at Ben. "She's doing well at her chef's course. Making lots of new friends."

Ben laughed with him. "So boneheaded Kyle is vacating, and you want us to move in there. I'm still not seeing a problem."

"Don't be obtuse, Ben. You know it'll mean Neridah will be dropping in all the time. Our fridge will constantly be filled with leftovers, and she can't cook nearly as well as Tahlia."

"It's still better than either you or I can cook. We won't need to cook anything ourselves."

"Neridah's ex, Brianna, is going to take my apartment. With the way Neridah's been talking about her lately, I think they're going to get back together."

Ben grimaced. "Neridah talks enough about sex when she's *not* getting any." Then he shrugged. "I'll deal. Still not a problem." Ben kept smiling at Jonathan like he'd never seen anything more beautiful.

Jonathan hated to do it, but he had to burst his bubble. "Neridah has quit smoking again."

Don't miss how the story began!

Just His Type

Just Life: Book One

By E E Montgomery

Daron's looking for a certain type: he loves tall, slim older men, and he's sure one of them will be his one true love, even though he doesn't truly believe he deserves it. His lack of confidence leads him to a series of meaningless encounters with strangers, convinced that eventually he'll find a relationship to last a lifetime. His best friend and coworker, Rebel, offers Daron the only stable relationship he's ever known. Rebel is younger than Daron and only slightly taller, so definitely not his type. Daron enjoys the time they spend together, but refuses to allow himself to think it could be anything more than friendship. He's never bothered to consider what Rebel thinks….

http://www.dreamspinnerpress.com

Just Like a Date

Just Life: Book Two

By E E Montgomery

Rebel Nguyen and Daron Boroughs both need to be loved, but when Rebel looks at Daron to fill that role, it mangles their friendship. Rebel tries a clean break and meets Jeremy. They hit it off, but Rebel is preoccupied with might-have-beens.

When Rebel doesn't contact him for days, Daron feels lost. He decides he'll never find love unless he can change, but the process of his makeover throws him into the arms of his last trick's ex-boyfriend. Shockingly, they work together—until Daron inevitably screws it up.

Rebel and Daron both need to learn that they don't have to change themselves for love—just the way they look for it.

http://www.dreamspinnerpress.com

Just in Time

Just Life: Book Three

By E E Montgomery

Mark Mendelson's life is close to perfect: he has good friends, a successful business, and a solid reputation in the jewelry industry. He fought hard to get what he has after nearly losing it all fifteen years ago, when his then boyfriend, Cole Porter, stole his designs.

When a handsome man enters Mark's store to request a commitment ring—a design Mark made specifically for Cole—Mark wants nothing to do with him. All he can think about is his rage at Cole's betrayal, something he thought he'd dealt with long ago. But Mark's would-be customer, Dr. Liam Watson, returns to the shop, thinking Mark might provide some answers. For years Liam has tried to convince his cousin Jon to leave Cole, who abuses him. As the relationship between Jon and Cole disintegrates, a fragile new one forms between Liam and Mark—but Mark can't move on until he confronts Cole once and for all.

http://www.dreamspinnerpress.com

E E MONTGOMERY wants the world to be a better place, with equality and acceptance for all. Her philosophy is: We can't change the world but we can change our small part of it and, in that way, influence the whole. Writing stories that show people finding their own "better place" is part of E E Montgomery's own small contribution.

Thankfully, there's never a shortage of inspiration for stories that show people growing in their acceptance and love of themselves and others. A dedicated people-watcher, E E finds stories everywhere. In a cafe, a cemetery, a book on space exploration, or on the news, there'll be a story of personal growth, love, and unconditional acceptance there somewhere.

E-mail: eemontgomery11@gmail.com
Blog: http://eemontgomery.blogspot.com/
Twitter: @EEMontgomery1
Website: http://www.eemontgomery.com/

The Courage to Love

By E E Montgomery

In 1915, after his beloved Carl died from a vicious beating, David Harrison enlisted in the Army and went to war. He returns home to find a world seemingly unchanged, while he will never be the same. At Mrs. Gill's boarding house, he meets Bernard Donnelly, a young man suffering the aftereffects of his own war experiences. David finds himself increasingly attracted to Bernard, but that terrifies him. He blames himself for Carl's horrific death and fears he isn't strong enough to lose another love to violence.

Bernard needs David to help him face each day and find a way they can be together without stigma—and without putting them in legal and physical danger—but David clings to his idea that the only way to keep a lover safe is not to have one. His fears threaten to destroy everything, unless he learns that sometimes the risk is worth it and finds the courage to love.

http://www.dreamspinnerpress.com

Ordinary People

By E E Montgomery

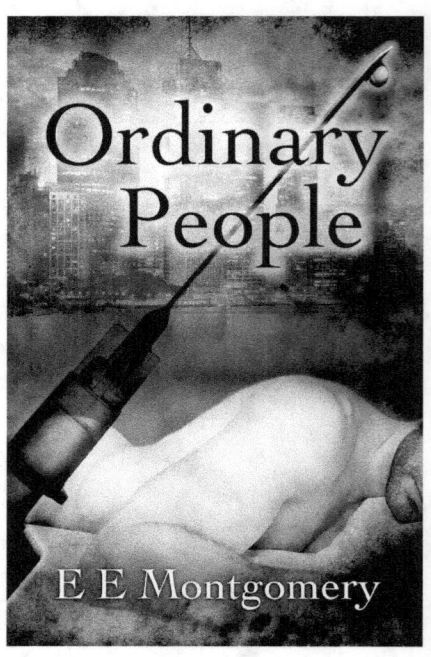

When Queensland Police Force Constable James Laramee raids a hotel room, he finds Vinnie Canterbury on top of a naked, dead man, covered in blood. Vinnie promptly vomits all over James's shoes.

Thanks to a cocktail of horse sedatives and Hendra vaccine, Vinnie's memories of his ordeal are fractured. Finding the culprits and the reasons behind his abduction will be a challenge. With his apartment trashed, his building set on fire, and his clothes, phone and wallet gone, Vinnie needs a place to stay. To his surprise, James not only takes him in, but also lets him cry on his shoulder. It must be true love. Vinnie has plans for his future with James all mapped out, and he hopes he can get James on the same page.

http://www.dreamspinnerpress.com

What About Him

By E E Montgomery

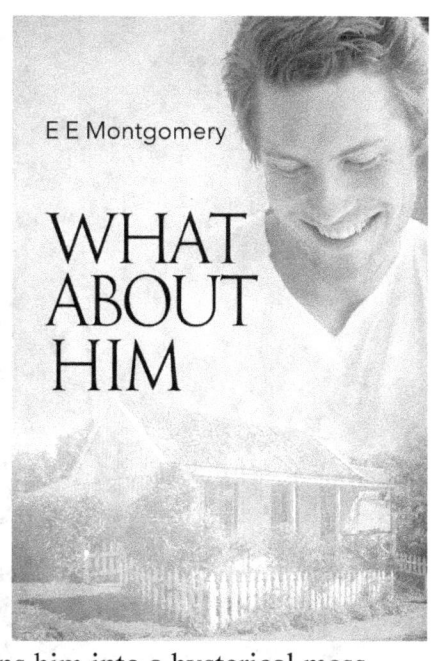

E E Montgomery

WHAT
ABOUT
HIM

There's a snake in Aidan's bed, but it's not the kind he wants. A nest of snakes under his house heralds the kind of disruption that Aidan has been trying to avoid all his life and turns him into a hysterical mess. First he sleeps with his best friend, Baxter. Until their one-night-stand, Aidan was happy with his life and their friendship. Now he's lonely and craves a relationship Baxter doesn't want.

Then Aidan meets Detective Sam Walters while consulting on a murder investigation and his dreams are suddenly invaded by a man who makes Aidan want to strip faster than an attack by green ants. Too bad Sam is straight.

When snakes take over Aidan's home and a gorgeous snake catcher comes to his rescue, Aidan's confusion is complete. To add to the mess Aidan's life has become, a man ends up dead on his living room floor, Baxter confesses to his murder, and calm, cheerful Sam yells at Aidan. It's enough to make a quiet professor of sociology prefer the snakes.

http://www.dreamspinnerpress.com

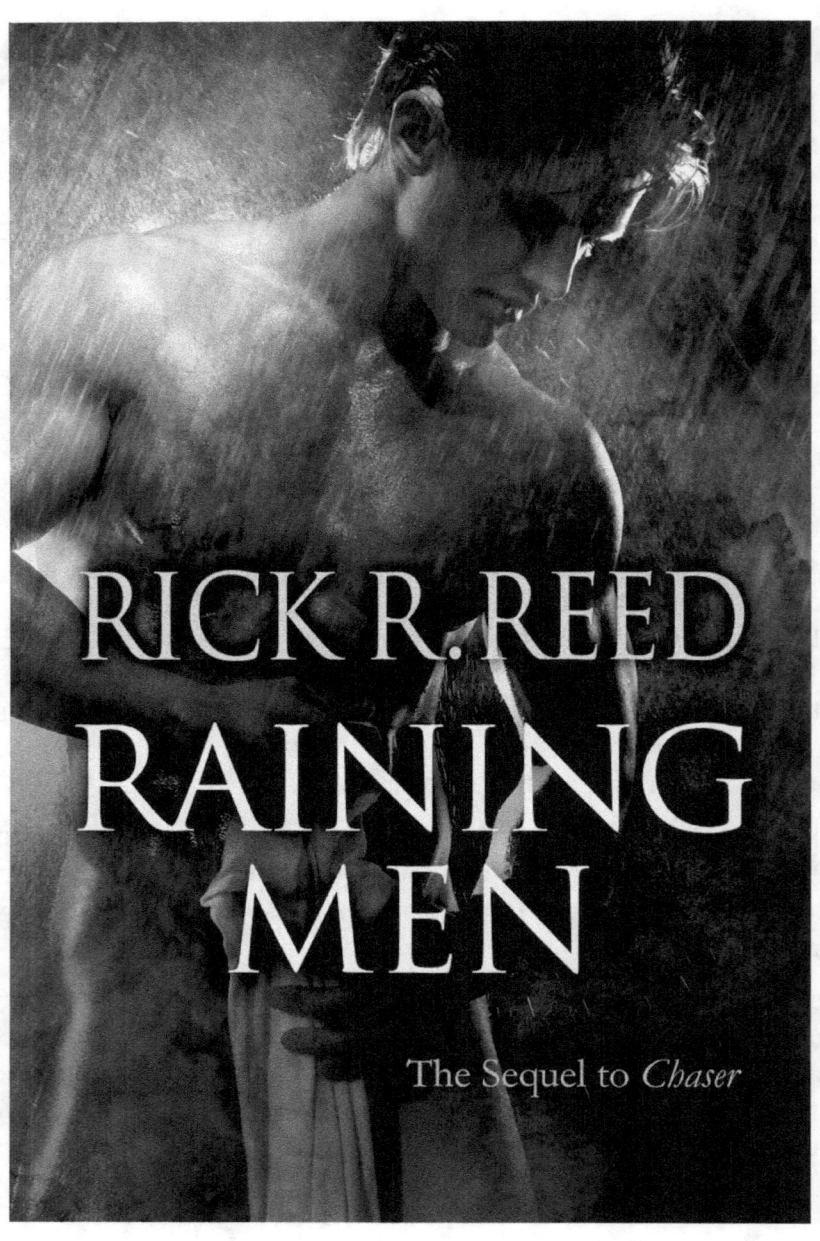

RICK R. REED
RAINING MEN

The Sequel to *Chaser*

http://www.dreamspinnerpress.com

http://www.dreamspinnerpress.com

A HARD WINTER RAIN

John Inman

http://www.dreamspinnerpress.com

http://www.dreamspinnerpress.com

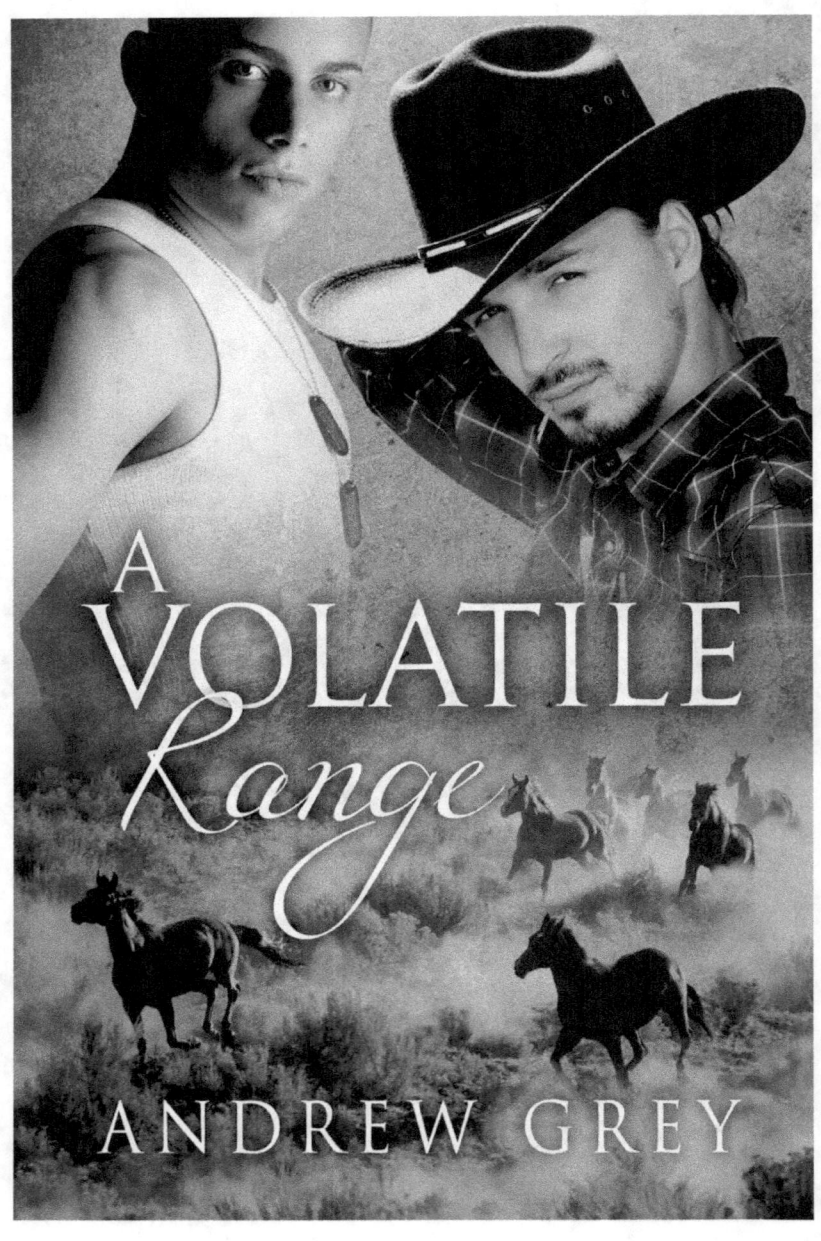

A VOLATILE Range

ANDREW GREY

http://www.dreamspinnerpress.com

RENAE KAYE

SAFE IN HIS ARMS

http://www.dreamspinnerpress.com

FOR **MORE** OF THE **BEST GAY** ROMANCE

DREAMSPINNER
PRESS
dreamspinnerpress.com

www.ingramcontent.com/pod-product-compliance
Lightning Source LLC
Chambersburg PA
CBHW070114260626
47160CB00004B/1464